THE ANCIENTS

Gregory M. Tucker

iUniverse, Inc.
New York   Bloomington

The Ancients

iUniverse books may be ordered through booksellers or by contacting:

iUniverse
1663 Liberty Drive
Bloomington, IN 47403
www.iuniverse.com
1-800-Authors (1-800-288-4677)

Because of the dynamic nature of the Internet, any Web addresses or links contained in this book may have changed since publication and may no longer be valid. The views expressed in this work are solely those of the author and do not necessarily reflect the views of the publisher, and the publisher hereby disclaims any responsibility for them.
Printed in the United States of America

ISBN: 978-1-4401-0965-2 (sc)
ISBN: 978-1-4401-0967-6 (dj)
ISBN: 978-1-4401-0966-9 (ebook)

Library of Congress Control Number: 2009920066

iUniverse rev. date: 01/05/2008

Acknowledgments and Dedications

This book is dedicated to all my friends, the most
precious of treasures.

Special thanks to:
My parents
Anne Foust
Jennifer Yoder
Josh Payne
Mark Wulfert
Jason Beasley
Audrie Bennett
Matt Broten
Tina Mould
And
My lovely Stacie

PREFACE

In the early 1930's a group of Mexican investors illegally smuggled seventeen tons of gold into the Four Corners area of the United States to take advantage of the exchange rate caused by the passing of the Gold Act. The gold was never exchanged, and despite a lengthy investigation conducted by the United States Treasury Department, and many searches and excavations by civilians, the gold remains unfound to present day. This part of the story is true...the following is fiction.

CHAPTER 1

The old man, fifty years ago, would have gone unnoticed in the small oilfield town in Northern New Mexico. His clothes were dusty and dry, his leather cowboy hat worn and cracked from the relentless beating of the sun's rays. He strolled slowly and deliberately down Main Street, appearing dull and lifeless, like he had stepped out of an old painting, clashing with the more colorful world that surrounded him. People stared at the man; he paid them no mind.

He stopped for a moment at the corner of Main and Fourth Streets surrounded by old buildings that appeared to have all been built at different times exhibiting inconsistent themes of architecture. The buildings were of varied heights made with a strange combination of stucco, brick and stone, as diverse as snowflakes. He was looking for the town's first modern micro-brewery, assuming, like the other buildings, it would have some kind of fake antique sign written in calligraphy, something nearly impossible for him to read. After a few frustrating minutes of wandering, he was standing only a few yards from the entrance. He entered the brewery and was greeted by a young hostess who led him to the bar. The antique building had obviously received a modern makeover. The old oak hardwood floors, the pressed brass ceiling, and the exposed brick walls seemed dormant, overtaken by computer cash registers and ergonomically correct tables and chairs.

He sat at the bar and waited as the overweight greasy bartender tried fervently to strike up a conversation with a very young attractive girl who sat at the bar. She gained entrance by using the fake identification card she kept in the back pocket of her tight blue jeans. She deliberately refused to look at the bartender as he talked to her and seemed interested only in his leaving her alone. The old man tried to keep his mind focused on the task at hand but could not help observing the pair to see if the bartender really thought he could interest the girl. He wore a white T-shirt badly stained with grease and other unidentifiable stains which was several sizes too small for his build. His large belly hung suspended by his overworked belt, the white flesh and hair of his belly exposed below the shirt he pulled at repeatedly as if some miracle would occur and the shirt would remain stretched far enough down to hide his girth. The fat bartender shrugged his shoulder, more experienced in being turned down than flipping burgers, and came to the old man.

"What can I get you?" he asked, pulling again at his shirt.

"You can get me the owner," the old man replied.

The bartender smirked at the old man. "Can I tell him your name?"

"He won't know it, but he'll want to," the old man replied.

The bartender swaggered due to his weight as he walked away, stopping again to attempt more small talk with the girl. After another failed attempt, he climbed a long wooden stairway in the back of the brewery and went through a heavy wooden door at the top. The old man waited patiently as the bartender came back down the stairs followed by a man in his twenties dressed in very clean, pressed clothing. The owner stopped at every table on his way to the front of the brewery. He shook customers' hands and greeted them as he passed. When he reached the bar, he picked up a half-empty bowl of pretzels that sat on the bar-top and filled it up, winking at the girl sitting at the bar as he placed the pretzels in front of her. She blushed, trying unsuccessfully to fight off an awkward smile.

The owner approached the old man, smiling. "What can I do for you, sir?"

"Is there somewhere we can go to talk?" the old man asked.

"I guess that depends on who you are and what you want to talk about," the owner replied.

"Most who know me, which there are few these days, call me Lowery," the old man said.

"Nice to meet you, Lowery. My name is Sam Hewett," the owner said, shaking the old man's hand.

"What I want to talk about may not be good barstool talk with so many ears around," the old man said.

"Well, I know most everyone in here and they won't pay mind to …."

The old man cleared his throat and looked the young owner in the eyes. "When you were in high school you worked for a radio station and came across a tape recording of an interview with a Navy pilot…"

Sam interrupted the man, "Let's go up to my office?" Sam turned to the bartender and patted him on the back as he walked past him. Curious if anyone had heard the old man's statement, Sam looked around. Satisfied that his customers seemed busy in conversation, he moved away from behind the bar and motioned for Lowery to follow him.

The smell of yeast and hops got progressively stronger as the two climbed the long wooden stairway at the end of the brewery. Lowery stopped for a moment at the top of the stairs to catch his breath as Sam opened the large wooden door. Once through the door, Lowery could see a storage room filled with bags of yeast, hops, and beer bottles. At one end of the room was a large metal desk that reminded Lowery of the one he sat behind for years when he was in the Army.

Sam grabbed two beers from a large cooling unit and handed one to Lowery. He pulled his chair from behind the large metal desk and placed it next to another chair that sat in front of the desk. Sam sat down and opened his beer. The old man pressed his thumb against the top of his beer until it shot off in a loud pop and smiled as he took off his hat and placed it in on his knee.

"I am 78 years old. I'm too damn tired and frankly don't have the time to play grab-ass. Do you still have the tape?" Lowery said before he took a long drink of his beer.

Sam wondered if the old man's mouth and tongue would soak the beer in before he could swallow. Everything about the man seemed dry. Even his eyes seemed waterless, slowly closing as the cold beer ran down his throat.

Sam sauntered to the desk and opened a drawer with a broken lock. He thumbed through some items, and without much delay, pulled a single cassette tape from the drawer. He sat back down in front of Lowery and handed the tape to him.

Lowery's eyes widened, and Sam wondered what thoughts were dancing through his head. He knew what Lowery was looking for but doubted that the tape would provide any help. Sam could almost feel the old man's excitement vibrating through him. A feeling Sam had not experienced in years began again to simmer.

"You know, about every other year a man comes into this town looking for it, but nobody has found a thing," Sam said.

The old man took one last look at the tape before sliding it into the chest pocket of his shirt. "I suppose I'd be just like the rest if I told you that I was the one who was going to find it. That I had spent a life time collecting information and knowledge so that one day I would be the one. I suppose I'm not the first to receive a copy of the tape from you, and not the first to say I'll be the one who'll know what to listen for."

The old man finished his beer and stood. "I'm not really sure what I would do with it if I found it. Not sure I care. The fact that this tape exists, and the fact that it's still out there, well ... what the hell else is there to do?"

Sam sat drinking his beer as the old man approached the stairs. Suddenly the old man stopped, locked the door, and turned around holding a gun. Sam's immediate thoughts were not of terror but of disbelief. He could see the pistol was small, black, and had a silencer attached to the barrel. This last fact is what bothered him the most. It would not be the first time a man pulled a gun after asking for the tape, but this gun ... it was out of place. He would have expected a large 45 six shooter to match the whole cowboy appearance, or that maybe the old man would have lunged at him with an old rusty bowie knife, but to have him pull a black semi-automatic with a silencer? This bothered him.

The old man cleared his throat. "I also suppose I'd not be aware of the other tape. That this tape, without the other, is as useless as my ex-wife."

"I don't...."

The old man raised the pistol. "I hope you don't take me as a bluffer, son. Like I said, I didn't come here to play grab-ass."

The desk was only a few feet away from Sam. He wondered if he could dive behind the desk and get his 35 out of the drawer. The man would fire, Sam knew he was not a bluffer, but maybe he would miss. He only had to miss once then the desk would protect him long enough to get his gun.

Then what? Sam thought. *I would be pinned down behind the desk by an old dusty cowboy with a silencer.*

"Look," Sam said, calculating when the best time to dive for the desk, "I have it somewhere else."

"Where?"

"It's in a safe deposit box at the community bank," Sam said, feeling his muscles twitch as if to send him airborne but willing the shaking to stop as he noticed the gun aimed between his eyes. He began to sweat.

"That won't do, son. That won't do."

The man began calculating a new plan in his head.

The gun lowered to Sam's chest, and without giving it anymore thought, he dove for the desk. Sam felt two quick snaps of pain before he hit the floor, their location not immediately known. Sam knew he'd been hit, but was terrified when he felt that he had been hit twice. The realization of how fast the old man was made his hands tremble uncontrollably. He had no time. Sam quickly reached for a drawer to the desk, and once opened, grasped his 35 with his right hand. He felt pain in his left arm, and his right calf began to throb. He could feel that his left arm was broken as he tried to use it to press himself into an upright position. Quickly, he spun into a sitting position and pressed his back against the desk. He raised the gun above the top of the desk to show the old man that he had one, and quickly lowered it so his hand did not get shot off.

"Son-bitch," the old man said. "You stupid, son-bitch."

"Get the fuck out of here, old man. Get the fuck out before I blast your goddamn ass off!" Sam grimaced with pain. He felt himself begin to black out and shook his head trying to stop it. If he passed out, he was dead.

The old man chuckled and reached for an old bar stool. He wiped the seat of the stool off with his sleeve and slowly propped himself onto it. He exhaled deeply as he took his hat off again, placing it back on his knee.

The old man pulled a Marlboro Red out of his pocket and lit it with a book of matches he had taken from the bar downstairs. "There was this girl I met in Weslaco, Texas. She was something. At first, ya know, all I wanted was to knock the plum fur off of her. But, she could smile. Oh, could she smile."

Sam turned his leg a bit so that he could see the wound to his calf. He was bleeding badly from the two wounds, and he knew that he had to get to the hospital soon. He wondered if the old man somehow knew this and was stalling, waiting for him to die. Sam promised himself that he would not simply sit against the desk and allow himself to bleed to death. It would be a gun fight. If the old man wanted the O.K. Corral, he'd get it.

"I bet you'd be hard pressed to find a man who loved a woman more, my friend. Hard pressed." The old man ran his fingers along a small feather that was held to his hat by a leather hat band. "She's gone, Sam. Gone from this earth, son. The only time I will see her again is when I die. That is, of course, if the book is true."

The old man heard Sam grunt with pain. He knew the boy would make his move soon.

"So, Sam, I don't think it bothers me too much for a young man to tell me that he is going to shoot my ass off. If you cut me down, Sam, good for you. You must know this though - all your suspicions about me are true. You won't win. You can't win."

"So what … I just bleed to death?" Sam nearly coughed but fought the urge.

"Over a goddamned tape? You want to die over a tape that leads to something that can't be found? What are you … stuck on stupid?"

Sam grimaced again. He was running out of time, and the old man was right. He had made a promise to protect the tapes, but to give his life? He wanted the tapes destroyed. He didn't see the reason for keeping the tapes around, but the others... they wanted to keep them. No, he wanted to keep the tapes...or did he? His mind was cloudy and losing focus.

"Okay," Sam said and pulled a key out of his pocket.

A key slid skidding along the ground toward Lowery from under the desk.

"Behind the painting behind you is a safe. The key unlocks the dial, and the combination is 34-2-17. The tape is in the safe."

The old man put on his hat and slid himself off the barstool. He thought briefly that Sam might try and shoot him in the back as he was unlocking the safe, but dismissed the thought, doubting Sam had the strength. The safe opened, revealing stacks of cash, some legal documents and a single cassette tape. Lowery took only the tape and closed the safe.

"On my way out, I'll tell one of your girls to call an ambulance."

Sam felt himself very close to unconsciousness. He bit his bottom lip hoping to keep himself awake. "Don't go after it, Lowery. You don't want to find it."

The old man smiled and slid the small silencer between his belt and the small of his back. "And why is that?"

Sam knew he did not have the strength to explain. "Just don't…." Sam's head fell limp as darkness overcame him.

CHAPTER 2

Michael O'Brian sat alone at the bar. He tried to appear pre-occupied and uninterested in his surroundings as he tapped his fake wedding ring on the side of his crystal martini glass. He had told his colleagues at the law firm that the tap of the wedding ring had to be very calculated, not too loud, but loud enough so that the women would notice it; however, they should not know that he intended them to notice it. He proclaimed that women were far more immoral than men. A man without a wedding ring was not desirable, but a married man must have something that would keep a girl around. Most men in these types of clubs did not care if a woman was married or not, but the women seemed to be attracted more to the committed. He happily allowed the women to take advantage of his fake and apparently troubled marriage.

Michael squinted his eyes through his fake eyeglasses at a black, plastic clock with hands made out of glass that hung above the bar. His friend was already fifteen minutes late; this was expected. The new trendy club was very exclusive, and he doubted his friend was on the short list. He took a moment to see if he knew anyone in the bar, and noticed that some of the people were familiar, but none he could call by name. All the clubs in New York City would most likely be packed at eleven o'clock on Saturday night but this one would be especially so - this was *the* new club. A must-go for all the who's who of the New York elite, and although *the* club may change over time, he assumed that the elite do not. Soon this club would be yesterday's hot-spot, and he, along with most of the others in the bar that night, would snub their noses at anyone who would even suggest such a lame atmosphere.

He took advantage of his friend's tardiness and began to engage in one of his favorite pastimes - people watching. Not knowing exactly why he enjoyed the art so much, he knew he was quite good at it. He remembered many occasions at parties in high school when he spent nearly the entire night in the background refusing to participate in gossip, to get into a fight, or even trying to land a girl. He found himself curious if anyone in the bar could break free from the unimportant, lifeless form they were taking in his mind. Despite the large crowd of people all gathered under the same roof, he was simply an observer like someone in an empty movie theater watching animated figures move about the club engaging in conversation and insignificant acts of movement for his simple entertainment. Perhaps someone else in the bar would be looking at him, and dismissing him in the same flippant way that he did to all those around him. It was a joke, really, the same routine with the same dense people, all trying their best to sound unique and interesting to the other hollow souls.

Michael surveyed the new club, wondering if all of these kinds of clubs are designed by the same uninspired architect. The bar was placed in the middle, and all the track lighting, the Italian marble countertops, and even the obvious display of an unlimited supply of top shelf liquor could not hide the fact that the two snotty bartenders could never serve the hundreds of people surrounding the bar. Just as the difficulty of getting a drink was expected, so too were the private tables that always found themselves in the supposedly desirable locations in the club. If one had the means to purchase a bottle of vodka for the same price as a monthly mortgage payment, the table was yours. Between these same tables, and those like Michael who were lucky enough to get a spot at the bar, was the chaotic stream of peasants who were squished so tightly together that their movements were not voluntary but rather caused by the current of the crowd. Spilled martinis would be the ruin of many items of clothing that night.

His tardy friend was named Bill Bryant and was the only man in New York whom Michael called a friend. They both knew that they were nothing more than acquaintances, but they were good compliments for each other when it was time to go trolling for women. Michael was a tall slender man with thick blond hair worn intentionally messy which was inconsistent with his very clean shaven face and slick hand-tailored Japanese suit. He took great pride in his appearance and was not modest at all when it came to showing his wealth, which was the reason he wore the Japanese designer that night. Certainly he would agree that Versace or Armani made very nice and expensive suits, but for the super sophisticated, or those wishing to appear so, there was the even more desirable Japanese suits. Most girls in the bar that night may not know the difference, but those girls would not be worth his time. The Italian suits were his casual wear, and this was a special night.

Bill, on the other hand, was a stocky brunette who cared little for clothing. He liked to dump his money on expensive cars and vacations, which never made any sense to Michael. You cannot bring your Ferrari into a bar, and nobody gives a shit if you have been to Italy eight times. His appearance was boring, and if it were not for Michael, they both admitted that no women would believe that he was a lawyer at one of the largest, most prestigious law firms in the country. He looked more like a linebacker for the New York Giants than a lawyer. In fact, they had used the roll a few times in the past; convincing young college girls that Michael was a sports agent in town to land a big deal for the dim-witted linebacker.

Together they covered all their bets. If a woman were looking for a stocky strong guy, she could pursue Bill. If she wanted a wealthy, elite model-type, she had Michael. It was rare that the two would hit the town and find themselves going home alone, and despite the numerous tales they created, they both knew they were not friends.

Michael had already decided on the story for the night. They would use one of Michael's favorites. He would be the owner of a medium-sized computer company based in San Francisco who was in town to visit an old college buddy. He discovered recently that his fake wife was having an affair, and despite her demands for wanting to make the marriage work and go to counseling, he just didn't know if he had it in him. She continuously proclaimed her love for him, and knew that she betrayed the best man she had ever met. If he told her he wanted a divorce, she may even kill herself.

The story never failed. It gave the woman everything she was looking for, drama, for one, but also the voice of a woman that demonstrated how wonderful this loyal hard-working man really was. Bill got lots of credit as well. He was a good man who would do anything for his friend, and despite the fact that he had a deadline at work and would have to pull an all-nighter, he was the guy who puts his life on hold when there is a friend in need.

The Versace suit Michael noticed Bill wearing as he approached was a good choice.

"Sorry, man," Bill said as he sat at an empty bar stool next to Michael, "cost me an extra c-note to get through the line."

Michael smiled and motioned with his fake wedding finger in the direction of two girls who sat at a table close to the bar. One was a slender blond wearing a tight white halter-top dress and stiletto heels. The shoes were expensive. Being able to notice this was knowledge that Michael took seriously and spent a great deal of time learning. The heels, he noted, would make her calves look defined, but he could see that her legs would look good in any shoe, chiseled from hours spent on a stair-stepper and the latest kick-boxing aerobics class. She laughed and smiled as she pretended to be interested in her friend's stories, but with each flick of her hair, Michael noticed her noticing him. She would be easy. Out on the town on a rich father's credit card trying to find a man who would keep her accustomed to the lifestyle she was brought up in before being told by daddy that she had to start thinking about her future.

The other girl would be impossible for Michael to land but perfect for Bill. She wore non-designer clothes, tan pants and a cotton sweater, and showed signs of being a bit annoyed by the trendy bar. She also had blond hair, but it was very short and messy, not unlike Michael's hair. Despite her counterpart pressing her thick red lipstick lips to an apple martini, she drank a dark English lager without a trace of make-up on her face. This was obviously not her choice of clubs. She would rather be watching the Yankees' game at the sports bar down the street, and would be cheering loudly as Alex Rodriquez just hit a home run in the 4th inning, something Michael just learned as he received a text message on his phone from the sports updater website.

"Very nice," Bill said and then ordered a tonic water and lime. He promised Michael that he would not drink the next night out since the last time he passed out at the bar and ruined a very good set-up.

"How's my contract coming?" Bill said loud enough for the girls to hear.

Michael waited to make sure the girls were not looking in their direction and nodded his head. Once he noticed the dress looking his way, he took off his fake wedding ring and slammed it on the bar. Bill did not miss a beat. Bill let the wedding ring sit on the bar, knowing that he was not to touch it or hand it back. It was a prop that would drive the women crazy. Their heads would be filled with curiosity. Would he put the ring back on? Why did he take it off? What if it gets knocked off the bar and he loses it? The curiosity that killed the cat. The cats would be slain.

"She loves you, Paul," Bill said using the name that meant Bill's roommate Paul was at Bill's apartment, and it would have to be either Michael's or a hotel.

"How long have I known you?" Michael replied, trying his best to secure the academy award.

'Long' was code for Long Island. This meant that Michael had the keys to one of the partner's beach houses in Long Island. Bill's next drink order would have caffeine in it, as he knew it would be a late night.

"Long enough to know you and Trish were meant to be together," Bill responded and grimaced, not knowing why he picked such a strange name.

Michael fought the urge to smile, and raised his drink to his mouth in case one slipped out. The dress had looked at the ring several times. This was good. Michael shot the girl a flirtatious glance as she turned her body slightly toward them, crossing her legs and pointing the tip of her expensive shoes in their direction. Body language was everything. Michael was sent to a seven-day seminar called, "Understanding the Unspoken Language in a Deposition" which was taught by psychologists on reading body language. He knew from his studies that when a person positions himself to face another, he is either interested in what the person is saying, or what he might have to offer. She wanted Michael to notice her shoes, which meant she wanted Michael to notice her. He would look at her just long enough for her to catch his eye, and then look away as if he were slightly embarrassed and ashamed that he had potentially evil thoughts.

Michael had heard the term, "it's like shooting fish in a barrel," but he did not like the analogy. He liked to call it a gimmie, like if Tiger Woods had a six-inch putt. There was no need to actually make him go through the motions, but to make it official, he had to hit the shot. In Michael's mind it was a gimmie at this point. The night was unfolding as it should.....until.

Bill saw her first, but in hopes that she would pass the table by, he did not alert Michael to the beast. She was a heavy-set woman wearing a suede mini skirt that could hardly be called mini in all practical circumstances. She had jet black hair, short on one side, and long on the other, combed, not brushed, tightly against her pudgy pale face. She paused for a moment at the edge of the table, taking a moment as she hammered away at the keys on her Blackberry, and both Michael and Bill prayed she would pass on by. But, as she sat next to the dress, Michael reached for the ring.

"What are you doing?" Bill asked quietly.

"It's over," Michael said.

"We can do it! No, it's not over," Bill protested.

Michael lowered his voice, "It's over and you know it. No two men on this planet have ever been successful in penetrating a threesome when mean bitch is the third wheel."

"Just wait a second," Bill pleaded, and breaking all code, turned to look directly at the table to survey the situation.

"Stop it," Michael said. "We need to move on."

"It can be done," Bill said turning back toward Michael.

"No, it can't," Michael said.

"Why?"

Michael exhaled deeply, "Our game clock is winding down and you want me to waste what we have left explaining the situation?"

Bill motioned for the bartender and ordered a double Crown and Coke.

"Oblige me," Bill said.

"Look, there's nothing we can say, or do, that will get past the ugly mean bitch. They have their own code, and it's simple. Since they have a miserable existence and never get hit on by any guys, they will shoot down any attempts that any guy makes toward the hot friends. That is clubbing 101. It wouldn't matter if Brad Pitt approached one of those girls, mean bitch will shoot him down bad!"

"We're pros," Bill added.

"Doesn't matter," Michael said putting his fake wedding ring back on his finger. "There's only one way to take down mean bitch. You have to have a guy who's willing to jump on the grenade. A guy who's willing to show full attention to mean bitch so one of the hot girls can be busted away. The hot girls have a life. They are somewhat internally happy, and if they go home alone, it's fine. Unusual, but fine. Mean bitch always goes home alone, and she is sick and tired of going out with her hot friends and nobody showing any interest in her."

"So," Bill said taking a drink of his double Crown and Coke, "you want me to jump on the grenade?"

"No, we need to move on. We can find a better opportunity. A two-some we can do, even a four-some or more, but a threesome, no way."

Bill turned to look at the girls again. He spent a considerable amount of time looking at mean bitch. She was not bad looking. A bit heavy, and with a chip on her shoulder, but a chip that Bill felt a strange desire to knock off.

"I'll jump on the grenade … I'm a trooper," Bill said with a strange smile.

Michael laughed and placed his hand on Bill's shoulder. He knew Bill was not kidding, which is why he always asked him to go out trolling. Bill had slept with the ugliest and prettiest girls Michael had ever seen. When he once asked

Bill why he slept with anything, Bill responded, "If you hit the entire spectrum, you'll never have expectations and never feel ashamed. Complacency, my friend. Complacency."

Michael noticed his Blackberry was vibrating on the bar, and looked to see if it was a score update on the Yankees game. He saw that it was an incoming call from a 505 area code. He picked up the phone and placed his thumb on the receive button, but realized it was far too loud in the bar to hear a conversation and put his phone back down on the bar.

"Who was that?" Bill asked. "Perhaps a grenade jumper?"

"No," Michael said still looking at his phone waiting for the prompt that would tell him a voicemail was sent. "It was a 505 number calling me. That is New Mexico."

"New Mexico?" Bill responded. "Foreign client?"

"No," Michael replied, speaking with a sarcastic impression of an idiot. "New Mexico is a state ... part of the United States. It has running water and everything down there. It's great!"

Bill lowered his eyebrows with a strange expression on his face.

"That's where I grew up," Michael added.

"I didn't know you grew up in Mexico," Bill said.

"New..." Michael said. "New Mexico. Not a lot different from the old one, but new all the same."

"You know any twosomes in New Mexico?"

"No," Michael said.

Bill turned back to look at the three girls, and Michael glanced at his phone wondering who would have called him, and why. It had been over ten years since he had been back to New Mexico to attend his mother's funeral. The anger he had felt as he looked around the densely populated church, and more noticeably the absence of the friends he had when he was growing up, had faded over the years but was not something that had ever left him completely. He carried his disgust for the town around with him, locked tightly in the leather briefcase of his mind. When he left his mother's funeral, he found himself looking at his phone, expecting at least a phone call from a former friend. He did this often at first, and as the first year passed, he consciously noticed that he was checking his phone for that call less frequently, until the desire slowly faded away as an afterthought. Yet, like the eye in the Tell Tale Heart, his cell phone sat quietly beside him with a rhythmic blinking red light that informed him that he had a voicemail from New Mexico.

"Hey!" Bill said, startling Michael. "Are you going to call that number back, or stare at your phone all night? We have business to attend to."

"I don't need to call back. They left a voicemail."

"Ok," Bill replied. "Then put that thing away and let's get busy. That is, of course, unless you think it may be important."

"It's not important. Don't really care for anyone back there anymore."

CHAPTER 3

To the north of Farmington, New Mexico are towering green mountains that start the southern border of the Rocky Mountains appearing statuesque, spreading northward into Colorado. In all other directions the land is very barren desert with sparse population. If one were suspended miles above the town, a small patch of green with rivers cutting into the landscape would be visible; a small town seeming to sprout from an endless horizon of dirt like a desert flower with no natural reason for existing. On the bank of the Animas River, tucked deep within the cottonwood trees and Russian olives, was an estate.

Sam Hewitt inherited his small estate when his parents died in a helicopter crash while on a skiing trip near Telluride, Colorado. At the time of their death, Sam was unemployed and living in a small run-down apartment with two roommates who had few more worries in the world than a ten-year-old boy on summer vacation. It was not unusual when one noticed devastation at the tragic loss of a parent, but what was unusual was a persistent refusal to inherit anything from his parents. Sam would look as if someone were trying to feed him a spoonful of poison anytime anyone would ask him why he kept avoiding showing up to the probate of his parents' estate. He would not accept his parents' demise, and felt as though he were celebrating it if he were somehow to prosper. But, as sorrow turned to dark depression, and with the help of drugs and alcohol – and the need to support the habit – he eventually succumbed to the inheritance and quickly found himself a millionaire, living, or existing as many would say, in the large estate his parents built and that he despised. The only money he had spent was to open his bar which was his escape from the estate and an excuse to support his drinking.

Visitors to the estate were not unusual. Sam would leave the doors unlocked and the keys in his vast collection of vehicles for anyone who wanted to come in and enjoy the estate. However, as he watched an infomercial on Shop-TV, barely sober enough to understand what was going on around him, a very unlikely guest arrived.

Kevin Day was a close friend of Sam's growing up. They attended school together from kindergarten through high school graduation. They would go to great lengths to ensure that they had the same classes, played the same sports, and spent most of their free time hanging out together. However, as time went on they slowly drifted apart. With Kevin's leaving town to try and make a living in professional baseball, and Sam's leaving reality to try and drown out sorrow with vices, they slowly lost touch and eventually complete knowledge of each other's lives. Even when Kevin returned to town after his accident, he made no effort to contact his friend. They were not boys anymore, and what once they had in common was gone.

Kevin did not have to knock when he came to Sam's door because it was open, displaying the large family room that was twice the size of Kevin's entire house. He paused for a moment as he reached the entryway. The large flat-screen TV was the source of the very loud ramblings Kevin had heard as he exited his car near the guest house. Sam was lying sprawled out on a large red sectional couch, and Kevin could not tell if he was awake or not. He expected Sam to be unconscious as he approached his limp former friend.

Sam turned his head slowly to look at him, and then reached for a remote control. He spent a few moments pushing buttons on the remote then set it down and picked up another one. It would have been comical had Kevin not known into what bad shape his former friend had fallen. Just as Kevin started toward the TV in hopes of finding an off switch, the TV turned off and the large room echoed with silence.

"Kev-n," Sam slurred. "What the hell did I do to deserve your visit?"

Kevin shook his head and went to the kitchen. He opened a large double-door refrigerator and took out a bottle of water and an energy drink called "Lightening Bolt." When he returned to where Sam had been lying, he was surprised to see that he was gone.

"Out here," Sam yelled from a patio opposite the front door.

Kevin exited to the patio and handed the water and the energy drink to Sam. Sam took the drinks from Kevin and sat them next to a clear drink Kevin assumed was some type of vodka mixture.

"Sorry, dude. I was almost asleep," Sam said, sounding a bit better.

"Didn't mean to come unannounced, but I don't know your phone number."

"You know you don't have to announce yourself in my house," Sam said, taking a sip of his clear drink.

Sam sat on a large wooden bench suspended by chains attached to the ceiling of the patio. He patted the bench, inviting his friend to sit next to him. Kevin smiled, picked up the water Sam was obviously not going to drink, and sat on a wicker chair adjacent to the swing-bench.

"Just wanted to check on you," Kevin said.

"Thanks, bud. I'm doing pretty well. I was wondering when you'd come by here. It's been awhile."

Kevin unscrewed the lid to the bottled water and Sam noticed something written on Kevin's wrist.

"What's that on your wrist?" Sam asked.

Kevin turned his wrist as if he didn't know what Sam was talking about, displaying the word "Proverbs."

"It's a tattoo," Kevin replied.

"Proverbs?" Sam asked.

"Yes. It's a book in the Bible."

"I know it's a book in the Bible. Why did you tattoo it on your wrist?"

Kevin thought for a moment of ignoring the question, but figured he couldn't avoid it. "There's some pretty sound knowledge in Proverbs. I wanted it on my wrist to remind me of a few things. You know I'm religious."

Even though he was well under the influence of strong pain killers and alcohol, Sam knew that he should probably leave the subject alone. Kevin was known for his short temper, his strong religious beliefs, but also for his desire to keep people out of his business. Sam also knew that the reason for the tattoo on his wrist was not just because of the convenience of being able to see the word Proverbs all the time, but also to help cover up the scar that once disfigured his wrist. To anyone who did not know Kevin, it appeared that he had tried to take his own life judging the large scar, but Sam was with him that night: The night Kevin's father came home drunk and told him that he was a pussy if he could not take a knife away from a drunken bum. Kevin took the knife away from his father, and when his father was released from prison, Kevin's wounds had healed into scars. Despite knowing all this, Sam found himself intrigued by the tattoo.

A cool breeze blew from the south, over the river, and Sam reached for a throw blanket as if he were snuggling up for a bedtime story.

"What is it about Proverbs?" Sam asked.

"I came to talk about your situation, not my tattoo." Kevin was feeling a bit annoyed as he glanced at his wrist. He came to talk to his troubled friend and did not want Sam to try and make the conversation about him and his tattoo. He had brought his Bible and intended to talk to Sam about a few things he thought might help, so beginning with Proverbs may not be a bad start.

"I know," Sam replied, "please, I'm curious. We have all night to talk about me."

"You should read Proverbs sometime. It's like taking a lesson from a wise man."

Sam smiled, "You know I'm not really that into religion. In fact, not at all."

"Well, if you want to understand it, you have to read it. There's too much in there to explain easily. Besides, you don't have to believe in anything to read a book about knowledge."

Sam smiled, "But you don't even go to church. You never did, and I hear you still refuse."

Kevin returned the smile as if he were pitched a lob-ball in a home run derby. "You can find that reason in Mathew 6:5. There are good passages about hypocrites that preach and act holy in synagogues and on street corners to look righteous to everyone while the truly righteous actually follow the word of God in private. I have yet to find a church that was no more than a place for men to try and exploit their own self interests, gossip, and contradict nearly everything that the Bible and God are all about."

"That's very interesting," Sam said as he pulled a prescription bottle out of his pocket. "I actually want to read Proverbs now."

"You sure you should take one of those?" Kevin asked. "It looks as though you've been drinking. Not sure you're supposed to take things like that and drink."

"Nonsense," Sam said and struggled to read the bottle. "It says right here, 'alcohol may intensify the effects of the medication.' I'm just helping the pill do its work, buddy."

As Sam struggled to get a pill out of the bottle, Kevin admired the estate. They were sitting outside on a large covered patio with numerous pieces of outdoor furniture and stone statues that Kevin assumed were purchased by Sam's parents. The bushes, trees, and grass were badly neglected, and Kevin doubted that Sam had done a minute of yard work since he moved into the house. The house, however, was very clean. That was probably due to the handy work of a maid, or maids. The marble floors were clean and polished, the maple cabinets freshly oiled, and everything seemed to be placed away making the house look more like a large hotel than someone's home. What caught Kevin's attention the most was that there were no pictures of any family members or friends. It was a beautiful house but it was cold and empty.

"You seeing anyone?" Kevin asked.

"Not really," Sam replied and swallowed the second pill with his vodka drink. "Dated one for about a year, but all she wanted to do was bitch at me. I couldn't take it anymore."

Kevin picked up the book that sat on his lap. It was an old Bible with a worn leather cover. On the back side of the Bible the leather was black and cracking, delicate like old parchment. The black burnt leather was a result of Kevin's father holding the Bible over a candle at dinner one night. He told Kevin that if the Bible were true that certainly they would hear the cries of all the prophets demanding that he stop, or witness the will of God blow out the candle. The corners had teeth marks where it had been badly chewed when Kevin's father used it to play tug-of-war with their dog, Killer. Despite the damage and worthless appearance of the book, Sam knew that this was Kevin's most valuable possession. It was worth far more to him than anything else in the world.

Kevin flipped through some pages and handed the Bible to Sam.

"You've tried this before," Sam said as he waved away the Bible.

"Just read, Proverbs 21:19," Kevin replied.

Sam reluctantly took the Bible, and after spending a few moments trying to find the verse and focus on the words, he cleared his throat of toxins, and read, "It is better to live alone in the desert than with a crabby, complaining wife."

Sam read the verse again, and when he was done, he smiled and read it a third time to himself.

"Let's go to the tattoo parlor," Sam said. "I want 'Proverbs 21:19' tattooed on my chest."

"See," Kevin said, "pretty good knowledge in there."

"Wicked knowledge," Sam added. "I thought this thing was filled with stories about Jesus and stuff."

"It is, but there's a lot more in that book about life and how to live."

"Interesting God-talk," Sam said and handed the book back to Kevin. "What does it say about Vodka and pain pills?"

Kevin doubted that Sam would ever again read a verse in the Bible. He would prefer that Sam try and live a life of righteousness, but he would make no more overt efforts to try and lead him down that path. He despised the church-goers who spent tireless hours trying to convert people to their religion. Kevin believed that they did this simply to increase the church's revenues so they could purchase bigger facilities, repave parking lots, or increase the salaries of the church's staff. He considered himself a man of God and did not need a congregation of people to tell him that he was. His relationship with God was personal, and the most private and cherished part of his life.

"Did they find the man who shot you?" Kevin asked.

"No, still looking," Sam replied shrugging his shoulders. "There's three hundred miles of desert around us. The guy is gone."

"Why'd he do it?"

Sam shifted uneasily in his swing-bench, and despite being well on his way to la-la land, he could not cover-up the fact that he was hiding something. "I don't know. He was just a crazy old man looking for money, I guess."

"He didn't take your money."

Sam opened a wicker box that sat on a large glass table and pulled out a bottle of vodka. He poured the vodka into his glass, managing to spill only a bit of it, and settled back into his swing.

"Quite the little detective," Sam said.

"Sam, I was your friend…I am your friend. I've been your friend for a very long time, and despite our losing touch for some time, I love you, and would never do anything to hurt you. This conversation is between us."

"You love me?" Sam replied. "You really love me? Oh, Kevin, I knew it. Let's consummate."

Kevin failed to see the humor and took off his hat, rubbing his hand over his light brown buzzed hair. As he did this, Sam knew that Kevin was getting irritated. Kevin was one guy that Sam knew you did not want to piss off. Kevin was tense as the well-defined muscles in his arms were tight; the veins bulged under his skin. Sam told people that Kevin was the one guy he would never want to fight, and if Kevin ever wanted to fight him, he would turn and run as fast as he could. Sam knew, however, that he stood no chance of outrunning Kevin.

"He came for the tapes," Sam said, slumping his head back to rest it on the bench.

"The tapes?" Kevin asked.

"I wanted to wait until Michael got here to tell you guys."

"What tapes?" Kevin asked.

"The tapes, Kevin. He came for the tapes, and got them both."

Kevin sat his worn Bible on his lap and leaned forward, placing his elbows on the table. "We destroyed the tapes."

"No, *we* didn't."

Kevin stood and began to pace around the patio. Sam thought for a moment that his friend looked like a cage-fighter pumping himself up before a big fight. He wondered if he had taken enough painkillers so that he would not feel the damage Kevin may inflict on him at any moment.

"You told us that you destroyed the tapes!"

"I lied," Sam replied, shrugging.

"You fucking promised you'd destroy the tapes!"

"I lied," Sam replied, shrugging again. "That's not very nice language for a Bible reader. Blasphemy."

"That's not what blasphemy means. Fuck is not even in the Bible," Kevin replied, "You Fuck!"

If it were not for the promise Kevin made his wife, he would have yanked the scrawny druggie out of his swing, grabbed him by his girly long brown hair, and beat his face into the concrete until he was unconscious; a promise he would not have had to make less than a year ago if his wife had not bailed him out of jail for the third time. He wondered if there were exceptions to the rule. Surely she would whisper in his ear, 'kick that son-of-a-bitch around this house until the sun comes up.' But, she did not know about the tapes. She did not know about anything.

"I couldn't destroy them," Sam said.

"Why?"

"I couldn't destroy them because ..." Sam stopped himself from speaking. The truth was they reminded him of a life before his parents died. They reminded him of a better life filled with few worries, friends, and parents.

Kevin finished his water bottle and filled it half full of Sam's vodka. "Because why?" He asked.

"I guess they remind me of no worries," Sam replied.

"No worries," Kevin said. "Those tapes remind you of no worries? You must be crazy."

"I'm not talking about that night," Sam replied. "Do you remember the trip? Do you remember what it felt like to all be together on an adventure?"

"It was not an adventure … it was hell."

"Well, it ended in hell," Sam replied. "But that was just a small part of it. It was the last time I can remember being happy. The last time I had something to live for."

Kevin sat.

"Michael is coming?" Kevin asked.

"Yes, soon, I think."

"I'm going home," Kevin said. "You've opened a closet full of skeletons. How the hell am I supposed to explain this to Cindy?"

"You don't," Sam said.

Kevin shook his head and left his friend to fall deeper into intoxication.

"Besides, Cindy would understand," Sam slurred. "Remember, she was the one who found you in the maintenance shed at the baseball field when you were released by the Dodgers. What I heard is that you had all but given up on life. Drinking malt liquor every night, and sleeping on garden hoses and bags of manure."

"Word spreads in small towns," Kevin said. "Guess we both tried to escape into a bottle."

"Yep," Sam replied. "Cindy's friend told me that you were drunk and crying, telling her that you ruined your arm, and had nothing to live for. Cindy told you that you still had one good arm, and why not learn to pitch left handed. Girls are funny."

"Yes they are," Kevin said. "Look, I don't want her to know anything about this, okay?"

"*No problemo*," Sam said.

CHAPTER 4

In the center of the small town was a baseball field that most minor league players would envy. Once a year, the town hosted the high school aged summer league national championship, otherwise known as the Connie Mack World Series. Its success led to the metamorphosis of the nicest baseball field within five hundred miles.

Despite Michael's having not visited the park in a decade, he felt the comfort of home as he sat down in the bleachers. As the high school baseball team practiced, he absorbed all the wonders of the pristine park. The double-decker outfield wall covered with billboards displaying the names of oilfield related companies, the double cut grass that was second only to Augusta, the high-rise bleachers that could hold half the population of the town, and the dirt. The dirt was the most important characteristic of a baseball park to an infielder, and since Michael played second base, he treated the infield dirt as if it were a cherished heirloom that needed precise, detailed cleaning on a frequent basis. He was always aware of the importance of the dirt having few rocks. Rocks caused bad hops and black eyes.

He had spent many hours walking the infield dirt picking out the occasional rock and tossing it off the field. It was his second home, and he had to keep it clean. He promised himself that when the team had all left the park, he would walk the infield looking for rocks.

A young coach exited the dugout to talk to a boy playing first base. He talked to the first-baseman for a moment, occasionally pointing around the infield giving what appeared to be instructions. Michael immediately recognized the coach. His name was Kevin Day, and to Michael, he looked exactly the same as he did in high school.

Kevin Day was once a friend of Michael's, but when Kevin struck Michael out in the Connie Mack World Series in front of the entire town, they became rivals. They had seen each other only a hand full of times since the strike-out, and each time the tension lessened but never subsided.

Despite his animosity toward Kevin, Michael was very upset when he heard the news of Kevin's injury. Once every five years or so, despite baseball being the only thing for young boys to do, the town produced only one true professional quality player. Kevin was one of them. At the age of eighteen Kevin could throw a fastball in the high nineties and a low-eighties breaking ball that led to his being accused of throwing spitballs on numerous occasions.

After high school, Kevin signed immediately with the Dodgers and played minor league for only two years before being called up to the majors. Only twenty games into his first year, Kevin threw the pitch that would end his career as a professional baseball player. All the years of being the best, and being the one who was always called on to throw, finally caught up to Kevin. When the doctor told him his tendons would never heal completely, and that he will probably never be able to throw again, Kevin wept.

Kevin had known only one thing in life - baseball. He did not collect baseball cards and could not tell you many professional players' names; he simply loved to play the game. Michael had seen Kevin on numerous occasions sitting in the dugout with a blank stare on his face, smelling the pine tar on his bat or the oil in his glove. He absorbed everything about the game. Michael wondered if you said the word baseball to Kevin if he would actually salivate. Michael believed that when Kevin played the game, he could actually taste it.

Michael, on the other hand, never had a chance with a baseball career. Not unlike most of the other boys in the town, he was good, but not in the same league as Kevin. Michael did not spend his time in the dugout smelling the pine tar on his bat. He spent his time looking into the bleachers trying to decide which girl he was going to put the moves on after the game.

Kevin waved in a boy from centerfield to home plate so the kid could practice hitting. Michael sat in the bleachers in a lounging position with his elbows on the bench seat behind him. He sat up and leaned forward as Kevin grabbed a bag of baseballs and stood on the pitching mound.

Kevin reached into the bag pulling out a baseball with his left hand. He took the mound, set up like a left handed pitcher, and stood there waiting for the boy to get ready in the batter's box. Once the boy was ready, Kevin rocked back, and as if he was a natural lefty, he threw the baseball toward home plate.

As the ball made its way to the plate, Michael whispered to himself, "Jesus Christ."

Michael sat in the bleachers for over an hour, amazed every time Kevin rocked back and pitched the ball left-handed to the boys. He could see in Kevin's eyes that this was not batting practice. Kevin was in a world of his own. Despite not striking the boys out, or even trying for that matter, he existed not in a practice, but rather some fantasy game. The bleachers would be full of cheering fans. At bat next would be the feared all-star from Somewhere, USA who made a living devouring the likes of pitchers such as Kevin Day. He was the conductor of the game. It all began and ended with him. The smell of pine tar and freshly cut grass was thick now.

When practice was over, Michael approached as the last high school player had left the dugout. As Michael entered the dugout, Kevin was stuffing baseball bats into a large bag. Just as Michael began to speak to Kevin, a skinny baseball player ran into the dugout and approached Kevin.

The last time Michael had watched Kevin pitch was the night they set off for the location the tapes disclosed. He remembered sitting in the stands, anxiously awaiting Kevin's inevitable winning of the game so that they could start their camping trip, and despite Kevin throwing a near perfect game and a no hitter, Michael spent every inning wishing Kevin would somehow speed things up. This time he found himself watching with no anticipation, but rather enjoying every pitch despite it just being batting practice.

"Hey, coach," the young kid said, "the boys were telling me that you used to throw an overhand screw ball in high school. They said that it was unhittable. Is that true?"

"I did throw that pitch," Kevin said as he continued to stuff equipment into the large duffle bags. "I don't know if it was unhittable. This guy right here took it out of this park a few times."

The young boy looked at Michael, uninterested in him. "Could you teach me to throw that pitch?"

"I could," Kevin replied. "But I won't. That pitch cost me my career, and I promised myself never to teach it to anyone. Sorry. Stick to fastballs and traditional curves, and you will have a long career."

"I need a pitch like that or I won't have a career in baseball, coach," the young boy added.

"Sorry," Kevin said. "I won't teach anyone that pitch."

The young boy shrugged his shoulders and ran out of the dugout.

"I bet you feel pretty good that I'm nothing but a small-town coach," Kevin said, not looking at Michael.

"Jesus, how the hell did you teach yourself to pitch left-handed?" Michael asked.

Kevin sat exhausted on the bench in the dugout, wiped his forehead, and responded, "It was just batting practice."

"I bet you were throwing mid-seventies,"

Kevin looked up to Michael for the first time. "What do you want, Michael?"

"Look, I've gotten over the strike-out thing. You were better, fuck it. I'm not mad at you anymore," Michael said.

"Not mad at me anymore. Hmmm. Well then, I guess I should forget about your trying to screw my girlfriend? I guess your trying to strike me out with her should be forgotten too."

Michael smiled and walked closer to Kevin. "Trust me dude, you are better off since you left her. She is one crazy bitch."

"I didn't think so," Kevin said.

"I didn't either. She came to my house a few days later and went totally psycho on me. Broke all my shit. She even broke my Wade Boggs bat. What kinda sick bitch breaks a Wade Boggs bat?"

Kevin smiled. "Whatever, man. Like you said, fuck it. Why ya in town?"

Kevin knew exactly why Michael had come to town. His belligerent friend had told him about the tapes, and told him that Michael was on his way to town. What he really wanted to know is what Michael thought he could add to the situation.

"Sam," Michael said. "I'm here for Sam."

Kevin stood and pulled the draw string to the large bat bag and threw it over his left shoulder. He walked up the steps of the dug out and threw the bag onto a stack of several other bags. Kevin looked around the baseball field, and Michael wondered if Kevin was thinking of baseball or Sam.

"Sam is fine. In fact, we're meeting at the Drip Tank tonight for some beers."

Michael walked up the steps of the dug out and stood next to Kevin. "The tapes? Where are the tapes?"

"Gone," Kevin said and handed two of the bags to Michael. Kevin picked up the remaining three and went to his truck.

It was getting dark when Michael pulled into the parking lot of a local dive, the Drip Tank Bar and Cantina. He quickly pulled into a parking spot in the back area of the parking lot, hoping that nobody had seen him driving the airport rental sedan. He was a successful tax attorney in New York City and did not want anyone who might know him thinking for a moment that he was back living in the small town, some poor loser driving a four door Chevy sedan.

He knew he would stand out in the bar. He doubted that anyone else was wearing Versace. But, after all, he should stand out. He was not a small town oil field redneck who drank light beer in blue jeans and spit chewing tobacco on his cowboy boots. He had overcome obstacles that he doubted anyone in the town had ever even dared to try. Certainly his friends would feel jealous when he informed them of his position in life. He already knew Kevin did. He truly felt bad for Kevin's bad luck, but he could not help feeling amazed that Kevin had taught himself how to throw left-handed. Michael carried a combination of pride and jealousy toward his friend.

Kevin and Sam sat at a small table toward the back of the bar as Michael came their way. Michael did stand out in the bar. He appeared timid and nervous as he searched around the bar while approaching his friends. He was frail and sickly, not the baseball player Kevin and Sam remembered from high school. The funny silk clothes, Kevin thought, would probably get Michael into a fight tonight. Kevin pondered whether he would help Michael or let him try and fight it out himself. He would decide later.

Michael sat at the table with an awkward smile on his face. "Pretty crowded tonight," he said looking around at the people at the bar. Somewhere in New York right now, Bill would be at a night club surrounded by upscale people with money and purpose, and probably working on landing a girl or two. Michael, on the other hand, was surrounded by guys in T-shirts with oil stains, and girls in tight blue jeans who probably did not care who they slept with that night.

The Drip Tank Bar and Cantina was filthy. Aside from the occasional wipe of the countertop with a dirty wet cloth, the bar was disgusting. The floor was made of wood that was stained with spilled beer and chew spit, and despite all the windows being open, the bar smelled like stale beer and musty mold. Unlike the upscale bars Michael had become accustomed to, this bar had only a small selection of alcohol, mostly beer and cheap whiskey. Behind the bar were a few neon beer lights that buzzed and flickered, their plastic broken and cracked. Standing below the lights behind the bar was a fat lady with a cigarette hanging out of her mouth who spent more time talking to the men at the bar than she did pouring drinks for the customers.

Sam reached across the table with his good arm and patted Michael on the shoulder, "wet t-shirt night."

Michael rolled his eyes, "Of course."

Kevin took a drink of his beer and looked out over the crowd. "You still like girls, don't you?"

"I do. It's just kind of tacky…"

"I think the girls that do it like to show off their stuff. I think the guys that watch, like to see their stuff. No harm, no foul." Sam said.

The waitress came to the table and asked for their orders. Kevin ordered another pitcher of Bud Light and Michael tried to ask for a wine list. Before the waitress could even begin to laugh, Michael quickly asked for a glass to share the pitcher.

"So, how have you guys been doing?" Michael asked.

Sam pointed to his arm that rested against his chest held in a sling and smiled. "I was doing better until I got shot in the arm and leg."

"I bet you were," Michael said.

Kevin added, "Doing better? Hell, Sam owns his own bar, lives in a large estate, and gets a different girl every night. I'd say he's doing better than better..."

"Better than better. Wow, Sam. Good for you." Michael said, putting his elbows on the table as if he were letting them in on a secret. "I am a tax lawyer for the largest tax firm in New York City. I was the youngest...."

"You're a bean counter?" Kevin asked.

"No, I am not an accountant. I am a lawyer who deals with tax issues."

Kevin took a long drink of his beer. "Sorry, dude."

"Sorry?" Michael responded. "It's one of the most prestigious law firms in the country, and one of the hardest jobs to get."

"Hey, I didn't mean to get you mad," Kevin said, "I was just thinking how boring that ... must ... never mind. Hey, here comes our pitcher."

What an ignorant hick, Michael thought. *He is so stupid he can't even comprehend what I have accomplished.*

Sam grabbed the pitcher and poured himself a beer. "Who cares about our jobs, what else you been up to, Michael?"

Michael knew the question Sam asked was not intended to be insulting, but as he pondered his answer he realized there was nothing else he had done. He was prepared to talk about NYU Law School, his landing the big job with the firm, and a few important cases. That is what he expected them to ask him. That is what he expected them to be interested in. Michael took a sip of his beer and smiled, trying to portray to his former friends that he was up to all sorts of stuff that was too wild and obscene for their virgin ears to hear.

After several pitchers of beer and some reminiscing about some high school stories, Sam brought up what they had all been trying to delay. "What do we do?" Sam said nearly sobering up as the words left his mouth.

Michael finished his beer and poured another glass from the pitcher as he said, "I told you guys we should have gotten rid of those fucking tapes."

Sam looked at Kevin as if to get concurrence on reaching across the table and ripping Michael's head off. "You've got to be joking. I held the goddamn things over the campfire and you stopped me."

Kevin looked at Michael, "It's true. You wanted to keep them."

"Bullshit," Michael replied. "Why would I want to keep those things around? Besides, Sam, you told us that you destroyed the tapes."

"Well, I didn't," Sam said. "And, why the fuck did you want to keep those things around?

Kevin interrupted, "Forget all that. We didn't destroy them and now some crazy old man has them. That's our problem."

"Is it?" Sam replied. "I know we promised each other that we'd stop anyone from finding it, but it's been over ten years now. What can happen?"

Michael shook his head in disbelief. "I live in New York. I should be the least concerned, but certainly you guys remember the warning."

Kevin raised his finger to his lips telling his friends to be quiet. "We should probably finish this somewhere else, guys."

Sam replied softly, "The warning? What about Jake?"

"We don't know a thing about Jake….."

Kevin stood quickly from the table, "Alright, that's enough. I'm going home, and I suggest you two do the same. We'll talk more later."

CHAPTER 5

The three men sat around the campfire somewhere in the desolate desert where the New Mexico and Arizona border runs undefined on the vast Navajo reservation. Despite the three being related either through blood or marriage, they were oddly unknown to each other. They sat quietly, absorbing the sounds and scenery around them as the sun began to set. Their camp was on a small ridge in a valley with a dried-out river wash of cracked red clay below them, and above them a hill covered in pinon and cedar trees. In both directions of the valley were numerous sandstone formations that protruded from the red sand appearing as though nature had created statues and pillars to decorate the landscape.

Lowery sat comfortably with his back against a sandstone rock as he pulled an old leather pouch from his coat pocket. The young man to Lowery's right placed a few cedar logs on the crackling fire, trying to watch Lowery out of the corner of his eye. Lowery opened the pouch, pulled out a bud of marijuana and placed the bud in a hand-carved pipe. The young man was filled with disbelief as Lowery smoked the marijuana like nobody he had ever seen. In college the young man smoked plenty of weed, but it was always done with a long inhale and then a pause as the lungs absorbed the smoke. Lowery smoked casually as if marijuana were as easily obtainable as tobacco.

The young man looked across the fire in the direction of the old Navajo man to see if he had any reaction to Lowery's casual smoking. The Navajo man seemed to pay no attention to anything except the flames that danced around the cedar logs in the fire pit. The youth looked at Lowery and smiled.

"I feel kind of weird asking this of my grandfather, but could I have a draw off that?" he said.

Lowery looked at his grandson returning the smile, "If you have something to smoke it out of, you can help yourself, but I'm not going to swap spit with you."

The young man began to look around for something to smoke out of when the Navajo man chuckled. The Navajo man pulled a small figurine out of his pocket and began to mumble something in a language the young man recognized as Navajo. After failing to think of a way to smoke his grandfather's marijuana, the young man opened a beer.

"Did you listen to the tapes?" the young man asked.

"I did," Lowery replied. "It was what we expected. The pilot gave approximate locations of the radar hit."

"Approximate?" the young man replied.

"The pilot was flying visual, not on instruments. He was probably just out of flight school. I think he was more interested in getting out of the La Plata Mountains than relaying the exact coordinates of what he'd seen."

The young man shook his head, "Not paying attention to such a significant find?"

Lowery took a long draw of his pipe. "He probably didn't know what he may have found. Not many people know, and the ones who do, don't believe. It's like an ocean of sand out there. There are some canyons, mesas, a few mountains to the west, but for the most part, not many landmarks. From a jet I suppose it would simply look like a brown blur."

The young man smirked as if to dismiss the ignorant. A navy pilot must have had some formal education, perhaps not as advanced as his magna cum laude honors in anthropology from Harvard, but some education. How hard could it be to figure out what he was picking up on radar? This all seemed interesting to the young man, but the truth was that his grandfather searched for something entirely different than what he was searching for. He thought of telling this to his grandfather, but decided against it. What was really important was that they both had the same goal - to find the site.

The young man's name was Sheldon. When his estranged grandfather, whom he called Lowery, sent him a letter asking him to go on this trip, he thought it was odd. He had spent his entire childhood only knowing Lowery's name, but despite his demands to meet him, he never did, until now. But what was even stranger about the trip, and especially the current situation, was that he was with Lowery, his father's father, and Ernest Benally, a medicine man, and also his mother's father.

Sheldon's father told him that Lowery did not want to meet him because he was busy searching for gold and treasure, but Sheldon knew that Lowery did not approve of his son marrying a Navajo. The truth, Sheldon believed, was his hick, wealthy grandfather did not approve of his father's wife, and resented his half-blooded grandson. Sheldon concluded this when Lowery replied to a note his father sent telling him of the good news about Sheldon getting into Harvard. Sheldon found his grandfather's reply stating that if he was asked for money to pay for the education, he would send five dollars: the exact amount that Lowery claimed the education was worth.

Sheldon was very excited and proud to attend Harvard, but was secretly more proud that he was attending the school on a full-ride scholarship. The faculty on the admission board also expressed their excitement for Sheldon to attend the college. Sheldon had stated in his application for admission that he was concerned that the Navajo part of his heritage was slowly slipping away to the modern development that surrounded the reservation. He did not hesitate to include his concern that the Navajo rarely spoke their native language anymore, and that most of the ancient traditions were being replaced by Christianity and technology. Sheldon was a unique applicant who actually had the desire to learn and research, and was not using Harvard as a stepping stone to get into Harvard Law School.

Sheldon asked, "Is it close to where we thought it was?"

"Sheldon?" the old Navajo man interrupted, placing a small figurine of a man on a small rock near the fire pit.

"Yes?" Sheldon replied.

"You are called Sheldon?" the Navajo man asked.

"Yes," Sheldon replied thinking how odd the question was. He had met his maternal grandfather on many occasions. "You don't remember me, Ernest?"

"I am not Ernest right now. I am your medicine man. I knew your father well," the medicine man said.

The medicine man pulled another figurine out of a bag that appeared to Sheldon to be the figure of a coyote. He looked at the medicine man oddly, wondering why he could not call him Ernest. He wondered why Ernest was wearing blue jeans, Velcro tennis shoes, and a cowboy shirt with snaps as buttons if he were supposed to be a medicine man that night. Sheldon would have had an easier time consenting to the medicine man story if Ernest had dressed in some kind of traditional Navajo clothing, worn feathers, or done something to indicate that he truly was a medicine man.

The medicine man studied the coyote for a moment and spoke softly. "Yes, I knew your father well. He was a very good man."

"Yes, he was." Sheldon replied.

"It wasn't long ago that we sat around a fire, as we do now. He was looking for the treasure you look for now. I will tell you what I told him. The spirits do not favor your journey."

"Do you know what happened to him?" Sheldon asked.

Lowery looked at Sheldon, scorning him with his expression. "You don't know what you ask. We're not here to ask those questions, Sheldon. We're here to be given guidance."

Sheldon looked briefly into his grandfather's eyes and quickly looked away into the fire. His grandfather's eyes were penetrating, not unlike his father's. He knew little about his grandfather. Most of his relationship with him was through stories his father would tell him. Of all the things he could recall about his grandfather there were very few certainties. He knew his grandfather was a hard-working oilfield hand who managed to acquire a few rigs, and eventually a small fortune. After selling his claims, he had disappeared into the Caribbean Sea searching for lost treasures. Occasionally, Sheldon would receive a coin or other small objects in the mail. These were never accompanied by a letter or photograph, but the small treasures Sheldon received told their own stories of adventure.

The only other thing he believed was that Sheldon's father always feared Lowery. The wealth that his grandfather had obtained never changed his disposition as being a roughneck oilfield hand. He was not a man for fooling around. All business, and he was the boss.

"Sorry, Lowery." Sheldon said, choosing not to call him grandfather.

The medicine man placed the coyote next to the other figurine and closed his eyes. He began to move his hands slowly in a figure eight pattern with his palms facing the fire. The smoke appeared to move obediently with the medicine man's hands. The fire seemed to gain strength, the flames getting larger.

"Your path will be crossed by the Skinwalker," the medicine man said continuing the motion with his hands.

Sheldon looked at his grandfather, concerned. "Why the Skinwalker?"

The medicine man stopped the motion of his hands and placed them on his knees. He exhaled deeply and looked up at Sheldon. "I do not like this journey."

"We must take this journey," Lowery added.

"You don't have to, but I know you will," the medicine man replied.

"What do you know of the Skinwalker?" Sheldon asked again. He had heard a few tales about Skinwalkers growing up, and on a few occasions found himself researching them in the Harvard library as a pastime.

The medicine man looked around the desert, his senses heightened. The fire caused the dark shadows of the surrounding cedar trees to dance across the desert sand. The sandstone walls of the canyon appeared to shift and move as if they were alive. "Not a good place to talk about Skinwalkers."

"Why?" Sheldon asked.

"If you speak of them, they come. We're in their territory. This wouldn't be a good place for the talk." The medicine man looked up at the sky and watched as the low clouds raced across the night's sky.

"He should know," Lowery said.

The medicine man exhaled as if confirming that Sheldon did need to know. He stalled for a moment, hoping a different question would be asked. None was asked. "The Skinwalkers are neither man nor animal. In ancient times, some of the witch doctors started practicing a very dark magic. They learned many abilities that were not of this world. They became evil witches that preyed on the souls of the good people."

The medicine man picked up the coyote figurine and wiped some dust away from its claws. "They learned the practice of turning their bodies into the shapes of wolves, coyotes … other animals. But, no matter how hard the Skinwalker tried this magic, he could not turn into the animal all the way. A

Skinwalker takes the shape of an unnatural animal. Not all wolf, but not all man. The prints they leave in the sand look like wolf prints, but are not wolf prints. They can howl, but the sound echoes bad magic like a demon's scream."

"They turn into animals?" Sheldon asked. He was now recalling from his study a small section he had read regarding the Navajo and their evil witches. He read a few studies about Skinwalkers, but did not recall any information about shapeshifting into animals.

The medicine man continued, "Yes, but their eyes. Their eyes are red, always red. They are red as elk blood, and follow you like the demon ghost. The Skinwalkers move swiftly like the wind and hide in the shadows of the earth."

Sheldon began to look around as the medicine man did. His mind began to play tricks on him as he thought he saw various animals moving in the dancing shadows of the cedar trees.

Suddenly the medicine man stopped talking.

"What's wrong," Lowery asked.

"No more talk," the medicine man said very softly. His faced turned pale white, looking as if he was going to faint. He lowered his head and starred duly into the fire. "They are here. They are listening."

Sheldon sat his beer down and slowly put his hand on the butt of the revolver that rested between his belt and his right hip. Without moving his head, his eyes darted around looking into the shadows behind the medicine man.

"What should we do," Sheldon asked whispering.

"No more talk." The medicine man replied not moving his lips.

Lowery pulled a small bag out of his pocket and began to untie the ropes that kept it tightly closed.

"No," the medicine man said. "That is fake magic. It will do nothing."

Lowery put the bag down and nodded, confirming that he was passing authority to the medicine man to take charge of the situation. If the medicine man did not succeed soon, and proved himself to simply be Ernest, Lowery would pull the submachine gun out of his knapsack and take care of all the nearby animals.

The medicine man stood slowly. His face seemed to lose all the remaining color that it had. He appeared dead as he turned to face the cluster of trees just fifty feet behind him. A slight breeze blew through the canyon giving the fire new strength sending glowing ashes in a twisting flight high into the darkening sky. The shadow of the medicine man stretched along the desert ground, losing itself into the trees and bushes he was now facing.

The medicine man walked toward the trees mumbling again in Navajo. Sheldon and Lowery sat motionless as the man seemed to be consumed by the shadows. The fire crackled and the flames blew in the light wind shifting the shadows of the trees. When the shadows returned to where they once were, he was gone.

After sitting in silence for a few minutes, Sheldon whispered, "What do we do?"

Lowery emptied his pipe into the fire and refilled it with another bud of marijuana. He sat calmly smoking his pipe reflecting on what had just happened.

"We do nothing," Lowery finally replied.

"Is he coming back?" Sheldon asked with his hand still firmly on the butt of his gun.

"I don't know," Lowery said, smoking his pipe.

"Do you know him very well?" Sheldon asked.

"Today is the first time I have met him," Lowery responded.

"I have known him my entire life, but feel like I know nothing about him," Sheldon said. "I think he was just as ashamed of his daughter marrying a white man as you were ashamed about Dad marrying a Navajo."

"I never gave a shit," Lowery said. Sheldon sat quietly as Lowery smoked his pipe.

CHAPTER 6

Jake Blackman had called the meeting that was to be held in the bottom floor of the local library, but he was late. Kevin was also late, but Michael and Sam knew he would probably not show because he was at baseball practice getting ready for the big trip to visit several baseball scouts this up-coming weekend. Michael was hoping that Kevin would not show due to Kevin's embarrassing him by striking him out in front of the entire town less than a week ago. If it were not for Sam's tape, and what they thought they may have stumbled across, he would be just fine never talking to Kevin again. Just as Michael began to speak to adjourn the meeting, Kevin walked down the old concrete stairs and toward their table.

"Shit," Michael said just above a whisper.

"Relax," Sam said rising to pat Kevin on the back. "How's the arm, Kev?"

"Never been better, has it Michael?" Kevin said sitting at the table.

"Suck it, Kevin. I've taken you deep plenty of times over the years."

"But not the last time," Kevin said.

"Wow, Kevin. Not very good sportsmanship," Sam added.

Kevin shook his head, "How's trying to screw your friend's girlfriend for sportsmanship?"

"She hasn't been your girlfriend for two weeks," Michael said.

"Tell you what, Michael, how about you and I go outside and settle this."

Michael stood from the table. "Sounds like a good idea," Michael said, knowing it was a very bad idea as Kevin would probably destroy him in a matter of seconds.

Kevin stood staring into Michael's eyes when a voice came from the copy room, "Sit down. You guys need to hear what I have found out."

"Fuck that," Kevin said, "You guys go have fun. I am not going anywhere with that piece of shit."

"Yes you will," Jake Blackmon said, exiting the copy room with a stack of books and papers. "When you hear what I've discovered, you'll go."

"Bullshit," Kevin said and started walking back toward the stairs.

"Seventeen tons of gold," Jake said.

Kevin stopped and stared dumfounded at Jake. Michael quickly sat down at the table, seeming oblivious to what had just transpired. Sam smiled as if he knew what Jake was going to say and took a seat next to Michael. "Seventeen tons, Kevin," Jake added.

"Bullshit," Kevin said and walked up the stairs and out of sight.

Jake sat the books and paper on the table and took a seat next to his friends. "He'll be with us. I'll talk to him."

"Screw him," Michael said.

"He's in," Sam said.

"We're all in, or I will destroy this stuff and forget about it," Jake added.

"Fine, but fuck that guy," Michael said.

Michael and Sam sat anxiously as Jake shuffled papers trying to figure out how to start telling his friends what he had discovered. Jake was a peculiar guy, and nobody quite understood why Michael, Sam and Kevin were friends with him. They did not know the answer to that question either. They had known him since they were in grade school, and it was just a comfortable fit that was always around. He was skinny and badly dressed, unlike the rest of them, and despite all three of them being smart, Jake was intelligent. He told them what he had learned.

~

April 15, 1933

Rafael Borega sat on the side of a large stone fountain and waited patiently as one of his servants crushed mint leaves to put in Rafael's Mojito. He sat calmly with a strange smile on his face as he took long draws on his Cuban cigar, his hairy chest visible through his sweat drenched silk shirt. With him in the courtyard were the gentlemen he had invited to the meeting. Leon Trabuco, a wealthy miner, a rancher and a fortune inheritor from the Cihuahua District of Mexico. Also there were Ricardo Artega and Carlos Sepulvada both wealthy ranchers, but Rafael knew very little about their past or more importantly, their trustworthiness. This, however, would not be a problem because he had already decided to put Trabuco in charge of the shipment. The last man he had invited was not going to be an investor, but rather an advisor. His name was

Professor Morado from the Mexican economical counsel of the University of Mexico.

Aside from a few chosen details, only Professor Morado knew exactly what Rafael's plan was. The rest of the men did not specifically know why he had called the unusual meeting, but they sat patiently in the already hot April sun. Cuenavaca, Mexico was the location of Rafael's estate, so the calling of the meeting there was not unusual. It was, however, for most of the attendants, quite inconvenient. It was Rafael who called the meeting, though, and one did not miss a meeting such as this.

Rafael had decided to wait until he was handed his Mojito to begin speaking. He often used a cocktail as a prop in his investment pitches, stirring the drink to add suspense or taking a drink of the cocktail to pause, giving him time to think of a response to a question. When he was handed the cold drink he took a very small sip and took a moment to enjoy the flavors of lime and mint. What he was about to tell his new friends would taste far more sweet.

"I have just returned from Washington, D.C. where I have had the luxury of obtaining very valuable information," Rafael said stirring his Mojito. "The economic condition of the United States is still very grim. It appears that there is little hope amongst their government and citizens as they remain in a very dark depression."

Professor Morado nodded in agreement.

Rafael continued. "President Roosevelt has come up with a plan to strengthen the U.S. dollar. He is proposing a law to get their country off the gold standard by forbidding the hording of gold by U.S. citizens. The law will require that all gold be traded for an inflated amount of U.S. currency. Obviously, once this law is passed, they will not allow the importation of more gold from foreign countries."

"The implications of such a law…," Professor Morado began to say and looked to Rafael to confirm that it was alright for him to begin speaking. He saw that Rafael was pleased and raised his Mojito to his lips to take a sip. "The implications of such a law would mean the value of gold in the United States will rise significantly. Right now we can buy gold for about $15 U.S. dollars an ounce. I have predicted that the trade-in price, after the law is passed, will be close to $40 U.S. dollars an ounce."

Trabuco stood from a wooden chair and began to pace around the group. There was a moment of silence as Trabuco strolled aimlessly around the courtyard; the only sound was his turtle-skinned boots clacking against the stone ground. Trabuco was mysterious to all the men except Rafael Borego, who had known Trabuco for many years, referring to him as a friend. To the others, he was merely a tall handsome man who wore expensive clothes and who moved methodically, as if he were always calculating a situation. They did not trust him, but they did trust Rafael, and second guessing Rafael's judgment was not something that any of the men wanted to do.

Trabuco spoke softly as though he were simply thinking the words, his mouth betraying his choice to keep them secret. He said, "More than double my return in, how long?"

Professor Morado cleared his throat and responded. "We believe the economic condition is so drastic that President Roosevelt will pass the law within the year. So, more than double your investment in less than one year."

Trabuco nodded his head and raised his hand to his chin. Rafael felt the excitement tingle in him, allowing his new friends to plot the scheme in their heads. He wanted the plan to succeed without having to use much effort in persuading them. The plan was working. It also helped to know that Trabuco was sitting on tons of gold already. Information Rafael had paid a handsome fee to obtain.

Ricardo Artega unbuttoned part of his very large shirt allowing his body to receive some of the slight breeze that came through the courtyard. "How would we get the gold into the United States, and how would we sell it?"

Trabuco did not allow Rafael to respond. This was his project now, a fact that Rafael would soon realize. "We sell the gold to the U.S. government. The Professor already said that they are going to exchange currency for gold at an inflated price. Your other question is more valid."

Rafael smiled behind his Mojito, pleased that this would soon be Trabuco's hassle. Rafael would be an investor, and wanted nothing to do with the actual smuggling of the gold. He had enough problems with law enforcement and did not need to venture into another project.

"I'll find a way," Trabuco said. "I've been looking for a way to move some gold I've had for quite some time. This meeting, Rafael, was very good timing for me."

Professor Morado adjusted his eyeglasses and spoke softly, "I must say, however, that there is an element of risk. The law may not pass. The gold could be confiscated. The price may not increase enough to cover the cost of transportation."

"There's no such thing as an investment without risk," Carlos Sepulvada added.

"I'll take the risk," Trabuco said.

All nodded in agreement, and Rafael sat his Mojito down next to him on the fountain. He could not have hoped for the meeting to go more smoothly.

"We should pool our money, and I'll buy as much gold as possible," Rafael said. "I have many connections, and the price will be better if we are buying larger quantities."

Again the men nodded.

"Trabuco will be in charge of transporting and storing the gold in the United States," Rafael continued. "Professor Morado will monitor the passing of the law and the gold market.

Rafael clasped his hands together and held them against his lips, his elbows resting on his knees. He took a long exaggerated breath and let his eyes drift amongst the men. "Gentlemen," he said, pausing moments after the men were silent, the only sound was the water of the fountain splashing at his back. "I'm very serious when I say this; all gold is bad. All gold has some curse on it."

The men listened without comment or expression.

"I'm sure we have all heard stories of pirate gold, cursed gold, and unfortunate events that happened to people who found cursed gold," he continued. "Some of these stories I believe to be true. Some, of course, I don't believe. Trabuco is of full Spanish descent, so he'd probably agree with me that we must be careful. Make sure you all know the origin of all the gold you place in our horde. Does anyone have any bad gold?"

All the men, except Trabuco shook there heads.

Trabuco remembered the Bull. It was fifteen years prior when he found it in a market in Matamoras, Mexico. He strolled through a market drinking a beer, uninterested in the shops that all had the same assortment of cheap blankets, bullwhips, sombreros, and poorly crafted guitars. As the merchants started packing up their merchandise, he stopped and spoke with an old lady who held out a blanket for him to touch. The blanket was similar to all the blankets in the market, in fact the same blanket hung only feet away at a booth adjacent to them. It was not the blanket that made him stop, but rather an unusual wooden bull that rested on a table behind where she was sitting.

The Bull stood five inches high and seven inches long. It was carved out of a dark wood with black nails securing the legs into place. It was a crude carving, and like a small child's drawing, resembling the form of a bull just enough for an observer to ascertain what the artist had intended. The legs were not equal in length, the carving marks on its back visible and jagged, and the tail was broken.

Despite the plain, deformed appearance of the Bull, Trabuco found himself infatuated with the item. He asked the lady how much she would take for the Bull. She ignored his question and attempted to place the blanket in Trabuco's hands. He waved it away and pointed to the Bull. He explained that he wanted the Bull, and asked again how much she would take for it. She turned away from Trabuco and placed the blanket over the Bull and told him that it was not for sale.

He spent the next several minutes telling her he would pay her a fair price. The woman was poor, and Trabuco was dismayed that she would not entertain any of his offers. Eventually, Trabuco shrugged his shoulders and continued to stroll throughout the market.

The next day, Trabuco woke with his mind fixated on the Bull. He knew it was unsightly and probably carved by a young boy who had no talent, but he could not stop his mind from thinking about it. Later that day, he found himself in the market again, searching for the woman and her Bull. He had a pocket full of money and carried a sack full of various valuable items. When he found the lady, he tried again to purchase the Bull, offering her all the money he had on him. When that failed, he tried to offer her valuable pots, a glass bull created by a very talented artist, a few paintings, and a collection of expensive silk scarves. She refused them all.

The following week Trabuco would return with more money and items, and what started as fascination of the Bull was now an obsession. He would wake in the middle of the night thinking of the Bull, when he slept, he dreamt of it. He cleared the top of a mahogany table in his house and longed for the day he could display his Bull. However, every day he visited the woman she refused all of his offers, her aggravation steadily increasing at his every attempt.

On the eleventh day he returned to her booth, he carried an empty sack. He waited patiently behind her hidden by hanging blankets and ponchos. When she left her booth holding a blanket to follow a man who seemed interested in possibly buying the blanket, he reached into her booth and took the Bull. He quickly put it into the sack and jostled his way through the crowd, vowing to never return to the market.

The Bull sat on his table for over a year until one day he picked up the malformed carving and examined it. It was unusually heavy. When he inspected the belly of the Bull he noticed a tiny slit in the wood. Taking a small stiletto, he pushed the tip of the blade into the gap, heard a click, and a hatch sprung open. Inside it were a handful of gold coins. He spread the coins on the table and admired them, wondering why the woman, who was obviously very poor, did not use the gold to help take her out of the lifestyle she was living.

He spent only a moment observing the gold, and put the gold back into the belly of the Bull, pressing the hatch closed. He heard the clicking sound again, and satisfied that it was securely locked into place, he sat it back on the table. He sat in a chair a few feet away from the Bull and spent hours studying and experiencing the presence of his Bull.

Trabuco never opened the bull again.

"Trabuco?" Rafael asked, startling Trabuco from his daydream. "No bad gold."

Trabuco shrugged his shoulders and said, "No bad gold."

"Good," Rafael replied. "We will all meet again soon. Please stay as long as you like, and enjoy my estate. I know the journey here was tiresome."

~

August 1933

Trabuco was awakened by one of his employees as they drove down a dirt road in his new Dodge pick-up truck. Not yet awake, he thought they were facing difficulty crossing the border, but as his mind cleared he realized they had been in the United States for days now. The border crossing in Nogales, Arizona was in fact very uneventful.

"Wake up, sir," the worker said in English, distorted by a thick Mexican accent.

Trabuco opened his eyes and saw that it was dusk. He did not know where they were, but the landscape looked very familiar to his hometown and surrounding area.

"Where are we?" Trabuco said sitting upright in his seat.

"We are very close to Shiprock, New Mexico," the worker responded.

"I believe Shiprock is less than an hour from a town called Farmington. We should go to Farmington and get a hotel room. It is bigger, and we will have an easier time getting supplies."

"I'll wake you when we get there," the worker said, realizing that Trabuco had already closed his eyes and fallen back asleep.

When they arrived in Farmington, Trabuco immediately knew that he was correct in choosing this area of the country to hide his gold. It was a small town surrounded by desert to the south and west with Mountain ranges to the north. More importantly, it bordered the Indian reservation, which he knew through his research was declared a sovereign nation.

"That hotel looks fine," Trabuco said pointing to a rundown motel.

"*Bueno*," the worker said pulling the truck into the parking lot.

"English, Carlos. Remember, we speak English here," Trabuco demanded.

"Sorry, sir," the worker said parking the truck near the front office.

After checking into the motel room, Trabuco showered and changed into some clean clothes. The exhausted worker sat on one of the twin beds waiting for his next set of instructions. Trabuco told him to shower and then to sleep, and that he would return in time for dinner.

Trabuco was pleased by how easily they had passed through customs in Nogales, but did not like the amount of time it took them to drive all the way to the Four Corners area of the United States. The Border, he thought, may not be friendly in months to come. He had decided during the drive that the gold would have to be flown into the United States. It would take a plane that could carry such a load and one that would not draw attention. While passing through the smaller towns during the drive he consistently saw crop dusters flying low to the ground. He had decided that a crop duster would be the transport. He was there to find a plane and a pilot.

Trabuco knew that he could not begin his search by telling someone that he needed a plane and a pilot to smuggle gold across the Mexican/U.S. border. He was a foreigner and would raise enough suspicion without such conversation. He had decided that he would tell people that he was a wealthy land owner from Mexico that was looking for a pilot to take him and his business associates on hunting trips.

He received more strange stares than information from the people he spoke to until he met a farmer in a feed store. The farmer told Trabuco that he used a company out of Salt Lake City, Utah to dust his crops, and they always sent a pilot by the name of William C. Elliot. Trabuco's interest grew when he learned from the farmer that Elliot's plane had a large enough fuel capacity to make the trip from Salt Lake City to Farmington, as well as a very heavy pay load so that it could dust many crops in one day without having to land for restocking.

Setting up a meeting with Elliot was not difficult, as it was still crop-dusting season. The farmer told Trabuco that he would tell Elliot to go to the Flap Jack Diner after he was done with his daily work.

Trabuco spent the rest of the day in the library and county assessor's office looking over maps and literature about the surrounding area. He needed to create a landing strip that would not raise suspicion, and most importantly, a place to hide the gold. He made notes of roads and possible locations and decided that he would visit several spots before making a final decision.

Later that day he went alone to the Diner. He had given the worker some pocket money to go get something to eat, instructing him not to get too drunk and to stay out of trouble. He doubted that Carlos could prevent either from happening.

Trabuco sat in a booth in the diner sipping on coffee and waiting patiently. He did not ask the farmer what time the 'daily work' was done, so he decided he would wait until well after dark.

The moment Elliot walked into the Diner, Trabuco knew it was him. He wore a leather flight jacket and light brown pants. Aside from a scarf, goggles and a leather helmet, he dressed like all the pilots Trabuco had seen in photographs. It took Elliot about the same amount of time to notice Trabuco. The farmer had told him to go to the diner to speak with a Mexican businessman about a possible job. Trabuco was the only person that looked even remotely like a Mexican businessman.

Elliot winked at one of the waitresses as he walked toward Trabuco's table. The waitress nodded and asked him if he wanted the usual. He told her that he did as he slid into the seat across from Trabuco.

"Hunting trips - why do you need a pilot for hunting trips?" the pilot said, taking off his jacket.

"The season is almost over, William," Trabuco said. "What do you do during the off season?"

"Nobody calls me William," Elliot said, "not even my mother."

The waitress came to the table and sat a tall glass of lemonade in front of Elliot and kissed him on the cheek. "Here you go, William," she said and walked away.

William smiled and took a sip of his lemonade. "You can call me Bill or Elliot. Most call me Elliot."

"What do you do during the off season, Elliot?" Trabuco repeated.

"Not much," Elliot said appearing bored with the conversation.

"How would you like to help me and some friends in a few months?"

"Flights to and from Mexico will be very expensive."

Trabuco liked the man's cockiness. This was an asset he decided would help the investors. "I will pay for the fuel and all the meals, as well as pay you $2,500 per flight."

Elliot took his eyes off the waitress and looked at Trabuco. "That's a lot of money, sir."

"Yes, but our cargo is very valuable."

"These must be very important businessmen?"

Trabuco lowered his voice. "The cargo is very valuable and even more secret."

"I see," Elliot said.

"Once you agree, we will then talk about a possible bonus."

"You speak very good English," Elliot said, "so I assume you understand English as well."

"Of course," Trabuco replied.

"I don't want to know anymore until I've made my decision. Do you understand?"

"Of course."

"Good," Elliot said and looked around the diner to see who may be listening.

~

"Damn, what was $2,500 worth in 1933?" Michael asked.

"Enough to convince Elliot to take the job and to be very loyal," Jake responded.

"How long did it take them to move the gold?" Sam asked.

"The rest of the year, it is thought. 17 tons of gold is very heavy," Jake replied.

"But where did they store it?" Sam asked.

Jake pulled some paper from under one of the books and read quickly, verifying to himself that what he was going to say was in fact true. "The gold was moved by Trabuco and a worker, not Elliot, from the landing area to the hiding place over the course of only a few days. That is what Elliot testified to in the congressional hearings that the Treasury Department held."

Sam smiled, "the burial site cannot be far from the landing site."

"About as far as the coordinates given by the pilot," Jake added.

"No way," Michael said.

"I think so," Jake replied. "I think the pilot was flying an aircraft that was equipped with submarine detection equipment, and the sub-finder responded to the gold."

"Did they even have submarine detection equipment?" Sam asked.

"Yes. They had all sorts of jets equipped with radar-type devices, like the S-3B Viking that flew in and out of Farmington airport for training purposes. The airport is on the top of a cliff and not very long, so it was used as a good training aid to simulate aircraft carrier landings. Here, you can read about it if you want," Jake said pushing a book toward Sam that had a picture on the cover of a jet approaching to land on an aircraft carrier.

"So why didn't the government just go get the gold?" Sam asked.

"I thought that maybe they didn't put it all together like I did, but who am I? Shit, if I could figure it out in the basement of this old library, I am sure some freak in a think tank would have figured it out. I think there are several reasons. First, I don't need to tell you guys how desolate it is on the reservation. With the exception of a few hogans scattered about, there are miles upon miles of nothing but mesas, canyons, a few mountains, and so on. It would be like finding a treasure lost in the middle of the ocean. However, I believe the reason could also be conquest," Jake said.

"Conquest?" Michael asked leaning back in his chair.

"That's right. Conquest. When we took over the land in this part of the country, we worked very hard conquering the Indians or Native Americans…whatever we're supposed to call them. We drove them off of all the good land and gave them the reservations, land that happens to be some of the most worthless and desolate land from ocean to ocean, or so it seemed."

"So, that was long before this all happened," Sam said.

"Well, kind of. You see, you can't simply conquer; you must also keep your foot on their necks. Trabuco was no dummy. He knew not only about the United States Gold Act, but the Spanish Land Grants that would eventually be surrendered to the Navajo Nation. After World War II, the land grants were made, and the Navajo Nation gained a significant amount of property." Jake reached for another piece of paper.

"What does all this mean," Michael asked.

"The gold is not in the United States," Sam added.

Jake smiled. He was thrilled his friends seemed to understand his theory. "Nope. The gold is on the Navajo

Nation. A sovereign nation of which the land, and property on that land, is no longer the property of the United States."

"They know it's there but don't want the Navajo Nation to get it," Michael added.

Jake nodded, "Trabuco didn't want the U.S. to have it, and the U.S. does not want the Navajo to have it."

"Why?" Sam asked.

"Who knows? Who cares? Maybe they don't want to affect the gold market with the introduction of an additional 17 tons of gold. Maybe they don't want the Navajo to suddenly be showered with the gold. I don't know," Jake responded.

"Why not?" Sam asked. "How much is that?"

Sam started hammering on a calculator and when he was done he said, "seventeen tons is about 544,400 ounces. Assuming the current value of gold of about $900 an ounce, that is $489,600,000."

"Four-hundred and eighty-nine million dollars ... it's still out there?" Michael asked with his eyes widening.

"Let's go find out," Jake responded.

CHAPTER 7

Sheldon sat in a large leather chair gleaming with confidence as his professor read the last few pages of the first draft of his thesis paper. He had spent the past year researching and rewriting the document. He had audited creative writing classes for the sole purpose of making his thesis more dynamic and powerful than anything he hoped his professor had ever read. He anticipated the first remarks. His professor would be taken aback as if he had been enlightened by insight rarely bestowed upon a Harvard professor. He knew his professor would be pleased, a rewrite probably not necessary. His PhD would be granted and his paper published with great enthusiasm. His calendar would be booked with talks about the subject, and he would deliver the speeches with the same poetic language that was written in the papers the man on the other side of the desk thumbed through at a rapid pace.

His day dreaming was broken when his professor cleared his throat and slowly placed the pile of paper on the desk.

Professor Hynes was a large man with a kind face. If one saw him walking down the street and had to guess at his profession, school teacher would be the most likely response. However, he looked more like a fifth grade teacher than a Harvard genius. He had a glow about him that portrayed a gentle mannerism and unwavering patience. He had a full head of gray hair and grayish white facial hair that was thick and trimmed below his plump, aging cheeks. He was a man who looked as if he should be bouncing grandchildren on his knee rather than leading his field in anthropology.

"I must say," Professor Hynes said removing his glasses and laying them on top of the stack of paper, "I am a bit concerned about your thesis paper. Not the writing, as it is obvious that you have spent a considerable amount of time making sure it flows like a novel. I am concerned about the premise of the paper."

Sheldon's shoulders dropped. A year's worth of work was not good enough for this man. He wondered if the man he thought to be a genius was actually an idiot.

"It is very difficult for me to comprehend the basic theory that there is an ancient civilization that resides within the borders of the United States. I understand portions of the history you cite, but the possibility is very unlikely."

"I …" Sheldon leaned forward in his chair, "may I rebut?"

"Certainly," Professor Hynes said.

"Let me use an example," Sheldon said shocked that he had to defend what he thought was a fascinating examination of history, anthropology, and sociology. "After World War Two, the major countries of this world knew that another war was not an option. War meant total defeat. Total destruction. Countries fought each other by flexing their muscles. That is what led to the space exploration war. A country that proved its dominance in the space war demonstrated its dominance over the other countries. Russia sent a manned rocket into space, and we responded by sending men to the moon. It was a display of dominance, a war of propaganda and superiority; countries striving to prove they held a bigger stick, for the lack of a better term."

Professor Hynes rubbed his eyes. The light from the single window in his office was dimming, and he was tired and wanted to go home to his wife. He pulled a pipe out of a Crown Royal bag and packed it full of tobacco. He lit the pipe and smiled.

"I'm sure you're thinking that it is very cliché for your professor to smoke a pipe, but I used to smoke two packs a day. My wife, with the advice of my doctor, told me I have to stop smoking. For whatever reason, she has no problem with me smoking a pipe. Two years as a non-smoker."

Sheldon waited as the professor sucked the flame of his match into the pipe, the tobacco glowing more brilliant with every puff.

"What the hell are you talking about?" Professor Hynes continued as a large plume of smoke left his mouth.

"It was not that different when the Europeans came to the Americas," Sheldon said. "Europe was under the same pressures, but with different technology. The conquest was not space, as they certainly didn't have the ability to explore space. But, they did have the ability to venture out to discover the world. It was a time when man didn't know if the world was flat or round. When the first set of explorers ventured out across the ocean and found the Americas, they thought they circled the earth and landed in India. That is why the natives of the United States and Mexico call the Natives 'Indians.' In any event, they wanted to prove their dominance by exploring and achieving goals that weren't thought possible by man."

"I agree," Professor Hynes said.

Sheldon pointed at the stack of paper that lay in front of his mentor. "That is what my thesis is about."

"No, that is not what your thesis is about," Professor Hynes responded.

Sheldon sat back in his chair. He felt his whole life was on the line. All his work and reasons for attending Harvard, the reasons for his acceptance there, were now in the balance of a man he admired and thought he trusted.

"The Spanish sent Conquistadors to explore the new world. It was a race to discover and colonize in a world they didn't even know existed." Sheldon spoke confidently as if his future hinged on selling the pitch to the man who sat before him. "The Spanish tried to keep their men motivated. Cortez and the City of Gold was a story created to keep the men moving. To explore."

"I know,"

"And the men were distraught. Imagine, Professor, a time with no phones, no letters, no means of communicating with the people you loved. Walking through a land unknown to what was considered civilized society for years ... decades. They needed motivation, motivation that was, for the most part, false."

"But they ..."

"They sent their best men," Sheldon interrupted, refusing to allow this man to destroy all his efforts and work. "Conquistadors that carried magnificent swords, shields, helmets, made partially with gold. The best men of Spain were sent to find and conquer the new world. They were dressed to impress and awe."

"And the Spanish brought disease to Mexico and wiped out a significant portion of the population."

"They did," Sheldon agreed. "But, it did not stop there. The Spanish made their way north of Mexico. They traveled north into what became New Mexico. And, as the promises of the lost City of Gold started to wane, the men lost the desire to continue with the discovery."

"They started to colonize," Professor Hynes said taping the papers on his desk. "Believe me, I read your paper."

"They did," Sheldon concurred. "Some of them did colonize in places like Santa Fe, but some did not. Some pressed on, either on the belief that the City of Gold did exist or because they felt loyalty to orders they had received. Some, after losing hope, resorted to historic repetition. When the tale of a City of Gold raised doubt in their minds, they acted as they did in the Spanish Inquisition. As they failed to find this glorious city, they began trying to convert the natives of the land to Christianity. There is plenty of history documented to support that theory."

"I have read your footnotes. I have no problem with your thesis to that point."

"Then what is the problem?" Sheldon said sternly.

"All that you have stated has been done clearly and soundly in your thesis. It is very well researched and you have obviously put in a lot of work, but a lost civilization within the borders of the United States? That is a little hard to comprehend."

Sheldon exhaled. "Have you ever been to Northern New Mexico?"

"No, I have not," Professor Hynes said, mustering dignity as if it were far below him.

"With the exception of a few small towns, it is nothing but barren land. A vast area of .... well, nothing."

"That doesn't prove your theory," the Professor added.

"No, certainly not," Sheldon said and took a moment to think. The thought of starting over on his PhD was too much for him to consider. He felt that he must either sell the theory to his professor now, or quit. He was not ready to quit ... not yet.

"What if," Sheldon said, "a group of these Spanish men decided that the story of the city of gold was nonsense? And, what if they didn't have the drive or desire to try and convert the Navajo into Christians? What if they simply decided to live?"

"All very interesting questions," Professor Hynes replied. "Questions are the beginning of a thesis. However, the beginning of a thesis is just the start. It takes analysis, proof, a conclusion."

"And, I have provided you with evidence that a group of men left Santa Fe, and were never heard from again."

"So?"

"So," Sheldon said, trying not to mock the man. "So, the whole alleged purpose of the conquest was to document the history for competing countries to read, to prove Spanish dominance over the other European countries. Why the hell is there no documentation for these men?"

"Again, a question."

"The majority of Mexicans are a mix of the natives and the Spanish. Why is it so hard to believe?"

"And yet, another question," Professor Hynes said as he stood from his desk. "It is late." He pulled a large wool coat from a coat rack and exhaled loudly, dropping his shoulders a bit as if he was sharing in Sheldon's disappointment. "I think your thesis is interesting. The problem is that you pose a question with few supporting facts to prove a theory. However, your conclusion is based upon a missing element of proof. You have studied deductive reasoning, haven't you?"

"Of course," Sheldon replied, letting his hands fall limp on his lap in defeat.

"A syllogism is based upon sound reason. If A then B, if B then C, if C then D; therefore, if A then D. Simple logic. The problem with your theory is you have not proven the C. You are claiming that A exists, with which all historians would not disagree. Then you propose D ... your conclusion ... which, I must admit, is quite interesting. However, you assume C. The C element of your logic is not proven. You assume that since there is no documented history of C that you have the right to assert your own C and scholars are to accept it as fact. C is not a fact in your thesis. C is myth. You are so consumed in proving the conclusion, D, that you have neglected proving the base of the premise. You have posed a lot of questions where answers should be provided. You want questions?"

Professor Hynes put on his coat and buttoned it as he spoke, "Where are the people? Why have they not been discovered? Why? How? When? All questions that your thesis raises, and despite the fact that the questions may be compelling, they go unanswered."

Sheldon stood from his chair and felt his legs nearly give to the weight of his body.

Professor Hynes approached Sheldon and placed his hand on his shoulder. He placed his pipe in his pocket and said, "It is a good start. Please finish your work. It would be a fascinating find and an unprecedented discovery …. if you are right."

"I have spent a year on this thesis," Sheldon said, fighting a tear in his eye.

"It took me four," the professor said and patted Sheldon on his back. "Four frustrating, yet … enlightening years."

Sheldon fought the urge to vomit as professor Hynes walked out of the office, leaving Sheldon alone with his thoughts.

CHAPTER 8

Sheldon's grip on the gun gradually loosened until finally he replaced it with a beer. He sat strangely calm, watching the fire and occasionally looking over at his grandfather to see if he was still puffing on the marijuana. He thought of asking his grandfather if this were all some sort of joke to try and scare him, but what little he knew about his grandfather prevented him from asking what would sound like a ridiculous question. He further doubted that Lowery would form such a plot with Ernest the medicine man, a man Lowery most likely despised.

When Sheldon was a young boy, he would often wish his grandfather would fly into his town and snatch him up to go on some crazy adventure out at sea. He would read books about pirates and sailing, imagining his grandfather drinking rum and swinging a sword at the bow of a boat. He asked his father many times if he could go visit his grandfather, and was always told that one day he would be old enough to go an adventure with him.

Sheldon was old enough now, but he doubted he was ready. He never worked a hard day in his life, growing up in boarding school's libraries and then heading off to Harvard where he spent little time anywhere but the library. He was nothing like his grandfather. He sipped triple lattes at the age of eighteen while his grandfather drank cheap beer out of a can while wiping the oil from his forehead. He wondered if his grandfather knew the differences between them, and if his grandfather was ashamed of having such a sissy heir.

"How long are we going to wait?" Sheldon asked, placing more logs on the fire.

"All night, I guess," Lowery replied.

The thought of spending all night looking into the shadows for shape shifting monsters did not seem like a very pleasing prospect for Sheldon. He took a stick from the stacked firewood and began poking at the fire. Ashes jumped violently from under the logs as Sheldon poked. The fire hissed and crackled loudly, protesting the torment the young man was creating.

"Should I go look for him?" Sheldon asked, not knowing where the thought came from or how it escaped his mouth.

Lowery smiled from behind his pipe, seeing for the first time a little bit of the boy's father come out in him. "I don't know," he said, anxious for the boy's response.

"I will if you want me to."

"That is something you have to decide."

"Do you believe there really are Skinwalkers?" Sheldon asked.

Lowery sat pondering the question and then spoke, "I read a magazine story once about these kids in New York City who hid in the sewers and dressed up like vampires. I guess they were playing some kind of game and took it way too seriously. Hell, maybe they just liked vampires. They would run around at night, drink blood, perform rituals, you know, vampire stuff. It all went to hell when they started killing people. That's when the game was no longer a game. So, here is my point. If you ask me if I believe in vampires, my answer would be yes. That is my answer because there are people out there who run around acting like vampires and drinking blood."

"And Skinwalkers," Sheldon asked.

"Even more so, son. Skinwalkers are majestic creatures that the Navajo created based on their culture and their beliefs. The Navajo have strong beliefs. I know there are medicine men because I just watched one walk down the canyon just moments ago. Whether a Skinwalker can shift into the shape of an animal, I doubt. But I believe that there are Navajo who believe they're skinwalkers. They practice the dark magic and prey on people. Also, I've seen a Navajo man walking down a dirt road wearing a coyote skin."

"Wearing a coyote skin?"

"Before I owned my first rig, I set well heads. Believe me, son, there is no worse job on this planet than setting well heads. Imagine being in a pit of mud, acid, chemicals, and so on, reaching into the pool of shit trying to tie in the well head. All of this in the middle of winter, and right up the ass of nowhere. I was on my third night of work, and my body was shutting down. I was dead on my feet. It was late at night coming back from a rig on the south end of Largo Canyon. The snow started to come down in large soft flakes, and when they started to stick to the dirt road I was on, I had to drive very slowly. Trying to focus on where the road was, and trying even harder to see through the snow, I looked up and saw this man walking toward my truck kind of hunched over. On top of his head, wearing it like a hat was a coyote head with its skin draped down the man's back. I think he was hunching over to make it appear that the coyote was staring at me."

"What did you do?"

"Honked my horn and he moved out of the way. I don't know if it was a man trying to act like a skinwalker or what the Navajo would consider a Skinwalker, but either way, it was a man, not a creature. So, I guess you can say that I've seen one, and I do believe in them. They may not be able to enter your soul, but they would kill you. I believe they'd kill either of us."

Sheldon continued to poke at the fire for several minutes, absorbing all that he had heard, and suddenly stood. "Please do not let the fire die down. I'll need the light to find my way back."

"Sure," Lowery said, looking up at the figure that looked more like his son than his grandson now.

Sheldon paused at the base of the trees into which his medicine man grandfather had somehow disappeared. He could see a path that had not been visible from the campfire. It was narrow and twisted through the trees, and Sheldon began to understand why it appeared the medicine man had disappeared. A few feet down the path it turned sharply to the right, and the thick trees blocked any view someone back at the campfire would have of the path.

Sheldon began slowly making his way down the path when a horrible thought came to his mind. What if Ernest was the type of man who pretended to be a Skinwalker? Sheldon anticipated a crazy, screaming Navajo with a dead coyote on his head racing out of the trees with a spear or something. No attack came.

Sheldon wondered where he was going, why he was going, and fought the urge to turn back.

"Rattlesnakes are nocturnal," Sheldon said to himself as he reached for a small flashlight he kept in his back pocket. He quickly turned it on and pointed it at the path. There were no rattlesnakes. There were, however, shoe prints. Good. The medicine man did not disappear into the shadows or fly away.

He walked slowly at first, pausing at every step, but then gradually worked into a steady pace. He looked back and could just make out the fire through the twisted branches of the trees. He could hear the faint sound of the fire crackling and knew that he was still within yelling distance if it came to that. He pressed on.

The trail began to widen and eventually disappeared as the ground turned to sandstone and sand washes. The shoe prints where no longer visible and Sheldon stopped to survey the landscape. He stood in a large windblown bowl of sandstone with several cedar and pinon trees. He was far from the campsite now, out of sight and out of screaming distance. He lifted his head and noticed what the medicine man had looked up to see when they were sitting at the campfire. The clouds seemed only feet above the desert ground and raced across the sky, shifting shadows across the earth.

This would be something else if Lowery would have given me some of his weed, Sheldon thought.

Sheldon was trying to figure out which direction the Navajo man went when a cave across the canyon caught his eye. He gave it little thought before walking toward it. He did not see any light coming from the cave, and no noise came from that direction, but he sensed that the medicine man was there. He surveyed the area for Skinwalkers, or any animals that might look similar to one, but saw nothing. As he followed the sandstone formation that led to the cave, he turned and saw a very small speck of light far up the canyon in the direction from which he had just come. He assumed it was their campfire, but the distance was further than Sheldon thought he had gone.

"Shit," Sheldon said, feeling somewhat disoriented as he continued up to the cave.

The moon began to rise from the horizon, making the low clouds look like plumes of smoke blowing in the nonexistent wind. The moon also illuminated the sandstone formation, turning the brown sand into a pale gray. Sheldon stopped when he reached a ledge of the sandstone formation and then moved behind a small pinon tree. He was able to see several feet into the cave as the moon climbed higher into the sky.

Reluctantly, Sheldon left the protection of the pinon tree and walked toward the entrance to the cave; his hands beginning to shake nervously. It did not take him long to realize that he had made a bad decision. Not more than a hundred feet into the mouth of the cave were several shadowy figures moving about the darkness. The moon's light was not quite bright enough to penetrate the depth of the cave, but he could see that whatever the figures were, they did not appear to be like anything he had ever experienced. They moved slowly from one to the other, possibly conversing, but they did not look human. They walked on four legs and had unusually long snouts. Not as long as a dog or wolf, but longer than that of a man.

Sheldon reached for his revolver and saw one of the creatures turn to stare at him. Sheldon immediately knew that if he drew his gun that he would never see another day. He did not think that the creature would attack, but looked as though it could. Its eyes were barely visible and reflected the moon's rays. They were dark red, just as the medicine man had described them. He wondered if these things were Skinwalkers, and if they were, why they had not attacked?

He was not welcome. That was very clear to him, but what to do next, he did not know. He was not going to enter the cave in search of the medicine man. He thought of yelling out to the medicine man or to Lowery. He was bothered that his grandfather, a man he knew as Ernest his entire childhood, demanded that he call him the medicine man, and how he came to be in this situation. If he yelled, and Ernest was not there, he knew he would arouse the creatures. He felt the urge to turn and run, but he knew he had to leave. He had to leave immediately, but decided to retreat slowly.

Sheldon began to retreat, walking backwards deliberately and carefully, always aware of the creatures and the location of his revolver. When he made it back to his small pinon he felt a strange comfort. It provided little coverage, and was not tall enough to climb to escape an attack from the creatures; however, he took a moment to pause at the tree knowing that he soon had to turn his back to the cave to make his way down the sandstone formation.

He fought to stop his hands from trembling as he placed them on the sandstone so that he could shimmy down the rock. He told himself to calm down as he began the descent. If he started to slip, the sandstone would provide little help in stopping him, as it would crumble into handfuls of dirt as he grasped at it. Despite not knowing how far the drop into the darkness at the bottom would be, Sheldon knew that a fall would cause him significant injury.

After a slow deliberate descent and feeling his heart jump at every slight slip of his feet on the rock, he made it to the base of the rock formation. He looked up toward the cave and saw that nothing was following him. He breathed more normally again and turned to make his way back to the campfire. He found the path he came down, and kept his eyes on the ground to avoid stepping on a cactus or tripping on a rock.

When he looked up further down the path, though, he froze in terror. The sight of the creatures in the cave had frightened him, but what he now saw paralyzed him. About fifty yards down the path stood a tall Navajo man. The man did not look like any of the Navajo Sheldon had seen in his youth. He was unusually tall and wearing some type of ceremonial clothing.

Sheldon thought of turning and heading back up the sandstone cliff, but that path lead to unnatural creatures. He cursed his grandfathers, and wished one of them would come to him now. He did not know why the hell Ernest left the campfire causing Sheldon to end up trapped between the strange creatures and a mysterious Navajo man. Sheldon noticed that the tall Navajo man was just to the side of the path, and stood motionless, not looking at Sheldon. The man's head was tilted a bit backwards looking up at the cave. Sheldon did not know if the man knew he was there, the man was looking in the direction of the cave with the creatures, appearing to be oblivious to Sheldon's presence.

Despite his fear, Sheldon knew it was time to go and started down the path toward the tall Navajo man, anxious about what to expect when he reached him. The man stood just feet from the path and Sheldon prepared himself for the fact that he would have to walk right by him. As he neared him, he thought of speaking to him, but decided against it. He could not think of what to say, everything was too strange for his logical mind. The man was only ten yards away now.

Sheldon remembered the revolver. If the man moved toward him, he would have very little time to get to the gun. He knew the man could take him in a fight; it could not come down to that. He longed for his grandfathers as he crept closer to the anticipated confrontation.

At first Sheldon could barely make out the man's face, but as he inched toward him, it appeared stern and bold, and lightly covered by some type of ash. Sheldon quickly searched his brain for any recollection of Native American study that would help him determine who this man was and what the clothing and ash on his face meant. When he was only a few feet from the man, he noticed the man's chest expanded dramatically as he breathed. The man continued to stare up toward the cave not seeming to have any consciousness of Sheldon's presence.

Sheldon thought again of saying something, but he again decided against it. Soon he would be past the man and into the cover of the trees where he could run if necessary back to the campfire.

Just get back, Sheldon thought.

He passed the tall Navajo man thinking that the man may lunge toward him as he turned his back. He was into the trees before he realized that nothing had happened. He fought the desire to run, and continued the same cautious pace as he followed the path and back to the campfire. Soon, he thought, he would be able to see and hear the fire.

When Sheldon emerged into the clearing where the campfire was burning he saw both his grandfathers there smoking pipes as they sat by the fire. Sheldon stopped and looked back at the path he had traveled. No creatures, no tall Navajo man. He felt relieved that he was back in the presence of his two grandfathers, but was also enraged that they let him go to the cave. Fighting the two conflicting emotions, Sheldon wanted to collapse onto the ground and curl up in the fetal position. He placed his hands on his knees and lowered his head.

Medicine Man said, "You need to tell me what you think you saw so that I can help you understand what you actually saw."

"What was this, some spirit trip?" Sheldon said, refusing to sit down by the fire, trying to calm his breathing.

"Something like that," Lowery replied.

"Well screw this," Sheldon said walking toward the pickup truck parked near the camp site. "I'm leaving."

"Sit down, Sheldon. Sit down and calm down." Lowery said.

"We do not need this bullshit. We know where it is, and how to get there. Let's just go get it." Sheldon said as he sat frustrated next to his grandfather.

"You do not know how to get there," the Medicine Man replied. "Your journey takes you into very sacred land. Land that is still run the ancient way. Land forgotten by your people. Land where the dark magic is practiced."

"So, are you preparing us to face the dark magic?" Sheldon asked. "I thought we had to smoke peyote or something to go on a spirit ride? What difference does it make if I call you Ernest Benally or medicine man? You are my grandfather.

Quit talking to me in that trance of a voice! What the hell is going on?!"

"No, you do not have to take peyote," the Medicine Man replied. "That is not the true traditional way."

"Would have been more fun," Sheldon replied.

"I told you that I do not like your journey. I'll tell you what I told your father. Do not take this journey." The Medicine Man spoke a bit louder than he had all night.

"So what's the point of this?" Sheldon demanded.

"Knowledge," the Medicine Man replied.

"Sheldon," Lowery said in a low scratchy voice. "Forget what you think you know about this world. This is not a college course. You should forget logic and try and focus on knowledge. We need to know what you saw. Please, Sheldon, tell us what you saw."

"I saw some wolf-like creatures and a tall Navajo man," Sheldon said.

"Tell me about the Navajo man," the Medicine Man asked.

Sheldon paused, surprised by the question. He had just told his crazy old grandfathers that he saw some type of creatures and they want to know about the Navajo man. "Okay, he was bold. Like I said, tall…..dressed in ceremonial clothing….. some type of ash on his face…..he didn't acknowledge me. He just stared up at the cave where the wolf-things were."

The medicine man nodded his head as if to confirm a thought he had previously had. "What was in his hands?"

Sheldon paused again. He did not know. The fact that he did not know was suddenly a very unpleasant thought. He walked mere feet from this man and never thought to look to see what he may be holding. A terrible thought came to his mind that it was possible that the man did not have hands.

"I don't know. I did not see his hands………I did not see hands."

The medicine man again nodded. "You need ante," he said. "Ante is a dust you can flick at a Skinwalker to stop it from attacking you."

"That's what I have in this bag," Lowery said raising the bag he tried to open earlier but was told not to by the medicine man.

"No, that is worthless," the medicine man replied. "You must make ante out of the gallbladder of an eagle. The eagle must be caught and smothered. Killing the eagle any other way will make the magic useless."

"Catch and eagle and smother it," Sheldon repeated.

"Yes. There's no other magic I know of. You can't rely on a medicine man to protect you. My magic will only hold the Skinwalkers away for a short time."

Sheldon looked at Lowery but spoke to the medicine man. "Were you the man I saw?"

"Before many of our people decided to follow your God and read your book, the medicine man was considered good. Now, to many, we are evil," the medicine man said placing the two figurines into his pockets. "You can think I am evil or good, but know this of the medicine man; we are the only protectors from the Skinwalker. And the Skinwalker is evil."

"If that was you, where's the clothing?" Sheldon asked.

"There are many ways of the Navajo you will not understand. What you think you saw may not have been what you were actually seeing. This is a lesson you should remember. The Skinwalkers use the shadows of the earth to trick the eye. Sometimes you see things that are not. Sometimes you see nothing where something stands."

"I know what I saw," Sheldon responded.

"No you don't," the medicine man replied. "Now we rest."

Sheldon pulled a bottle of Crown Royal out of his backpack and took two large drinks. He settled his back against his sleeping bag and quietly admired his two grandfathers. He knew little about either one of them. Lowery had run off to search for treasure and had no contact with Sheldon other than sending him little trinkets from time to time. Ernest lived in a very remote part of the reservation, practicing the art of being a Navajo Medicine Man, refusing to come into town to visit his daughter as Sheldon grew up. Lowery smoked marijuana out of a pipe, and Ernest played with sage and other herbs, drawing a sand painting on the ground.

Sheldon was not close to either of his grandfathers, and he struggled thinking which one of them he would choose to hate for putting him through this. He turned his head away from them and decided to direct his anger at both. He wondered how the two had found one another.

Sheldon closed his eyes and slept.

CHAPTER 9

Michael was overwhelmed by the smell of honeysuckle when he exited the bar with Kevin and Sam. He paused for a moment and took in the summer night air. It was much different than downtown New York. It was nearly midnight and the sky was filled with stars. The full moon lit the town as if the sun were still hanging just below the horizon. He could not believe how much he had forgotten about his hometown in the short time that he had been away. His ears faintly rang, not accustomed to the quiet solitude and lack of big city noises. He had an urge to tell his friends how good he felt being home, but doubted they would understand. He closed his eyes and allowed his other senses to take over.

Suddenly, his peacefulness was interrupted by a terrible thought. He realized that if he walked directly to his car that his friends would see that he was driving an old piece of junk rental car. This could not happen.

"You still driving a truck, Kevin?" Michael asked.

"Same truck. Don't you recognize it?" Kevin responded as he approached an old Dodge Ram pickup truck.

"Sure I do," Michael said. "I spent many nights sitting on that tailgate drinking beer."

"I still sit on that tailgate drinking beer," Kevin said.

"What do you guys say we get a case of beer, head out to the hills, sit on that tailgate, and drink until the sun comes up?" Michael asked.

"It's getting late, but we do have things to talk about," Sam said.

"Damn right we do," Michael said, looking over at Kevin waiting for his consent.

"Sure," Kevin said and pulled the keys out of his pocket.

When they were in high school, they called it the well site. There were many reasons for this. When they decided to have a party out in the hills it was simply easier to pass around the word of a known location so that the word would spread and directions would not have to be given. There were many party locations, but the well site provided additional safeguards. It was high on the top of a bluff, reachable by only one road, and it was very difficult terrain. In high school, this was particularly helpful because it was easy to spot the approach of any police and made for a quick escape. This, however, had never happened, probably due to the generality of the name of the location. Only the people who had been to the well site knew how to find it. The name alone provided no clue to its location because the entire county was littered with well sites.

Many of the high school kids knew the location of the well site, in addition to other choice locations like Shirley's Rock, The Crevasse, The Beach, The Point, The Spot, and so on. However, the trick was to limit the amount of guys who knew which spot would be chosen. The party location was picked by the "enlightened," who was the guy who found someone old enough to fill the keg. He had the keg, so it was his call. He would pick the spot and slowly start telling his friends which location he had chosen. Guys spread the word to guys very cautiously.

For girls, however, it was a different story. Four wheel trucks were very popular because one guy could load up the entire back of his truck with many girls if he were lucky enough to convince them to get in. Kevin's truck was always filled with girls. What amazed Michael the most was that the girls were always random, varying from the entire varsity cheerleading squad to the choir girls. Kevin would often say, "Diversity leads to a better education."

Despite Kevin's success in filling up the bed of his truck, he always had the same passenger up front with him. Her name was Cindy. This fact not only confused Michael, but drove him crazy. He asked Kevin many times how he could get away with something like loading his truck up with girls, but Kevin would always respond the same way, with only a smile. He did not tell Michael that Cindy brought the girls for his friends, knowing that she would always be the girl sitting up front. She trusted Kevin, and was secretly proud to attend parties with the guy that brought a truck full of girls. She knew that those girls would not ever stand a chance with Kevin.

"This place looks as though it has not been used in a long time," Michael said as he climbed out of Kevin's truck at the well site.

Michael examined the fire pit and saw few signs of prior fires. The headlights on Kevin's truck lit up the area, and Michael scanned the trees and sandstone formations, failing to find any signs of teenage attendance. He heard the hum of a compressor and the twisting gears of a pump jack. His mind was full of memories. He felt lonely, older, thinking of the well site as it used to be, packed with his former high school classmates. He wondered what had happened to all those people, wishing that he could relive just one night.

Sam got out of the truck and opened a beer. "They party in houses now," he said as he opened the tailgate of Kevin's truck. "I think they get stoned and lounge around."

Kevin and Sam sat on the tail gate of the truck and Michael noticed that there was no room for him to sit. He grabbed a beer, and sat on a large sandstone rock at his friends' feet. He drank his beer quickly, like he used to do when he visited this place in the past, and felt calm. Watching his friends sit side-by-side on the tailgate of the truck drinking beer made Michael feel at home.

"Oh, I almost forgot," Kevin said jumping from the tailgate. "I got something for you, Michael."

"What?" Michael asked as Kevin went to the truck and pulled something from behind the seat.

"I thought you might want this back," Kevin said approaching Michael with a baseball bat.

Michael thought for a moment that Kevin might try and hit him with it, but quickly dismissed the thought. He had no idea what this was about.

"A bat?" Michael asked.

"Yep, a bat," Kevin said handing the bat to Michael then returning to the tailgate. "The crazy bitch didn't break it … she stole it."

Michael sat confused as Kevin let a crooked smile creep up one side of his face, and then took a long drink of his beer. Written on the bat was the autograph, "Wade Boggs." Michael no longer felt calm and at home. He felt small and defeated. He tried to speak, but could think of nothing to say.

Sam, who usually acted as the peacemaker in these situations, sat quietly. He wondered if Michael and Kevin would soon fight. Under ordinary circumstance Kevin would have no problem with Michael, but Kevin had just armed Michael with a bat.

Michael stood and Kevin sat his beer down preparing for an attack, but Michael walked in the opposite direction. He walked about twenty yards and stopped at the edge of the bluff. He knew that past the edge there was at least a two hundred foot drop. Michael took the bat in one hand and threw it over the edge of the cliff. Sam sat waiting for the sound of the bat hitting the rocks below, but no sound came.

Michael returned to his rock and opened another beer. "So, you struck me out and got the girl. Good for you."

Kevin did not have the anger he did a moment ago. Ashamed, he turned toward Sam hoping he was on his side. Sam appeared as he always did, neutral.

"I just thought you might want it back," Kevin said in a weak voice that neither Sam nor Michael had ever heard.

"Bullshit. You know exactly why you gave me that bat. You wanted to call me a liar and prove you are the better man, all without having to say a word. Well you said it." Michael began to speak softly. "I never loved her, okay. But when she wouldn't be with me, it devastated me. I am sure she told you she grabbed the bat to protect herself from my advances. That is bullshit. I would never do that to a girl, especially Cindy. I don't know why I lied about her breaking the bat. I guess I was just afraid of what story she would be making up about me. Yes, I tried to be with her, and maybe I got a little too aggressive. When she picked up the bat, I let her leave without incident. That was the last time I ever saw her."

"She said she went to your house to talk about me. That she was there to find out a way to get me back, and you tried to take advantage of the situation," Kevin said.

"I see," Michael said. "She's right, I guess. Why haven't you got over this yet? It's been nearly a decade."

"You were one of my best friends, and you tried to sleep with my girlfriend. A girl you knew I loved!"

"So," Michael mumbled, "what do you want?"

"We want you to get your shit together, Michael," Sam added. "Look at you. You've been acting like you are on parade. Guess what, there's no spotlight on you, bud. Nobody is watching and nobody gives a shit. Especially your friends. We don't care about your job and your money, you dumb ass, we care about you."

"Wow," Michael said. "Guess we are not holding any punches tonight. Well, do you even want to know why I tried to hook up with Cindy?"

"Sure," Kevin said feeling the tension return to his shoulders.

"Because I saw what you had, and wanted it. I was too young to understand love and relationships. I thought to have what you had, I'd have to have Cindy. It had nothing to do with the strike-out or revenge. It was envy."

"You had almost every girl in the school, why her?" Kevin asked.

"I couldn't find what you two had. I thought it was her, but I later found out that it was me," Michael said softly, worrying that he might tear-up. "I'm sorry. I feel like horse shit, and I'm sorry that I ruined it for you."

Kevin jumped off the tailgate and walked toward Michael. *This is it,* Sam thought preparing himself to jump into the middle of a fight with an arm in a sling and a bum leg. Kevin handed another beer to Michael and sat next to him on the sandstone rock. Michael took the beer from Kevin feeling defeated and embarrassed.

"You didn't ruin anything. You just delayed it a bit," Kevin said.

Michael looked at Kevin to see that he was holding up his hand, showing him his wedding ring.

Kevin lowered his hand and said, "Oh, you fucked it up pretty good. Took us several years to start dating again, but all is well."

"Is it the way it used to be?" Michael asked.

"It's better," Kevin replied. "We have a son and a girl on the way."

Michael raised his beer and tapped it against Kevin's beer. "Good for you," Michael said. "I can honestly say that for the first time it makes me happy to see you happy."

Sam sat quietly minding his own business, drinking the beer as fast as he could.

"That's the way it's supposed to be," Kevin said. "And I'm happy about your big job. Even happier to know, if the IRS ever comes after me, that I have someone to call."

"The IRS can suck it," Sam added slurring his words.

"Indeed," Michael said, feeling humiliated and taking no pride in himself or his job.

"Sorry about your bat, dude," Sam said. "What kind of sick bastard throws a Wade Boggs bat off a cliff?"

"We can go find it tomorrow," Kevin added.

"No need," Michael said opening a new beer. "I forged the name with a magic marker when I was twelve."

"I knew it," Kevin said. "I knew it was a fake, but didn't know if you had done it or bought it that way. I didn't want to tell you because I didn't want to break your spirits."

"Bullshit," Michael said. "It looked exactly like the real thing."

"No, it didn't," Sam slurred.

"All right, enough Michael is a turd talk. How about we talk about something else?"

"Like what?" Kevin asked.

"Like, Jake," Michael replied.

"Oh, shit," Sam said chugging his beer and reaching for another one. "Here we go."

"What?" Michael asked.

"He hasn't been the same," Kevin said. "You remember him, don't you? He was smart, liked to study weird things like the universe and physics. He was always a strange cat, but the kind of guy you would expect to go to an Ivy League school and end up in a think tank or something."

"So, what happened to him?" Michael asked.

"He never went to college," Kevin said. "He never went anywhere. He moved into some distant uncle's trailer up near Navajo Dam by the San Juan River, and spends his days fly fishing. I think he takes tourists fly fishing on the river. Sam and I visited him one summer and it was….."

Sam interrupted and spoke loudly, "Dude, let me tell this part."

Kevin smiled and said, "Calm down, go ahead."

Sam jumped from the tailgate and took stage in front of Kevin and Michael. "Okay, Kev and I had just spent all day at Navajo Lake. You know, drinking beer and fishing. This was before he broke up with me and left our friendship in shambles."

"Sure …okay," Michael said.

"And on our way down the dam, Kev says, 'Let's go see if Jake really lives in that trailer.' You know, because that's what we had heard."

"Okay," Michael added.

Sam sat his beer on the tailgate and took a deep breath preparing for the next part of the story. He raised his hands above his head and said, "Then out of nowhere comes this horse. I yelled at Kevin to hit the fucking breaks! Thank God he did, but my beer went flying into the dashboard. It was full, just opened it." Sam waved his arms dramatically, "Beer went everywhere. All over our clothes, our hair, the seats, the dashboard, the carpet…"

"It went everywhere," Michael said looking at Kevin who shrugged his shoulders.

"Oh, shit," Sam replied. "It went EVERYWHERE!" Sam paused to reach back and get his beer off the tailgate. "I don't know whose eyes were wider, Kevin's or the horse, but I can say this, and I am being honest, the horse was standing inches from the front bumper and, with wide eyes, shit right there in front of us. No shit."

"Shit or no shit," Michael asked.

"Shut up. So, we start laughing so hard we are crying as the horse walks away in shame. Beer EVERYWHERE! Suddenly, we hear a siren. Police siren."

Sam put his beer back on the tailgate, turned around and walked right in front of Michael. "Now! How many times have you seen a cop out at Navajo Dam?" Before Michael could respond, Sam threw his good arm into the sky and yelled, "EXACTLY! One day this police officer decides, fuck it, I am going to go for a ride up to Navajo Dam. You never know what kind of crazy shit can go down up at the Dam. And to this day, my friends, it kills me that the son-of-a-bitch was right. Hell, the guy has probably gone back to the Dam every day since, looking for the shitting wild-eyed horses."

"Who was driving?" Michael asked as he laughed.

"I don't know if you could say a whole lot of driving was going on, but if you're asking who was behind the wheel, Kevin was. Pay attention."

Michael and Sam took a moment to look at Kevin who was nodding his head.

"SO!" Sam continued. "The cop comes walking up to the window all tough and full of authority, you know what I mean. He taps on Kevin's window with his flashlight. Its three o'clock in the middle of the summer and he has his flashlight out. What a tool. Well, Kevin's window doesn't work."

"I remember that," Michael said.

"Do you remember that his door did not work either?" Sam asked.

"Oh, no."

Sam smiled. "Oh, yes. Oh yes, my friend. We both have to exit the truck from my side, and yes, we are both drenched in beer. Dumb-ass over there," Sam said pointing at Kevin, "left the truck in the middle of the road."

"I didn't want to run over the horse shit by pulling off to the side," Kevin said laughing into the mouth of his beer.

"Whatever," Sam said. "So trucks pulling fucking boats and shit are passing, trying not to burn out their brakes, as they try and go down the steep road down the dam. Beer EVERYWHERE! The cop asks, in his cop voice, "You guys alright?" And Kevin starts to laugh. And I don't mean chuckle, I mean laugh. Tears running down his face, grabbing his side, oh, it was a disaster. This may not surprise you, but, the cop; well, he didn't think any of this was very funny. And do you know what that smug shit did? He stood there and waited until Kevin stopped laughing. No, "what's so funny." No, "you think this is funny, son." No, "you better stop laughing or..." Nothing. Just stood there and stared at Kevin."

Kevin started laughing harder, "That's right. I forgot about that," he said.

"See," Sam said. "Like that. And Kevin must have laughed for fifteen minutes. It must have been quite a sight for the people passing in the trucks. SO! Once Kevin calmed down, the police officer told us that he smelt beer and saw what happened. I told the cop that the horse jumped out of nowhere and if it wasn't for Kevin's cat-like instincts, that me, Kevin, and the horse would all be dead. So, the cop points at the fat old horse that was huffing and puffing as it was walking away and asked, "that's the horse that 'jumped' out in front of you?" And Kevin, without batting an eye, says, "Yes sir, I love that damn horse."

"What?" Michael asked.

"That's what I thought," Sam said. "But, Kevin is a genius. He tells the cop that he is living in the trailer at the bottom of the hill and points to where we think Jake is living. He tells the cop that he noticed his horse somehow got to the road and that he had to get the horse before it caused and accident. "I didn't want to drive, officer, because it is dangerous and I am a Christian, but I don't think I could live another day if someone was hurt because Penny wondered into the road."

"Bullshit," Kevin said. "That is not what I said."

"Yes it was," Sam demanded.

"Not exactly," Kevin added. "Kind of close, but Penny ... come on."

Sam laughed, "You said Penny. I swear you called the horse Penny. So the cop is obviously not buying the story, but it is like 175 degrees outside and we are blocking traffic. The cop tells Kevin that he has to go straight to his trailer to sober up, and here's the kicker, he tells Kevin that before we can leave, he has to clean his horse's shit off the road. Oh, Jesus," Sam said with tears running down his face. "I watched Kevin kick Penny's shit off the road thinking that at any moment he was going to snap and tear the cop's head off."

"What does this have to do with Jake?" Michael asked.

"Calm down," Sam said. "So, the cop sits off to the side of the road and watches us drive to the trailer. We both know that if we do not go inside the trailer that we're going to jail. I reached to knock on the door and Kevin quickly stops me and reminds me that we told him that we lived there. Kev takes a deep breath and opens the door. We don't have a clue what we are going to find inside! But nothing could have prepared us for the horror we saw."

"It wasn't Jake's trailer," Michael added.

"Oh, it was Jake's trailer," Sam said. "But Jake wasn't home. We saw this old nasty toothless lady lying on a stinky pullout couch wearing lingerie that had chew spit stains and holes in it."

"What?" Michael asked.

"That is exactly what I said," Kevin added.

"You did!" Sam said laughing. "You did say, "what." Oh, man. So, she takes a large bite of her beef jerky and smiles at us. Kevin whimpers, 'Hi.' She replies in a deep sexy voice, 'hi.' It was beautiful. So, Kevin walks in and closes the door behind us, the trailer whore ecstatic that we had welcomed ourselves into her lovely abode."

"Trailer whore?" Michael asked.

"Yes, trailer whore," Kevin replied.

"So, anyways, the trailer whore takes the beef jerky out of her mouth and places it on a T.V. tray. Wipes her hand on her lingerie and asks, 'You guys here for a suck or a fuck?' I threw up a bit in my mouth and swallowed it. Kevin's eyes were wider than they were when we nearly hit the horse. We tell her, neither."

"Naturally," Michael added.

"Kev tells her that we are looking for a friend of ours named, Jake. She smiled wide and responded, "Oh, I like Jake."

"You've heard of coyote ugly. You know, she is so ugly that in the morning when you realize she is asleep and lying on one of your arms, you would be willing to gnaw your arm off like a coyote so you won't wake her," Kevin said. "Well, this lady was worse. If you woke up with this thing lying on your arm, you would gnaw your heart out because you would never be able to live with yourself."

"So, Jake was screwing the trailer whore?" Michael asked.

"Turns out, no. Jake, you see, is a business man," Sam responded. "Fed the trailer whore jerky and gave her drink, so she would stay. When the river got lonely, and the men needed a suck or a fuck, they knew which trailer to go to."

"Nice," Michael said. "Then what?"

"That's it," Sam said. "We hung out with the trailer whore until Jake got back, talked to Jake for a while, and then left."

"Well, how is he?" Michael asked.

"Seems to be the pimp of the San Juan River," Sam responded.

"No, seriously, how is he?"

Kevin cleared his throat and said, "Not well, Michael. I don't think he ever got over what he saw."

"Well, he's going to have to get over it," Michael demanded. "We need him for our trip."

"Our trip?" Sam asked.

"Yes, we have to go back," Michael responded.

"Bullshit," Sam said. "I'm never going back."

"We have to," Michael said. "Not just to stop this man from getting into what we got into, but because we were warned that if anyone returned, they would hunt us."

"I don't believe that shit," Sam replied. "Maybe when I was eighteen, but not now. I know you don't believe it either."

"I don't know what I believe," Michael said. "I do know that there's a man, and he's probably not alone, on his way to a horror that he does not expect."

"So," Sam replied.

Michael shook his head in disbelief.

"When we were eighteen we believed the threat," Kevin said. "I'm nearly thirty, and even now I can tell you, I still believe the threat. They know we're the ones with the tapes. They know if we had destroyed them that nobody would've ever returned. The man has the tapes, for Christ sakes, they'll know it came from us. Having said that, that's why we have to go."

"Because it's still out there," Michael added.

"No. Are you crazy?" Kevin said. "Jake told us that he was cursed. I don't believe in that kind of stuff, but he does. He told us that one of them put his hat in a jar and buried it. That the only way to lift the curse is to free the hat."

"What?" Michael asked.

"Hey, I don't believe it either," Kevin said. "But, Jake does. He hasn't been the same since."

CHAPTER 10

Michael was both relieved and disappointed when he found that the trailer whore was not sprawled out on the sofa in Jake's living room. He was not too surprised that there was in fact no trace of a trailer whore at all. He had doubted that Sam's story was true, but had enjoyed it anyway.

He could not find Jake in the old single-wide trailer. He had knocked on the front door, but when he did, it swung open due to the lack of a door knob or any latching device. The trailer looked as though it had never been cleaned. Beer cans and pizza boxes littered the floor leaving little room for someone to notice the filthy carpet underneath. He had called out Jake's name several times as he stood reluctantly in the entrance of the trailer. He got no response.

What was once supposed to be a kitchen had been converted into some sort of fly fishing laboratory. Spindles of yarn and thread were attached to a wooden device Michael assumed Jake had invented. It was attached to the Formica countertop next to the sink which was stained with remnants of fish blood and other liquids Michael doubted he wanted to know their identity. A single stool stood in the middle of the kitchen, and Michael imagined his old friend Jake sitting in it making flies.

On the refrigerator he noticed a dry erase board with a calendar of dates and what appeared to be clients' names. Written on the day's date and was "Johnson-3" with a line drawn through it, and under it was written, "Cancelled, Jake-1." Michael wondered if this calendar was intended for more people than just Jake. He assumed that all the trailers in the area were unlocked as Jake's was and that the people could and would come and go as they pleased. "Jake-1," Michael decided, meant that Jake had taken himself fishing.

Michael exited the trailer and followed a well worn path through the high grass that obliviously made its way down toward the San Juan River. He had never been fishing with Jake, even when they were young, so he had no idea where he might be, but the trail was as good a start as any.

The first couple of times that he stepped into mud he grimaced at the thought of ruining his expensive shoes, but the thought left him as he realized the damage had been done. He wondered how silly he would appear to Jake when he came out of the high grass to the river's bank dressed in slacks and an Armani turtle neck. It was the summer. It was San Juan County. He paused for and took in the wonders to his right, the large man-made dam that stood like a mountain of dirt and rock. There was only a small part of the dam that was made of concrete which was used as a spillway for the large lake above him. He recalled a story about a boy who tried to ride an inner tube down the spillway, but as he got older, and nobody could verify the name or when it occurred, he had chosen to believe it was a myth. Still, he could not help wondering what it would be like to ride an inner tube down the spillway, and what would happen to a person who tried.

As he made his way further down the path, the sound of the river got progressively louder. The hot summer air felt cooler the closer he got to the river. The dry towering hills that surrounded him gradually turned into a wet marsh with towering grass and brush.

Michael immediately knew it was Jake he was looking at when he got to the river's bank. Jake was tall and thin with wiry blond hair that appeared almost white, and light blue eyes and pale skin. Jake looked as though he had never spent a moment in the sun, and considering Jake lived every day of his life fishing a river under the sunny New Mexico sky, Michael found this odd.

Michael stopped at the end of the path. Jake stood knee high in the middle of the river wearing neoprene waders, a t-shirt, and a cowboy hat. He had his fly rod under his arm as he used his fingers and teeth to tie a new fly on the end of his fishing line. When he was finished tying the fly on the line, he took the handle of the rod in his right hand and began to slowly cast back and forth until the fly line was gradually extended. Soon there was a long trail of the line slicing through the air high above Jake's head. The faint rhythmic swooshing of the fly line over the river lasted for quite some time as Jake worked his cast.

Michael knew fly fishing, having gone many times with his father while he was growing up. He knew that the casting was in part for the positioning of the fly in the water, but mainly to dry the fly so that it floats naturally like a bug that has fallen into the water. Jake was far past positioning, and the fly would be dry after only several casts. Jake's eyes were closed. He was calm and content, visually unaware of his surroundings. He was listening.

Michael wondered what he was listening for. Michael could hear the fly line and the river, and despite the tranquility it provided, Michael felt that Jake was hearing something else. Jake continued to cast.

The rhythm was perfect. If you begin to cast forward before the line has flattened out in the air behind you, it will snap like a bull whip breaking your line and sending your fly into the brush. If you begin too late, the fly will approach your head, and you risk hooking yourself in the ear or head. But Jake was neither early nor late. He was perfect.

Michael began to wonder if Jake would ever complete the cast. He questioned whether Jake was even fishing at all, but thought he had to be because he watched him replace the fly. Jake turned slightly to his right, the fly line obediently following, and cast forward with an extended arm. The fly line looped and slowly began to settle toward the water. Michael saw that following the loop and the fly line was the leader, the tippet, and finally, like a dead bug that had fallen from a tree, the fly landed softly in the water floating high in the downstream.

Not two seconds passed when the fly was attacked by a fish. Jake quickly raised the fly rod high above his head setting the hook. The reel squealed as the fish darted downstream. Jake did not grab the reel as most rookie fly fisherman would do, knowing the very thin line would snap. He gently put the palm of his hand against the reel to provide slight resistance.

Jake turned to face downstream, his eyes still closed. His breathing was deep and slow. It was as though he was receiving some sort of blessing from a god, taking in powers and knowledge. He was the student and the river was his master.

It took over fifteen minutes for Jake to get the fish reeled in close enough so that he could touch him. When it finally did happen, Jake's eyes opened for the first time. He did not smile, but he looked pleased as he saw what he had caught. He changed hands, holding the fly rod in his left arm and ribs, and then put his right hand into the river. He did this so that he would not damage the fish's slim coat which helps to keep the fish healthy. After soaking his hand, he gently slid his hand under the belly of the fish and raised it slowly out of the water. He turned it slightly so that the fish and Jake could look eye to eye.

Michael was not certain, but he thought he saw Jake's mouth move, whispering something to the fish. Jake, very carefully, removed the hook from the fish's mouth, and lowered it back into the water. He held it so that the river was running into its mouth and out its gills. He did not let go of the fish until it was ready to swim off on its own. A moment later the fish kicked with its tail and was gone.

Jake remained crouched for a moment peering into the river's water. It was Sunday, Michael reminded himself, and this was Jake's church.

"Poor guy must be tired," Jake said as he stood and turned to face Michael. "I caught him yesterday too. Not on the same fly, but same place."

Jake stumbled toward Michael, trying hard not to lose his footing in the current of the river. Michael wondered how long Jake had known him to be watching, and if Jake knew who he was talking to. 'Poor guy must be tired' was not the strangest greeting Michael had received, but it was close.

"How are you Jake?" Michael asked.

"Damn good, Mike. Damn good." He said as he reached the bank of the river and shook Michael's hand. "Haven't seen you in, well, since high school."

"I know, I meant to come back sooner," Michael responded.

"Yah, we all mean to do things we never seem to get around to doing."

"Isn't that the truth."

Jake took the fly off the end of the tippet and pierced it through the side of his cowboy hat next to more than a dozen other flies. "I assume Kevin and Sam told you where I lived."

"Yes."

"Good. Well, let's go to my trailer and have a beer."

"Sure," Michael said and followed Jake down the marshy trail, worsening the damage to his Italian shoes.

When they got back to the trailer Jake got two beers out of cooler next to the couch, threw one to Michael and then sat down, transferring the river water and mud from his waders to the couch. Michael wondered if Jake were getting the couch dirtier or if the couch were getting Jake dirtier.

"Why'd you let it go?" Michael asked as he opened his beer.

"He's a good fish," Jake said.

"Good fish?"

"Yep, good fish."

"Okay, so you keep the bad fish?"

Jake smiled, "Sometimes. If I'm hungry for fish, I'll keep them and eat them."

Although Jake's physical appearance had changed a bit since high school, Michael could not believe the other remarkable ways in which he was different. He lived in a dump and talked and acted like an idiot. Or, was Michael the idiot? Michael suddenly realized he had nothing in common with his friend. He gazed around Jake's trailer. There was not a television or radio, no books, no puzzles, nor anything that could be used to pass the time. He assumed that Jake spent all his spare time sitting on the stool in the middle of the kitchen tying flies, thinking about fishing. Jake had nothing but fishing, and Michael came to talk about the tape; little else interested him, unless it was something related to fishing.

"We've lost the tapes," Michael said, deciding to get to the point.

Jake paused for a moment and then with a nervous look on his face, tried to smile. "Thought Sam was going to destroy them?"

"No. He kept them, and now some old man has them."

"How long ago?" Jake asked, looking quite concerned.

"About two weeks."

Jake stared at his can of beer and pressed the pop-top with his thumb then released it, causing a vibrating, buzz sound. He did this for several minutes, looking as though he was fascinated with his new toy.

"He'll find it in about another two weeks, I would say," Jake said.

"Sounds about right," Michael replied.

Jake sat back into his couch and began pressing the pop-top of his beer can harder and in shorter intervals. Michael stared dully at him for a moment trying to decide what to say next.

Jake cleared his throat and said, "I can't go with you."

"I know," Michael said.

Jake nodded, confirming that they both understood his condition and the cause of it. He could not wait for Michael to leave so that he could return to the river and close his eyes to the world.

"I also know about the jar," Michael said, not able to look Jake in the eyes. "Sam told me."

"You don't believe it, do you?" Jake asked.

"No," Michael said.

"Any time of my life prior to the night they found us, I would have said the same thing."

Michael felt pity for his friend as Jake sat in filth on his couch. Michael remembered the last night they were camping, Jake was being taught by Sam how to shotgun a beer. Jake punched a hole at the bottom of the can, and when Sam yelled, "now," Jake raised the beer, opened the top, and tried to swallow the beer as quickly as he could. Beer shot from his mouth and nose, covering his glasses with white foam. As Michael, Sam, and Kevin laughed, Jake stood dazed and defeated; drenched in beer. A moment passed, and Jake began to laugh along with his friends. He dropped his beer and held his hands out as if he was blind, the foam of the beer still covering the lens of his glasses. "You blinded me, Sam! You blinded me!"

"I remember who you were," Michael said looking into his beaten friend's eyes.

"I don't."

"I promise you that I'll find the jar and open it," Michael added, thinking the story was ridiculous.

Jake lifted his head to look at Michael; the energy and hope had been sucked from his soul. His eyes were tired and dull. His face was that of a much older man, a man no longer interested in living.

"Don't go," Jake pleaded, his voice tired and weary.

"Why?"

"They'll know you're coming. They'll not be as generous as the last time."

"Look at you, Jake. Do you think they were generous the last time?"

Jake pushed himself up from the couch and stood motionless for a moment. "I am tired, you should leave," he said.

Michael put his unfinished beer on a pizza box next to the chair and stood. He thought for a moment about giving Jake a hug or a pat on the back, but simply turned and walked out of the trailer.

Michael had just started the engine of his rental car when Jake came out of the trailer, holding something in his right hand that looked like a football. It wasn't until Jake got closer that he realized it was a wooden carving of some type of animal. Michael quickly got out of the car to meet Jake.

"What is that?" Michael asked.

"That night. I took it that night," Jake said, still approaching Michael.

Michael took the carving from Jake and was amazed at the weight. His other arm quickly rose as he needed both hands to support it. The carving resembled a bull, but Michael's impression was that it was very poorly crafted. Despite the poor artwork, he was mesmerized as he admired the bull.

Surrounded by a fortune of gold that night, Michael wondered why Jake had taken a carving of a bull.

"This must weigh forty pounds," Michael said.

"You're pretty close," Jake said not smiling. "There is gold in the belly of that thing."

"Gold?" Michael whispered. "Where?"

"In the belly," Jake responded. "There's a latch on the belly that opens a hatch. The belly is full of gold."

"Really?" Michael asked, turning the bull upside down to examine its belly. "Can I open it?"

"No!"

"Why?" Michael asked startled.

"I think it's cursed," Jake replied. "Please, never open it."

"Cursed? What are you talking about?"

"I don't want to talk about it anymore," Jake said, refusing to look at the bull.

"Well, here you go," Michael said trying to hand it back to Jake.

"No. You take it," Jake said.

Michael was very exited. He tried to do the math quickly in his head, but settled on knowing it was worth hundreds of thousands of dollars. And it was his.

"Take it back," Jake said still refusing to look at it.

"What?" Michael said.

"Take it back," Jake repeated.

"Give it back to those fuckers? You're crazy."

"I've been told I'm crazy," Jake said with a tear running down his cheek. "Michael, please take it back."

"But we could sell this thing and get you out of this trailer and…"

Jake raised his voice, "Please take it back!"

Michael's grin slowly lowered until his expression nearly mirrored that of Jake's. "You think you're cursed because you took this bull?"

"I don't know if it's because they put my hat in the jar or that I took that bull," Jake replied. "I was the only one they put into a jar. I was the only one that took anything. I'm the only one that is the way I am."

"Look, Jake. Maybe this is all in your head."

"It's all in my head, and I can't get it out," Jake said a tear falling from his other eye. "If you are really going back, I need you to please help me. There was a day when you were a boy that I could trust you to do this for me. Now all I have is faith you are still that same boy."

"You really believe you're cursed," Michael said.

"Yes," Jake said, lowering his head.

Michael reached into the back seat of his car and grabbed a backpack he used to carry around files. He took the files out. Files he really did not have any work to do on but wanted to use them as a prop to show his friends how important he was. He carefully put the bull into the backpack as if it were fragile glass.

"I won't tell anybody about the bull. And I promise, I'll return it to them."

Jake nodded, turned and walked away. Michael got back into the car and Jake picked up his fly fishing pole and ambled down the path to the river. Michael was eager to return to give Jake the good news that the curse had been broken. He wondered if Jake would snap out of the funk when he heard the news, or if he would finally discover that Jake had simply lost his mind. In any event, Michael would do what he promised his friend.

Jake heard Michael's car as it reached the end of the dirt road and turned back onto the highway. He fought the desire to look back. He walked in silence through the tall brush, allowing himself to absorb the crescendos of sounds of the river. When he reached the bank of the river, he sat his fly rod down, propping it against a bush carefully so that the fly line would not get tangled.

He crouched slowly and sat on his heels, placing his head in his hands. A small pool of water spiraled just inches from his feet. A leaf entered the pool, circled a few times, and returned to the current of the river. A slight breeze created small ripples of water in the pool to sparkle in the sun and reflect the bright blue sky and brilliant white cotton clouds above. He imagined himself to be much smaller. Small enough to make the little ripples appear like waves in the ocean.

He thought of his mother and a time at the beach when he was very young. The waves come toward him, and just before they crash into his body, his mother raises him by the arm, lifting him above the danger. He smells suntan lotion and salt water. A wave catches them by surprise, and he gets caught in its spiraling force, slamming him against the ocean floor in a twisting confusion of water and sand. He feels his mother grab his arm, but the next wave crashes into them and he feels her grasp slip from his arm. He tumbles in the water, not knowing which way was up, not caring. He knows his mother will pick him up. He knows she will not let him go.

~

June 1520

The lady stood at the dock holding the hand of her fourteen year-old son. She wore a cloth dress her mother had given her that was made out of wool, designed to look similar to the more prestigious Italian cloth of the time. The side of her dress had been crudely tailored with leather strands weaving through holes from her waist to her armpit. When she raised her left arm, the leather weave became visible, appearing like the back of a poorly crafted corset. The purpose of the leather strands was not for design, but rather so the dress could still fit her. Despite the odd style of the dress, it was the only one she owned. The other ladies in her small village envied the dress, and despite knowing that it was little more than rags to the people at the dock, she wore it with pride. This was a special day, and she had to look her best for her son.

She carried a wool sack with clothes for her son, some bread, and a wooden bull. She and the boy left the village in eastern Spain over a week prior. They walked most of the way, fortunate enough to ride on the back of a horse drawn carriage for part of the trip. Their retreat from the village was in the middle of the night and a secret from everyone. If the villagers knew where she was taking her son, and more importantly, that she had taken the Bull, they would have stoned both of them.

The village had been plagued with drought for nearly a decade. The crops were dead and worthless, and the winters a cold hell. When she sat next to her dying husband during the winter, she had formulated the plan to get her son out of the village and send him to the new world everyone was talking about. She knew that nobody in the village would approve of her plan, not even her dying husband. It was not until her husband passed away on a cold February night that she took his lifeless hand in hers and told him what she was going to do. Tears ran down her face as she explained to him that she was going to send their son to the Americas, and give him the Bull so that he could buy fertile land and start a better life for himself.

She did not know who carved the Bull. It was passed down through the history of the village, no one knowing who created it. The Bull, however, was not what the villagers were obsessed with, but rather what it carried in its belly. As far back as she could remember, when a person in her village was able to get gold for any reason, it would be placed in the belly of the bull. Over many years, the belly was finally full, and despite the droughts and disease that loomed over the village, they lacked the desire to spend any of the gold to help their troubled times or loved ones.

When she walked her son to the boarding plank of the boat, her hands trembled. She knew it would be difficult to put her son on the ship and never see him again, but letting the Bull go was unbearable. She hugged her son and kissed him on the forehead, her hand drifted down the wool sack feeling for the Bull. She fought the urge to take the sack from her son and run toward the village. Her legs were shaking and she felt sickly, her head faint and dizzy.

They cried as they said their goodbyes.

She stumbled as she made her way on top of a grassy hill, and fell exhausted on the ground, sobbing. When she heard the voices call out that they were casting off, she got into a sitting position, wrapping her arms around her legs as she pulled them tight against her chest. She continued to sob as she watched her son, the Bull, and the ship sail to the horizon. When the boat was little more than a speck on the water, and the sun began to set, she stopped crying. She reached into a small satchel and pulled out a broken tip of a sickle. She placed the index and forefinger of her left hand on her ribs that covered her heart and pressed the tip of the sickle between them. She pressed the blade into the gap of her ribs until it penetrated her skin. She grimaced at the pain and positioned herself on her knees. She prayed for her son, and pleaded with God to forgive her. She fell limp onto her chest, allowing her body weight to drive the blade into her heart.

On the fourth night on the boat, the boy sat on the deck listening to the ocean, the flapping of the sails, and the stretching of the ropes as the boat rocked gently. He had spent every night on the deck of the boat. Some of the men below were very ill, the stench was unbearable, but the main reason is that he had never been on a boat before, and being in the open air sailing across the vast dark ocean gave him cerebral feelings he had never experienced.

Two drunken men approached the boy and offered him a jug of wine. He smiled and took the wine from the men. They all sat drinking wine well into the night until one of the men asked the boy what he had in his bag. The boy explained that he was poor. He came from a distraught village, and was sent by his mother to start a new life in the Americas. He wanted to be a farmer, and had nothing but clothes and some bread. They demanded to see what was in the bag, and the boy reluctantly opened it for them.

The men rummaged through the boy's clothes, ate some of his bread, and one of the men held up the Bull. When he asked the boy what it was, the boy replied that it was just something he had carved.

The men made fun of the boy, referring to his bull as a toy. The boy nervously watched the men play with the Bull as they acted out bull fights, pretending a goblet was a matador. When the boy asked for the Bull back, the men only laughed. They taunted the boy with it making grotesque snorting sounds and ramming it into his chest. He pleaded with the men.

One of the men staggered to the edge of the boat and asked the boy if the Bull could float. The boy ran to the man and tried to grasp it from him. He begged the man not to throw it into the ocean. The man laughed and pushed the boy to the ground. Enraged, the boy stood and punched the man in face. The Bull fell on the deck of the boat.

The man stood shocked for a moment, and when he gained his senses, he grabbed the boy by the shoulders. The man stared the boy in the eyes, blood running from his nose. He told the boy that he would take good care of the Bull, and cast the boy into the cold dark ocean.

CHAPTER 11

Sheldon had been awake for quite some time, but remained motionless in his sleeping bag, listening to Lowery move about the campsite. He was thinking about the Navajo man he saw standing next to the trail when his other grandfather sent him to look for the creatures in the cave. He spent some time, as his mind slowly cleared from the fog of sleep, wondering if what had happened was real or simply a dream.

Lowery had already put fresh wood on the fire, and as the fire began to build, Sheldon was becoming uncomfortably hot. Soon he would have to leave his sleeping bag and begin the day, but he delayed, allowing himself to enjoy the desert smells and sounds. Assuming the fire had been made to cook breakfast, he was motivated to sit up. When Sheldon stretched to a sitting position, his grandfather was leaving slowly, holding a shovel. After his grandfather took a few more steps, the violent buzz of a rattlesnake's rattle permeated the silence. Sheldon quickly jumped out of his sleeping bag and ran to his grandfather.

"Wait," Sheldon said, grabbing the end of the shovel.

Lowery turned his head slowly to look his grandson in the eyes. "What the Hell do you think you're doing?"

"Don't," Sheldon said not letting go of the shovel.

"You wanna do it, fine," Lowery said letting go of the shovel and walking back to the campfire.

Sheldon looked down and realized how close the rattlesnake actually was to him. It was coiled tight with its head arched backwards. Venom and saliva sprayed from its mouth as it hissed at Sheldon, the rattle shaking so quickly now that it sounded like an electrical current.

"Shit," Sheldon said taking a tighter grip of the shovel.

"Well, smack it!" Lowery said sitting on a cooler near the fire.

"No," Sheldon said lowering the shovel. The rattlesnake's head followed the direction of the shovel's head, and for a moment Sheldon thought it would strike at it.

"Do you know what that thing could do to you if it bit you?" Lowery asked.

"Yes," Sheldon said softly. "But, I think it knows what I could do to it also. That is why it's prepared to strike. It's scared."

"It looks scary, I'll give you that, but it doesn't look scared."

"I've never killed one, Lowery," Sheldon said.

"Hell, we used to kill dozens of them a day out on the patch."

"Amazing," Sheldon said softly as he slowly started to crouch to take a closer look at the snake.

"You some kind of dumb-ass, or something?" Lowery asked, shaking his head.

"I won't hurt you," Sheldon whispered as he sat on his heels, looking directly into the snake's eyes.

The snake raised its head hissing louder, exposing its long fangs that glistened with venom.

"You fucking retarded, boy?" Lowery asked standing up from the cooler.

"Calm down and go away," Sheldon said to the snake.

"You better get away from that snake, Sheldon. You better get away from that thing right now or I'm going to knock you into next week."

The rattlesnake closed its mouth and the rattle began to slow.

"If it doesn't feel threatened, it will go away," Sheldon said.

"Who cares, goddamn it, just whack the stupid thing."

A few minutes passed when the snake's rattle slowed, and finally stopped, the rattle standing motionless in an erect position. Sheldon could see the muscles in the snake start to loosen as it started to uncoil its body. The snake eventually was lying flat, and began to slither away from Sheldon into the bushes, occasionally turning its head to see if Sheldon was about to attack it. Moments later the snake was gone.

"Wow," Lowery said. "You must feel pretty special."

"What do you mean?" Sheldon asked, returning to the fire and setting the shovel down.

"The gift of being able to talk to reptiles is…."

"Come on," Sheldon interrupted, "I just didn't see a reason to kill the thing."

"Next time you run across one of those things you whack it with a shovel. I'm not going to drive you to the hospital if you get bit while staring face-to-face to a goddamn rattlesnake."

"I've just never seen the reason to kill one," Sheldon said.

"Fine, you've seen one now," Lowery responded. "You hungry?"

"Yes."

Lowery took a pair of pliers and used them to pull a charred can out of the fire. He sat the can on a rock next to him and, holding the hot metal with a rag, opened it with a can opener.

Sheldon could see that the can was filled with boiling baked beans.

"Here," Lowery said, using the pliers to set the can on a rock next to Sheldon. "Don't touch the can; it's very hot."

"I can see," Sheldon said grabbing a spoon. "Beans?"

"You don't like beans?" Lowery asked.

"Sure, just that it's breakfast and, well, there's a lot of them."

"Thought you were hungry?"

"Okay, I'll just let them cool a bit."

"Good thinking," Lowery said and placed another can of beans into the fire.

Sheldon realized that his other grandfather, the self-proclaimed medicine man, was no longer with them. If he were missing, Sheldon decided he was not going to go look for him.

"Where is Ernest?" Sheldon asked.

"I don't know," Lowery responded.

"Are we done with him?"

"I am. Do you need more guidance?"

Sheldon pondered the question for a moment. He was not sure that he had received any guidance. He had more questions than answers. Had Ernest drugged him the night before? Was it a dream? He doubted that he actually saw unnatural creatures and a large Navajo man, but what was the explanation?

"I'm good for now," Sheldon said. "So, what's next?"

Lowery used the pliers to rotate the beans in the fire. "We need to get some more gear and a couple of horses."

"Horses? Won't it be faster to take the truck?"

"Two reasons we need horses," Lowery said. "First, the Bureau of Indian Affairs, BIA, is not going to allow us to drive all around the reservation without permits. We do not have time to get permits. So, we will stay off the roads on horses. Second, when you drive in a truck between two places you miss almost everything. We need to go slow so that we can look for the trail."

"I thought we had coordinates from the pilot?"

"We have approximate coordinates from the pilot. I would say we have a margin of error of about twenty square miles. Now, I don't know about you, but I don't have time to dig enough holes to cover twenty square miles."

Sheldon shook his head. "But, don't you think the government has sent more planes to pinpoint the location?"

"Almost certain of it," Lowery replied. "But, we don't have those taped interviews."

"Do you think it's still there?"

"I don't know. I've never gone after a treasure that I knew wouldn't be there."

Sheldon realized that all the times he wished to go on an adventure with his grandfather were about to come true. This was becoming far more interesting than he had ever expected.

"What trail are we looking for?" Sheldon asked.

"Trabuco's trail," Lowery said, pulling the other can of beans out of the fire.

Sheldon had spent some time researching the lost gold myth his grandfather had told him about. He knew a considerable amount about Trabuco and the Mexican investors. Despite his intelligence and his experience in research, Sheldon had the feeling that his grandfather knew considerably more about the legend.

"What are we looking for?" Sheldon asked.

"I don't know. You never know until you see it." Lowery could see that his grandson was not pleased with his answer. "It's called treasure hunting. You arm yourself with knowledge and you set out on the hunt. Same as oil. The ordinary person looks at a rock formation and sees just that, a rock formation. A geologist who specializes in oil and gas can see more than just rocks. He can see clues, history, signs of fortune. Ten years from now a person could find this campsite and see an old can of beans and think nothing of it. If a person were trying to follow the trail of Daniel Lowery, and knew that he loved beans for breakfast, that can of beans would tell a much different story, don't you think?"

"How many treasures have you found?" Sheldon asked.

Lowery laughed as he opened the can of his beans. "Oh, Sheldon, I have found plenty of treasures. Plenty of treasures, indeed."

"You also mentioned supplies," Sheldon said. "Do you mean ante? That's what Ernest suggested that we get to keep the Skinwalkers away."

"Catch and eagle and suffocate it?" Lowery chuckled and shoved a spoonful of beans into his mouth. "Catch and eagle and suffocate it," he repeated shaking his head.

"So, no ante," Sheldon said.

"Sheldon, I've heard all sorts of ghost stories. Most have been about mermaids, haunted pirate ships, evil ghosts that float on the waters of the ocean. Oh, I've heard many stories. I'd like to tell you that evil witches who can turn into animals is the most bizarre story I've heard, but I can't. Every culture has a boogeyman. Hell, you know this. You studied cultures, didn't you?"

"Yes. I wasn't suggesting that I believe in Skinwalkers, I was just…."

"That's fine. We don't need ante because there are no Skinwalkers that will be affected by the dried dust of an eagle's bladder. Now, we might run into a couple of crazy Navajo who pretend to be Skinwalkers, but I got a semi-automatic with night sights that will hold them at bay."

Sheldon began to eat his beans as Lowery twisted the can of beans on the fire with the pliers. Despite Sheldon being half Navajo, Lowery's face and arms were darker than Sheldon's, nearly black from years of sun exposure. The darkness of his skin made his light blue eyes glow, eerily fake. His face had several scars, and Sheldon thought that the only thing missing from Lowery to confirm that he was actually a modern-day pirate was a patch over one of his eyes. He was aware his grandfather was a treasure hunter, but also knew that he did not always get the treasure without using force. He also realized that Lowery would not be pleased when he told him why he was on the trip, and decided that the more he delayed the truth, the harder Lowery may take it.

"You know, Lowery, I'm not as interested in gold as I am about something else I hope to find," Sheldon said.

Lowery looked up at Sheldon appearing to be interested in what he had to say. "What do you mean?"

"I did my thesis paper on the mingling of ancient cultures. For example, what happened when Columbus first made contact with Native Americans? It's very interesting. Imagine two completely separate cultures, with little to no knowledge of the realities and beliefs of the other, colliding. It must have been very exciting," Sheldon said a bit too enthusiastically.

Sheldon sensed his grandfather thinking he was very odd and continued. "Sometimes the encounter was somewhat pleasant. Sometimes, as was the case for some of the tribes in South America when discovered by the Spanish, the encounter was not so pleasant. And, sometimes the encounter was unknown and there is no documented history."

"What are you talking about?" Lowery asked.

"The oldest town in the United States is not back east. It was not Jamestown or any other town in the new colonies. The oldest town is Santa Fe, New Mexico. The Spanish settled into the west by coming up through Mexico long before Manifest Destiny. As the Spanish migrated north, oddly enough searching for Cortez's City of Gold, they encountered various Native American cultures. Many of those encounters are well documented, while strangely, one in particular is not."

Sheldon took a few quick bites of his beans and saw that Lowery was being patient and seemed interested enough for him to continue.

"There is no history of the encounter between a group of Spanish Conquistadors and a Clan of Navajo that lived in this region."

"Why?" Lowery asked.

"Well, that was the question I asked in my thesis. Do you want to hear my conclusion?"

"Sure."

"As the Spanish searched for the City of Gold, many of the men decided to settle into the villages along the way. There were probably many reasons for this, they got sick, they fell in love, they were tired, and so on. I believe the last of the men made their way up into what is now the Four Corners area, and never left. I think they stayed and probably colonized with a tribe, or what the Navajo call a Clan."

"So?"

"So? So, there may be a Clan of people that is a mixed breed of Spanish and Navajo. An existing ancient civilization."

Lowery shook his head. "Hell, I don't know many people that aren't some kinda mix. Most Americans are mutts. You've heard the term, 'Heinz 57,' haven't you?"

"Yes," Sheldon said, "but that is not the point. It is not interesting what gene make-up a Spanish and Navajo would create; it is what their culture would become. What have the children been taught over the years? Do they have a deity, a god, Skinwalkers? What do they believe?"

Sheldon reached for his backpack and pulled out a large folded map. He unfolded a portion of the map and laid it on the ground between him and Lowery.

"In my research, I concluded that the lost men of Cortez made it as far as the Chuska Mountains. That is here," Sheldon said pointing to a mountain range on the map. Sheldon then raised his arm and pointed to the east. "Those are the Chuska Mountains."

Sheldon then moved his finger slightly down from the mountains and said, "And that is Shiprock."

Lowery smiled, "I never told you the coordinates the pilot gave on the tape."

"No, but last year when you were doing your research you said you thought we could find the gold near the Four Corners. I was finishing my thesis at the time, and was practically writing the words as you said it."

Lowery tested the side of his can of beans to make sure it was cool enough to pick up. Once satisfied, he picked it up and began to eat his beans quickly.

"Well," Lowery said with a mouth full of beans, "I wish I could tell you that we aren't going anywhere near the Chuska Mountains, but I'm afraid we are." Lowery raised his spoon and pointed it at Sheldon. "You listen very clear, boy. I take this treasure hunting very seriously. I'm not doing this to go find some Spanish Indians. Do you got that?"

Sheldon nodded his head confirming that he did.

"You'll concentrate on finding the gold or you'll go it alone. I don't give a worm shit about your thesis or ancient cultures. You can go farting around those mountains all you want after we get the gold. Am I being clear?"

"Yes, sir," Sheldon said sounding like he did when he was a boy.

"Your father died in those mountains because he didn't have his head on straight. You better get focused."

Sheldon suddenly lost his timidity. "You know what happened to him?"

Lowery threw the rest of his beans in the fire and nearly choked as anger filled his head. "Not for certain, goddamn it. Not for certain."

"What did you hear?"

"Forget about it, damn it," Lowery said, turning red with anger.

Sheldon's chest broadened, "Listen, Lowery, I am pretty sure you could take me in a fight, but you are talking about my father…and your son. I have been pretty damned patient with this over the years, and now I know what I have always suspected; that you know what happened to my father. Now, if you want to keep that from me, I swear, I will fight you. Right here and right now."

Lowery was slightly impressed with his grandson, but would dare not tell him that. It would not be much of a fight, he knew, but the boy was right. "I heard he was stabbed in those mountains," he said calmly.

"What was he doing in the Chuska Mountains?"

Lowery wiped his spoon violently on his sleeve and spat. "He went looking for Trabuco's gold. He wanted me to go, but I decided it was a waste of time."

Sheldon's head dropped. "You don't know for sure? Who killed him? Why?"

Lowery took a deep breath and said, "Sheldon, have you ever been game hunting?"

"You mean for deer?"

"Yes, deer, elk, anything."

"No," Sheldon replied.

"Well, you know that sometimes hunters where orange, right?"

"Yes," Sheldon replied.

"Do you know why?"

"I suppose it is because there are other hunters around and they do not want to be shot," Sheldon replied.

"That's right," Lowery said with an odd smile. "In treasure hunting, nobody wears orange."

Sheldon looked at his grandfather with a new form of respect and fear. His grandfather was a pirate, and his father died trying to follow in his footsteps. Now, here Sheldon was, knowing the path he was about to go down but possessing no desire to turn the other way. This had never been about the gold, but now he was beginning to see the extent of his grandfather's obsession.

"Then why are we going?" Sheldon asked, not wanting to turn back but rather wondering what drove his grandfather.

"Because your father was right about the gold. I think the gold is still there."

"Is that it?"

Lowery paused for a long moment.

"I need to find the son-of-a-bitch who killed my son."

~

April 1962

Daniel Lowery was exhausted. He was on the tail end of a four day continuous work shift. The boss told the men that they had an hour to sleep before they set the remaining two anchors on the derrick, but Lowery chose to spend his time eating some dry elk meat and resting. He believed that relaxing and getting food in his belly served him better than a mere hour's sleep.

He sat on the edge of large steel pipe on the top of a bluff, the setting sun painting the sky with brilliant colors of red and purple. More than a dozen pump jacks slowly worked up and down as they drove pressure down the hole to push the oil up hole. Occasionally, he could hear the compressors at each location turn on and join together in a rhythmic orchestra of humming engines. The pump jacks obediently rose and fell in unison, living beings playfully engaging in a contest to keep perfect time, not unlike finely tuned clocks.

Below the well site an old pickup truck rumbled its way relentlessly up the poorly maintained dirt road. The engine roared as the tires spun on the clay and mud of the roads, the bed of the truck violently rattling and shaking, the sound of twisted metal clanging through the basin.

He would be home at sunrise, and he would get there with two weeks' pay. A year and a half ago when he first got this job, the seven dollars an hour seemed like a fortune. However, as he slaved night after night in freezing conditions, he became acutely aware that the 'suits' were the only men who were really benefiting from his labor. He knew that his time as a jobber was short lived. His wife was very disappointed in the poor lifestyle they were living. She did not understand that he was making a good salary, and yet, he always told her that they did not have money to buy anything. What she did not know is that Lowery had decided very early on that he would save every penny he made to buy his own rig. Then he could use his knowledge and experience to make real money. That Money would give her the life she deserved, and get Lowery out of the pit so that he could spend more time with her and their newborn son.

Lowery chewed a piece of the jerky off and filled his mouth with water so that he had enough liquid to chew the food. He was badly dehydrated; spending most of his time on breaks drinking whiskey straight out of the bottle. He had been unable to spit for days, saliva more like little cotton balls than spit. He needed the water now simply to chew the salted elk meat so that he could swallow it.

The truck pulled into the well site very quickly. In fact, it sped up far too quickly considering the safety standards that Conoco enforced without exception. The truck pulled up in front of a foreman, and when a suit exited the vehicle and spoke briefly to one of the hands, Lowery saw that the hand pointed in his direction. The suit walked directly toward Lowery. Lowery remained sitting on the large steel pipe, taking another bite of his elk jerky.

"Daniel Lowery?" the suit asked as he struggled to walk up the dirt hill to Lowery's perch.

"Yes, sir," Lowery responded and took another drink of water noticing that he did not have enough saliva to make the words sound coherent.

"Sir," the suit said as he stood trying to catch his breath. "Your wife has had an accident."

Lowery slid himself off the pipe and walked quickly to where the suit was standing, throwing his jerky to the ground.

"What do you mean she had an accident?" Lowery asked staring the man in the eyes.

The suit's shoulders slumped. He realized that he did not want to be the one to deliver the news to this man. Daniel Lowery was in his mid-twenties, and was built of pure muscle and grit. The suit feared that when he told him what corporate had instructed him to say, Daniel Lowery would throw him around like a rag doll.

The suit took a nervous deep breath and said, "Your wife fell off the roof of your barn. It was raining and she…"

"Is she okay," Lowery said, his hands shaking.

"No," the suit replied. "She has passed on."

"Passed on!" Lowery shouted. "Passed the fuck on!? You mean my wife is dead?"

"She is," the suit replied and took a step back toward the truck.

Lowery stood motionless for a moment, his face reddened, his breathing exaggerated and deep.

"I am so sorry," the suit said.

Lowery looked around the well site in desperation, his breathing deeper and more violent. The suit wondered what Lowery was looking for.

"YOU!" Lowery said as he pointed to a laborer who was standing next to the well head holding a large wrench.

The worker looked at Lowery and turned toward him, not knowing what news Lowery had just received.

"You got a problem?" the laborer asked.

"Don't, Lowery," the suit said, but was too late.

Lowery briskly strode down the hill directly toward the man. A few feet away from the man, Lowery said, "You called me a puss when I couldn't set that anchor last week!"

"You are a puss," the man said, standing a good five inches taller than Lowery.

When Lowery reached the man, the man raised the wrench as if to hit Lowery with it. Lowery grabbed the wrench, twisted it in the man's hand, and tossed it aside as though it was made out of balsawood. The man took a swing at Lowery, and Lowery made no effort to block the punch. A few more punches were thrown by the man, Lowery not attempting to block any of them.

Lowery's face was bleeding badly as the man continued to deliver blow after blow, the men at the site began to gather to watch the fight. But, it was not a fight at all. Lowery was not fighting back. He was taking the punches, some of them knocking him to his knees, and with every landed punch, Lowery cried out. His cries were not that of pain from the punches, but deeper, more disturbing cries. It was obvious to everyone watching, everyone but the man throwing the punches, that Lowery was not trying to fight. He wanted to be beat, and wanted to be beat badly. The physical pain was used to cover the pain brewing in his mind.

Lowery felt his nose snap, the bones shattered like a fragile piece of china being thrown at a brick fireplace. The jolt of pain burned like a welder's flame throughout his body. He could see his wife smiling, leaning forward to kiss him on the forehead. Another punch landed in the middle of his throat forcing him to gasp for air as he buckled to the ground. "You are my, everything," Lowery heard her voice whisper in his ear. "You are my man, and I will dedicate my life to you."

Lowery stood, trying to focus on the figure that was fighting him. The image of the man was blurry, not immediately identifiable. The man swung again, landing a punch on the side of Lowery's face. He did not feel a thing. Another punch followed, it had the same effect. Then the man sent his steel-toed boot into Lowery's stomach and he buckled forward, grasping at his stomach. Not able to get air into his lungs, Lowery fell to the ground again. Blood dripped from his nose and eye onto the mud below his trembling face. He remembered a blanket they spread on the bank of the La Plata River. He asked her to marry him. She said yes.

He stood slowly, swaying from side to side as he tried to gain his footing. He raised his fists to beg for more. More came. With every punch and kick that followed, the pain replaced the pain. With every blow came a snapshot of memory, the smell of her hair, the way her eyes sparkled like emeralds when she smiled, her laugh, … the way she laid herself on his chest and fell asleep, comfortable as her head raised and lowered with his every breath.

A derrick hand jumped into the fight, grabbing the man who was throwing the punches at Lowery. Lowery quickly threw his first punch, but it was at the man breaking up the fight. Lowery's punch landed hard and square, knocking the derrick hand out with a single punch. The man fighting Lowery stopped and watched as the derrick hand lay limp on the ground. His face turned from aggression to utter fear.

The man fighting Lowery stood awkwardly next to the limp derrick hand, lowering his hands and shaking his head. He spoke in a trembling voice, "I don't want to fight. I have nothing against you, Lowery."

Lowery turned away from the men and fell to his knees. He covered his face in his hands and began to cry. The cries turned to yells as Lowery screamed out his wife's name, his body shaking uncontrollably, his voice echoing throughout the basin. All the men standing around the once entertaining fight looked at each other dumbfounded. The last thing any of them wanted to do was to approach Lowery, a man they all feared could hold his own, but in this situation, may kill someone. A few uncomfortable moments passed and the men slowly started to walk away from the situation, going about their jobs as if nothing had happened.

Lowery finally stood and took in a deep breath. He walked to the man in the suit, and when he approached, the man winced as if he was going to be punched.

"Your keys," Lowery said.

"My what?"

"Give me your fucking keys!" Lowery shouted.

The man handed the keys to Lowery with trembling hands, and watched as he got in the truck and drove away. The man in the suit found himself standing at the well site surrounded by the sound of pump jacks and compressors as he watched his truck speed down the dirt road, leaving a large plume of dust behind.

~

September 1933

Trabuco's face was numb. He wondered how long his face had sliced through the cool summer night's air, but certainly Elliot would have to land to refuel soon and Trabuco could try and warm his face. A large tank was the asset he had found so appealing, but now he wondered how long he could tolerate the reserve.

Trabuco admired the beauty of the scenery below. They flew low, as he had instructed, so the ground was clearly visible. With the bright moon above to illuminate it, the ground was gray as the surface of the moon. He thought about Carlos somewhere below driving his Dodge pick-up back across the border. He hoped that Carlos would have no trouble explaining why two men had crossed and only one had returned. He doubted that customs would be that organized, but everything seemed to worry him lately.

He and the investors had managed to gather seventeen tons of gold. He had about eight tons himself. The other investors were feeding Rafael with money, and Rafael had delivered, producing the rest of the gold at a very modest price. It all fell on his shoulders now, his and his new friend Elliot, the pilot. Still, Trabuco could not help allowing himself to be consumed by the tranquility of the summer night.

"We'll start our descent soon!" Elliot yelled.

"Are we there?" Trabuco yelled back.

"Yes!"

Trabuco was happy to see that the group of men waiting along-side the runway was made up of Rafael and some of his trusted workers. He was a bit concerned when he saw the figures during the descent, fearing they may be *federalies*, but his concern turned to pride as the wheels touched down on the runway. This was his chariot. It was his flagship that would transport the riches into the United States. Certainly the investors would be impressed by his swift return and his ingenious idea.

When Trabuco deplaned, the workers scrambled to unload his gear for him. He stretched his legs and back for a moment, trying to get the blood to re-circulate through his body, his face still numb from the relentless beating of the wind.

"Trabuco, my friend," Rafael said, placing both his hands on Trabuco's shoulders. "A long journey."

"A very long journey," Trabuco said.

"Last time I was in Mexico, I had a cute little senorita under my arm," Elliot said strolling up to the two men.

"Rafael, this is Bill Elliot, our pilot," Trabuco said, presenting Elliot.

"Nice to meet you, friend," Elliot said, extending his hand.

"Yes, nice to meet you," Rafael replied. "I am sure we can arrange a senorita for you."

Elliot smiled.

"Rest is what we need for now," Trabuco added.

"You rest," Elliot replied, "I'll go with Rafael."

Rafael laughed. "There will be plenty of time for women and rest."

Elliot woke the next morning watching the thin lace curtains of his window blow gently in and out of his room. This is how he would spend his fall. Instead of raking fallen leaves, and then shoveling snow, he would be flying valuable cargo to and from paradise. He stretched his arms over his head and allowed himself to let out a very loud yawn. The yawn awoke the beautiful young woman who slept by his side. He brushed her hair gently and whispered in her ear that it was morning. They made love again.

After washing his face in a water basin, he changed into clean clothes and ventured out of his room and into the halls of the estate. The wooden floors creaked slightly as he walked down the hallway lined with solid brick walls. Below him in the courtyard Trabuco and Rafael were having breakfast near a large fountain.

"What's for breakfast?" Elliot asked as he approached the men.

"Whatever you desire, Bill," Rafael responded.

"Just call me Elliot, sir, everybody does."

"What would you like, Elliot?" Rafael asked.

"Just coffee and toast," he replied, sitting at a chair next to his new associates.

"Elliot," Trabuco said, "we have been discussing your compensation."

Elliot thought Trabuco's offer of $2,500 per flight was high, and wondered when the deal would be modified. This was expected, but he did not fly all this way for pocket change. "I thought we had a deal?"

"Relax," Trabuco said, "you will still get what we agreed to, but we want to offer you something extra."

"Something extra?" Elliot asked.

"Certainly you must know that what we have offered you is a lot of money for flights," Rafael said. "If what we were doing were legal, we could ship the goods for far less money than what we are going to pay you."

"I figured as much."

"We are not transporting anything dangerous," Rafael continued. "It's not guns or anything."

"Okay," Elliot said taking his cup of coffee from a young woman. "Do I even need to know?"

"We think it cannot be done any other way," Trabuco added.

"Gentlemen, I have committed to you that I'll do the job. You should just come out and tell me what's going on so that we can quit beating around the bush."

"Fine," Rafael said. "We're transporting just over seventeen tons of gold."

Elliot did not know how to react. He assumed seventeen tons of gold was a lot, but how much it really was, he had no idea. He wondered how big the load was and how many trips would it take to transport that much gold.

"You look concerned," Trabuco said.

"No," Elliot responded. "I am just trying to do some figuring in my head, payload and stuff like that."

"Well, that's your responsibility," Rafael said.

"I understand," Elliot replied. "It'll take some time to come up with flight plans and the balancing of the plane."

"There's time for that," Trabuco replied. "However, due to the amount of responsibility you have, we've decided to add a bonus. We're transporting the gold and plan to sell it in about a year's time. We would like to offer you 5% of the net profits for your services."

"What are my services?" Elliot asked.

"Transport and aid in hiding the gold," Trabuco replied.

Elliot smiled and moved his eyes back and forth to look at the men. He did this without moving his head and with an expression that looked more like he was consenting to some kind of conspiracy than one of concern.

"Whom are we hiding the gold from?" Elliot whispered.

"Everyone," Rafael added. "Secrecy is what you're being compensated for."

"Everyone ... got it."

"We have a lot of planning to do," Trabuco said. "That's if you are willing to accept the job."

"Sure," Elliot replied.

"Good," Rafael said taking note in his mind to compliment Trabuco on his successful recruitment.

"Yes, good," Trabuco said. "There are several things you should start working on. Come up with a schedule of flights. How many and when they will occur. You need to go back to the area and make a landing strip that is both concealed and easily accessible. We will also need to find a temporary storage site until I can come up and transport the gold to the final hiding spot. We need to establish a plan that involves only the investors and a few workers whom I trust. All the gold must be transported and at the final hiding spot by the end of this year."

"You both have invested a considerable amount of money in this project," Elliot said, "so I assume you know what you're doing. To be honest, it matters little to me if you do or not. But, I must ask why it must be done by the end of the year?"

"Certainly you must ask," Rafael replied, "and as you probably expected, we will decline to give you that answer."

Trabuco left the men to talk. He walked out of the estate and into the countryside, consumed with his thoughts about the transport. He had yet to decide whether he would take the bull with him. He knew he would not exchange the gold contained in its belly. The thought alone was not even a consideration. It was his bull. It was his gold. However, he needed it safe. A hiding spot secure enough for all their gold surely would be safe enough for his bull. There would be many trips, and he struggled with the thought of bringing the bull or leaving it behind. In either situation, the bull would be out of his possession. These thoughts troubled him the most about the plan.

CHAPTER 12

It was dark when Michael pulled into the driveway of his father's house. He knew that he would not be home because every Sunday night for the past thirty years he had gone to the local Baptist Church to play bingo. He was curious what all exactly went on during these bingo games that caused his father to return home smelling like whiskey. His mother never seemed to mind. It gave her time to work on little projects, knit, paint, or do other things she enjoyed without Michael's father bothering her. His father, however, was all alone now, his mother having died four years earlier.

His father seemed to be getting along fine by himself. The boys down the street kept the front yard looking very clean and trimmed in exchange for some money, lemonade and cookies. The house had recently been painted blue, a color Michael knew his mother would never had allowed. And, the house was just as clean as it had always been.

He was somewhat relieved to see his father's car was not in the driveway. He enjoyed talking to him, but he needed time to clear his mind. He had just promised an old friend that he would venture back into the Chuska Mountains to return an ugly wooden bull. He had considered several times during the drive back from the river of opening the bull, keeping the gold, and simply telling Jake that he had returned it. How would Jake ever know? Michael did not believe in curses, and maybe Jake would return to his normal self after being told the bull was returned without his actually returning it.

Michael reached into the back seat of the rental car and picked up the backpack, and although he was used to carrying a heavy load of files in it, it was far heavier now. He unlocked the front door and walked into the dark living room, setting the backpack on his father's old recliner. He turned on the hallway light and made his way to the kitchen.

He froze in terror when he saw the man standing next to the refrigerator.

The man was tall with a cleanly shaved head. He wore a cheap black suit with a white shirt and an even cheaper red power tie. He had an odd smile on his face when he saw Michael walk into the kitchen and raised a small pistol so that it pointed at Michael's chest.

"Relax," the man said, "the gun is just so you wouldn't run off when you first saw me. I'm going to put it away now, but don't think I can't pull it back out very quickly if I need to. You don't want to end up like your friend Sam, do you?" The man slid the pistol into a shoulder harness.

The man opened the refrigerator and pulled out a jar of olives. "These Spanish olives are fine, but I like those Greek ones. What are they called, Kalamata, or something?"

"Who are you?" Michael said, standing motionless at the entrance of the kitchen.

"Oh, this will go a lot smoother if you don't know the answer to that question. Please, sit down," the man said, pointing to a chair at the kitchen table. Michael sat as he was told.

The man pulled an olive from the jar and put it in his mouth. "You have done very well for yourself, Michael. Senior associate at Jackson, Thomas and Clark is something you should be very proud of. You're handling the Ventmo deal, aren't you?"

"I'm one of the attorneys working on that case, yes. Why?"

"You know," the man said crushing an olive in his teeth, "I know of a loophole. Offshore contracts out of Puerto Rico could make the deal go very smoothly. I would think if you could get your hands on some of those contracts that your client could gain about three-quarters of a billion in shipping business over the next several years."

"The Puerto Rico contracts are government contracts. I've looked into it already."

"Oh course you have. It would just take a committee member from say the Energy Department to give just a slight nod." The man chuckled, taking his glasses off and rubbing them on his sleeve. "I would think that getting such a contract would make your firm very happy. Hell, you would probably make partner. The youngest partner in the history of the firm. Wow!"

"What is this all…"

"And the street smarts you have as well. You see, they like men like you. Not just the nerdy type who spends their lives in the library, but the social ones. The rainmakers, I think they call them. You can wine and dine. You could bring in new clients."

The man put the olives back into the refrigerator and took out a Diet Coke.

"There was that time in Houston, though," the man continued. "Skinny dipping in the fraternity pool. Damn, who would have known that the police would be called on a false alarm next door? Damn. I have seen the pictures, and I must admit she appeared mature enough. And I cannot believe to this day that she was under age. She was hot, Michael."

"May I talk?"

"Pretty impressive lawyer you had. Lude and lascivious conduct with a minor was all you got. Five days in a county jail and a slap on the wrist. Whew!"

The man opened the Diet Coke and took a drink.

"Funny, the incident was never mentioned in your application to the New York Board of Bar Examiners, or your law firm application. Odd."

Michael adjusted himself uneasily in his chair.

"What is that word that is above the entrance of your firm, "honesty"? No, "Integrity," I believe."

"I didn't think a stupid college stunt was worth mentioning."

"Maybe not," the man said and leaned against the counter, "maybe not."

"What do you want?"

"Why are you in town, Michael?"

"I haven't been back in years. I wanted to visit my friends."

"Ah. It didn't have anything to do with Sam losing the tape?"

Michael did not know if the man was a cop, but he assumed that he was with some government agency. It would do little good to lie to him.

"It concerned me, yes," Michael responded.

"Concerned you, why?"

A vision came to Michael. His hands were tied high above his head and he struggled to keep from passing out. He looked to his left and saw Sam, his body covered in white ash. There was screaming. A distorted figure walked slowly toward him with wild eyes. The figure raised a long stick with a glowing tip and extended it forward toward Michael's stomach.

"I heard Sam had been shot," Michael chose to say.

"I see," the man said, tapping a finger on the side of the Diet Coke can. "Here's the deal, Michael. I know that you know where the gold is, so let's just get past that. I know where it is, as well. I work for some individuals who are very interested in obtaining the gold, but circumstances prevent them from going and getting it."

"What circumstances?"

"So, we would like you and your friends to get the gold and bring it to us."

"You want me to bring you seventeen tons of gold?"

"Yes."

"How do you suppose that can be done?"

The man reached into his coat pocket and pulled out some keys with a bottle opener for a key chain. He tossed them on the kitchen table.

The man paused for a moment, looking at Michael and then said, "Those are keys to a very large oil transport truck. The truck can carry well over seventeen tons. The truck, you will find, is quite nice. It is decorated in BIA permits and tags. You will have free range of the reservation with no questions asked. You see, simple."

"Simple," Michael said looking at the keys.

"You cannot get the contracts without me, and I cannot get the gold without you. A trade you might say. And that Houston incident, well, I am not sure there are any records of that. Well, at least not in anyone's possession except mine."

"The gold is worth far more than the contracts to me," Michael responded.

"You think so," the man said walking closer to Michael and taking a seat in front of him. "How would you sell seventeen tons of gold without being discovered? The moment you tried to move one bar of that gold you would have the Treasury Department crawling up your back like a crazed cat. The Navajo Nation would file a federal lawsuit that would get tied up in litigation for more than your lifetime. You would see nothing. You would be a man without gold, a job, or a license to practice law due to your false bar application. If that's what you meant by more, I guess you're right."

Michael lowered his head. "There is more than just getting the gold."

"Oh, yes. You are scared of the Indian witches. Skinwalkers I think they call them. It is a very scary legend."

Michael looked up at the man. "These people are out there."

"The people out there are not as frightening as the people I work for, trust me."

Michael watched as the man leaned a bit forward, his coat opening slightly, revealing his pistol. This was not an argument Michael was going to win, nor one that he wanted to continue.

"I'll try," Michael said softly.

"Good," the man said, standing up from the table. "There is the issue of the old man who took the tape. You need not worry about him; he is my problem."

"Hey, he's going after the gold, why not have him get it for you?"

"My people have chosen you. Their reasons are their own."

The man walked to the side door of the kitchen that exited to the side yard.

"Michael, you shouldn't tell anyone about this. Your friends are hicks. They do not understand the world the way we do. There are no heroes here, got it?"

"Yes," Michael said as the man sauntered slowly out of the house.

CHAPTER 13

Elliot sat on the tailgate of a pick up truck as Trabuco's workers unloaded the first shipment of gold. He thought of helping the men, but kept reminding himself that he was being paid to fly the plane, not to lift gold.

He had told the men that he needed a landing strip on the top of a mesa where he could see in all directions, wanting the benefit of remoteness as well as the ability to see if anyone were approaching. The spot they had chosen was perfect, at least for his part of the job. In a few months, Trabuco would be moving the gold to a location that only Trabuco and one other worker would know. How Trabuco would move the gold was not Elliot's problem, and despite telling himself this, he knew if he did not help Trabuco figure out a way to get the gold off the mesa, it would become his problem.

One of the workers sat down on a stack of gold bars and wiped his brow. Elliot watched him for a moment and began to realize how much work the Mexicans had done at the landing site. They had taken down what was once an old Anasazi hogan and used the adobe bricks to construct a tower near the landing strip. They were told to tie a white cloth to a stick and place it on the top of the tower so that when Elliot was on approach to the runway, he could see what direction the wind was blowing. They had also taken apart half of another Hogan and used the adobe bricks to outline a runway. In the center of the hogan that had been partially taken down was a large pit where the workers had begun to store the gold temporarily.

Just past the disassembled hogan the Mexicans had set up camp. They had several tarps they used as tents and had constructed a fenced corral for their horses. Nearly a mile away, one of the men sat motionless on a horse on the highest peak of the mesa. Nobody had discussed what they were supposed to do in the event that someone approached the mesa while they were unloading the gold. Elliot wondered if the men had a plan to cover the gold with a tarp and hide, or to dig in their heels and fight it out. Elliot knew what he would do, and that was to jump in his plane, never to return to the mesa. He could live just fine on the advance Trabuco had paid him.

Elliot waved at one of the resting workers to come to him. The worker did so obediently.

"How do you think Trabuco will get the gold off the Mesa?" Elliot asked, knowing this worker could speak some English.

"We've been working on this," the worker said with a thick accent.

"What have you been doing?"

"We are making a road off the back side of la mesa ... over there by the man on the horse. Very steep. But, we will finish."

~

Lowery placed his foot on the remnants of the hogan's wall and leaned forward looking down into the dark pit below. He stared motionless for a moment, allowing his eyes to distinguish the difference between the darkness and the floor of the pit. He was not surprised when he could see that there was nothing but sand at the bottom.

Sheldon dismounted his horse.

"Why don't we just go to where the pilot thought he got a radar blip?" Sheldon asked.

Lowery pushed on his knee to help himself return to the standing position and exhaled deeply.

"You in some kind of hurry?" Lowery asked.

"No, just don't know why we're here."

Lowery shook his head and sat on the edge of the wall. "I told you, there's too much guess work in the pilot's coordinates. That is why everyone has failed. They want the quick prize. They want to go straight to the X on the ground and find treasure. Well, like most things, you have to work hard for big return."

"Fine, but why are we here?"

"This is the starting point. This is where we begin our journey. Many years ago, Trabuco and Elliot stood at this location. This is where the gold was first flown in by Elliot and stored by the workers."

Sheldon looked around briefly. "How do you know?"

Lowery pointed to a strange stack of adobe bricks and said, "In your study of the Anasazi or any Indian culture, do you recall ever seeing a structure like that?"

Sheldon looked at the structure and replied, "No."

"That is because the Indian did not have airplanes and had no need for a wind tower."

Sheldon took his horse by the reigns and walked toward the structure.

Lowery continued, "These hogans were taken down and the adobe bricks used to construct that tower. Tall enough for a plane to spot, and it probably had some type of cloth at the top to allow the pilot to know the direction of the wind."

Sheldon reached the tower and placed a hand on one of the bricks. Lowery was right, this was not a structure any Indian tribe he had ever studied would build. It had no use other than what Lowery was telling him. For the first time since he discussed this trip with his grandfather, he actually believed the story to be true. Here was proof. A tower built by the men who smuggled the gold into the United States. Still standing.

Sheldon turned to his grandfather.

"Holy shit," Sheldon said. "You really know what you're doing, don't you?"

"Well, thanks son. I am glad you suddenly realized that I didn't just bring you out here to walk around the desert for awhile."

"They landed that plane right here," Sheldon said pointing to the ground. "And you can see forever up here. This place is perfect."

"Perfect," Lowery repeated.

"They probably hid the gold in one of those pits until Trabuco could transport it. Just like Elliot said in the Congressional hearings," Sheldon said.

"Yes," Lowery said, enjoying his grandson's deliberation.

"But how did they get it off this mesa?" Sheldon looked around pondering his own question. "No way they got down the way we came up."

"No," Lowery said, turning to face the eastern side of the mesa.

Toward the east, Lowery could see the large mass of rock called Shiprock. The dust and pollution from the power plants further to the east made the rock look as though it was a giant pirate ship sailing through fog on top the desert sands. He turned to the west and could see the peaks of the Chuska Mountains. Between the mesa and the Chuskas were numerous valleys, sand washes, and more mesas. Lowery closed his eyes and began to do what he always did during the beginning of a treasure hunt; he tried to think as Trabuco would have. He envisioned that he was the one who just landed on the mesa with the gold, and tried to think where he would take it.

"There are a lot of digs going on in Largo Canyon in an effort to find this gold," Lowery said turning to Sheldon. "Come here, son," he told Sheldon as he walked to the east edge of the mesa.

When Sheldon got to his side, Lowery pointed to the large rock formation called Shiprock and said, "That is Shiprock. Elliot's only disclosure regarding his job for Trabuco was that the landing site was near a famous New Mexico landmark near the Four Corners. Not much out here but that, I would say."

"Yes, I agree," Sheldon said staring at the large rock.

"Continue east, and you come to Shiprock, the town, and then Kirtland, and further east, Farmington," Sheldon said moving his finger to point toward the eastern horizon. "If you continue east, you come to Bloomfield and the beginning of Largo Canyon."

Lowery smiled at his grandson, "several years ago, some oil field workers found a few Spanish swords in Largo Canyon near a well site. It got some local folks very excited as they made the connection to Trabuco and his gold. Now, people are spending thousands of dollars excavating that area trying to find the gold. This is why we start here."

Sheldon thought he understood, but asked regardless, "Why?"

"Like I said, you don't start with the finish line. This is the starting point, Sheldon. Now that you are here, do you think there is any way the gold would be buried an hour from here in Largo Canyon? Do you think they would land here and then drive all that gold through several towns to bury it in Largo Canyon? Why not land east of all the towns and bury it there, if that was the final hiding spot?"

Sheldon knew that despite his education and intelligence, there were many things he could learn from his grandfather.

Lowery turned to face west and pointed toward the Chuska Mountains, and said, "They would go that direction. There are no towns, plenty of hiding spots, and nobody around to see what they were up to. Look around and all you see is canyons, mesas, and a mountain to the west. Not a living soul for miles."

"The Chuska Mountains," Sheldon added.

"I believe that the gold is either at the base of the mountains, or somewhere along the way. The radar hit is approximately there," Lowery said making a large circle with a pointed finger. "See, twenty mile radius is not that helpful. When a ship wrecks, it's hard enough to find any treasure even if you can find the approximate location of the ship. We sometimes search in a radius of hundreds of feet and can't find anything. Imagine this area as an ocean. We are searching in a radius of twenty miles in an ocean of dirt, trees, cliffs, and caves. We don't stand a chance unless we can follow the trail."

Sheldon walked to the west side of the mesa, occasionally looking up at the Chuska Mountains and feeling himself forget about the possibility of a lost civilization. He was consumed with the thoughts of gold. He caught himself whispering aloud, questioning where it was and how Trabuco got it off this mesa. When he reached the west edge of the mesa, discouragement overcame him as looked down at the cliffs and steep descent below him.

He noticed that Lowery had sat back down on the remnants of the Anasazi ruin, understanding that it was his time to go to work as Lowery rested. Sheldon started walking north along the west edge of the mesa. He had been on numerous digs with his archeology classes, and as he walked, instinctively he looked for ancient arrowheads. The presence of the Anasazi site made it very unlikely that he would find an arrowhead that dated into the paleo period, but still he looked.

He wove his way through what is called a blow-out, where the sand is either blown by the wind or swept away by running water. He saw several flakes of non-native rocks that were signs that there could be an arrowhead from the Folsom or Eden time period. He picked up the occasional flake and rubbed it with his fingers.

The day was drawing to an end as he proceeded to the furthest northern point of the mesa. He found an old oil can lying on the sand and picked it up to examine it. It was much larger that a Coke or soup can and had a hole punched in the top with little holes along the side of the can just below the larger hole. It was rusted to the point where he had no hope of reading anything on the can, but he immediately determined that it was an old oil can. An old oil can on the top of a mesa that could not be reached by vehicle.

He examined the ground for tire tracks, but laughed at himself. Tire tracks would have been blown away in a few days, and he was looking for clues that would have to been left for decades. He yelled at his grandfather to tell him about the oil can, but he was well out of range for Lowery to hear.

His attention was drawn to the edge of the mesa, and he took a few steps backward to see if what he thought he had seen was actually there. As he slowly backed away, he saw a widening between two large sandstone formations. One of the larger stones had fallen over. He examined the rock through squinted eyes and decided that it had not fallen over but rather had been pushed over.

He approached the fallen sandstone formation, and realized that a very steep clearing had been made that twisted its way down mesa. Stumps remained where trees had been removed to broaden the path, and as the path twisted down the mesa, more sandstone formations had been pushed down. It did not look like a road, but it did not look natural. There was a clearing near the bottom that was wide enough for a vehicle to drive through, and although it looked very steep and dangerous to drive on, he concluded that it had to be the way Trabuco got the gold off the mesa.

He stood at the beginning of the path and studied it as he examined every inch of the path. *There could be no other reason for this path,* he thought. *There was no well site on top of the mesa, no home, no sign of human impact, nothing but dirt. There was nothing but dirt, and at one time, gold.*

Looking down the path as it twisted its way down the mesa, Sheldon squinted as he saw something crawling hundreds of yards away. It was crawling toward him, but he could not make out what it was. He thought of running back to get Lowery, but did not feel threatened because the creature looked injured. It was crawling very slowly.

Sheldon found himself walking down the path toward the creature without having consciously chosen to do so. He was drawn to it, and felt an uncalculated desire to help it. He could not figure out what the thing was, despite the gap narrowing between them. It looked like a sick, unnaturally large dog, very skinny and very long.

Sheldon circled a large rock, losing sight of the creature for a moment, but when he cleared the rock, he saw that the creature was only twenty yards away from him. It sat panting and staring at him.

"You okay?" Sheldon asked still not knowing what the creature was. "You don't look so good."

The creature raised its head to look at Sheldon. It did not appear to understand, but seemed curious at the sound of Sheldon's voice. Sheldon doubted that the thing had ever heard such a sound. He continued to walk toward the creature, not knowing why or what he planned to do when he got to it.

"I won't hurt you," Sheldon said reaching his hand out toward the thing.

The red eyes of the creature looked into Sheldon's eyes. It looked helpless and battered. It panted heavily, showing signs of exhaustion and dehydration.

Sheldon was close now, close enough to the creature that he could touch it. He reached for it, not knowing exactly why he wanted to touch it. The creature snarled, displaying long yellow fangs covered in blood and flesh. Sheldon fearfully continued to reach for the animal.

"Looks like you found it," Sheldon heard a voice say from behind him.

Confused, Sheldon withdrew his hand from the animal. "What?" Sheldon asked the creature.

"Good job, son," Sheldon heard.

Sheldon took a step back, awakening from some type of trance. He suddenly realized the situation he had put himself in, and cautiously continued to back away. The creature snarled again and began to follow Sheldon.

"Lowery," Sheldon yelled, "I think I need help!"

Lowery rode his horse down the path, and when he came up behind Sheldon, Sheldon turned to look at him, his lips quivering.

"What's wrong?" Lowery said holding the machine gun in his hands.

Sheldon pointed at the creature and moved behind Lowery's horse, unable to speak.

"What, son?"

Sheldon peered out from behind Lowery's horse to see the creature again, but it was no longer there.

"You ok?" Lowery asked. "You look like shit, boy."

Sheldon continued to point to the where the creature had been but could not find the strength to speak. He was petrified with fear, but he was not sure why he was so afraid. He shook his head, attempting to clear it, and when he did, he found himself standing at the top of the path again, looking down its steep descent.

Sheldon turned south and saw that Lowery was sitting on the ruin and not in fact near him at all. He felt faint. He squinted again at the path to find the creature, but saw nothing. His knees were weak and he knew that he should go back to his grandfather soon. He took a few steps and collapsed.

Chapter 14

Michael was surprised at how easily he drove the oil rig transport truck. It was big and slow, but he felt comfortable behind the wheel. He had decided that there was no way he was going to be able to talk Sam and Kevin into helping him get the gold. So, he spent much of the time he was driving deciding when he was going to tell them what he planned to do.

He was an attorney driving a transport truck, preparing to load up wealth and fortune, proving to his friends that he was there only for the money. This would certainly cause a fight.

He worked a few summers during high school on the rigs. He could not design a derrick or run a swabbing truck, but he knew the general set up and process of drilling. He was a grunt, but he was an intelligent grunt. He had spent the long hours in the sun setting anchors or mixing mud, watching and listening to the bosses. It had been interesting to him at the time, but now, he felt that he was way above that kind of work.

He talked to some acquaintances from his past who still worked for some of the big jobbers, and learned that one of the companies had fallen on some difficult times. As a result of a booming oil and gas market, they had leveraged themselves as a big time player in the market. Unfortunately, the company also learned that no matter how good the market may be, cash is still cash. Buying up trucks, compressors, and rigs put the company in a position of being financed to the hilt. Now, with the cash gone, and without liquid assets, it was time to sell some assets.

As a result, Michael learned that Triple J and Sons had numerous inactive well sites scattered across the San Juan Basin. The presence of a rig transport truck at one of the sites would not be unusual, and he doubted anyone would notice.

After spending some time in the office of the Bureau of Land Management (BLM), he found a few sites fairly close to where he knew the burial site to be. It would be quite a hike from the site, but there was no way he would be able to drive the large truck any closer to where he believed the gold to be. He doubted the truck could handle the rough roads that would get him closer, and getting the large truck stuck was the last thing Michael wanted.

After passing through Shiprock, New Mexico, Michael turned down highway 504, a small-two lane road that wound its way through the Navajo reservation from Shiprock through the Four Corners area. Michael looked at the driver's side window and saw the various stickers and permits stuck to the glass, and rehearsed again in his mind what he would tell the BIA or Transportation Department if he were pulled over. He was prepared to be an employee for Triple J and Sons who was taking the truck to a rig that will be dismantled in a few weeks' time. This was a story he thought would carry a lot of credibility. When things went bad for an oil and gas company, word spread like a brush fire through the basin.

He dressed the part as well. He wore a baseball cap that had a logo for John Deere Tractor, a white Skoal T-shirt that he spent some time getting dirty with mud and oil, blue jeans, and steel-toed boots. Papers and job orders that he created the night before were stacked on top of a metal clipboard that sat in the passenger's seat.

As he drove, he tried to remember the turn-off. It was a dirt road several miles down Highway 504 that was not marked with a sign. The problem was that there were many dirt roads that led to nowhere. It had been years since he drove down the road, years spent trying to forget everything that happened the last time he drove down it. After getting as close to the location as he could, he would leave the truck and hitchhike back to town.

"What am I doing?" he said softly as he pressed on.

He stopped the truck in the middle of a dirt road and took a moment trying to figure out which way to turn. He calculated how far the Shiprock formation was from the campsite. He turned his head to look at the mountains to the west, and what was once a beautiful sight, made a cold chill run through his body. He reached down reluctantly and shifted the truck back into gear, and after a few jerks from the transmission, he started down the road again.

If this plan failed, he prayed his back-up one would not. He hated relying on other people, and both options depended almost entirely on the actions of others.

Cindy sat on the couch with a glass of water resting on her stomach. "Look, babe," she said to Kevin, "the baby's moving the cup of water.

Kevin looked up from the sports page of the news paper and smiled. "That is pretty weird," he replied. "It must feel funny to have something alive inside of you."

"It does, babe," she said as she watched the cup twitch. "I like being pregnant, though. Most of my friends said they were miserable when they were pregnant, but I don't mind it at all."

"Well, don't like it too much babe," Kevin replied. "I just hope we can afford this one."

"We'll figure it out. As long as you and I are together, we'll figure it all out."

Kevin turned back to the sports page and pretended to read the articles. He knew what he was about to tell her would not cause a fight. She did not seem to mind much what he did with his spare time, but he knew that he would have to lie to her. He never told her about what happened to them in high school, and doubted that he ever would.

"Michael's in town," he said still staring at the news paper.

"Really," she said, still interested in the moving cup of water.

"Yah, he seems to be doing pretty good. He's got some fancy job in New York."

"Do you think the baby can hear us talk?" she asked, trying to change the subject.

"I don't know? Maybe. Probably sounds pretty muffled," Kevin said putting the paper down on the kitchen table. "Are you not interested in Michael?"

"Interested in him?" she said smiling. "No, not really. I'm sure he turned out exactly the way I thought he would."

"Yeah, he did."

Kevin walked over to the couch and sat down next to Cindy, being careful as he sat not to tip the glass of water on Cindy's stomach.

"Sam and Michael want to go camping and hiking tomorrow," he said putting his hand on top of hers.

"Oh, that sounds fun. For how long?"

"I don't know. They want to go for like a week or so," he said.

"Wow. That's a lot of camping and hiking. You haven't been gone that long since you went hunting with your father."

"I know, babe," he said gently rubbing her hand. "We haven't all been together in a long time, and they want to do some catching up."

"Okay, babe. It sounds fun," she said holding his hand.

"I don't know if we will have a lot to talk about. It may be the longest week I have ever spent camping."

"I'm sure you will figure out ways to entertain yourselves."

Kevin ran through his mind the things he feared he was going to have to do and felt very uncomfortable.

Does not sound much like entertainment, Kevin thought.

"I'll miss you," he said softly.

"I know, babe. I'll miss you too. But, you have been working so hard lately. You need a break."

"Please ... not that talk again," he replied.

"I know. But, you told me that you would be able to stop working for the construction company nights and weekends once we refinanced our house. Your family misses you."

"And I miss them, Cindy. I miss you. It's just ... without you working, it has made it real hard lately. Once the baby comes, I promise you that I will quit working construction and just be a coach."

Cindy smiled and said, "Just a coach?"

"Just a coach."

"You are not just a coach. You are the best coach I know," she said and sat the cup of water down on the ground. "And, by far, the cutest coach."

"Getting kind of fat," he replied.

"I don't like scrawny little guys. I like big tough guys, like you."

"Really, cause I could probably easily put on some extra weight, if you want me to."

Cindy laughed, "I like you just the way you are."

"You know how much I love you, right?" Kevin said, praying this was not their last conversation.

"Of course," she said and kissed him on the cheek.

Kevin stood up from the couch and walked toward the kitchen with no real purpose. If it were just him that he was worried about, he would tell his friends that he would take on all the monsters that lived in the hills, but he had a family, a family who lived less than fifty miles from the god-forsaken place.

What if the threat were real? What if they came after his family? He had to end his fear of the curse once and for all.

Kevin whispered, "and if I don't come back, please tell the kids about their father."

"What?" Cindy said placing the cup of water on her stomach again.

"Nothing, babe. Just talking to myself."

Cindy flipped through some channels on the television as Kevin longed to tell her about where he had to go, and what was probably waiting for him. He knew, however, that if she knew even half the story, she would not let him leave the house. He poured a glass of lemonade, and sat at the folding card table they used as their dinner table.

"Hey, babe," Cindy said motioning for Kevin to come to her.

"Yes," Kevin said and made his way back to the couch.

"Look at this," she said pointing to the television. "They're cloning people's pets now. This lady in England missed her dog so much that she had it cloned. So weird."

"Science is pretty strange," Kevin said glancing at the television.

They sat watching the program for a while when Cindy broke the silence again.

"What if they clone Jesus?" she said.

"What?"

"What if they clone Jesus?" she repeated.

"I don't think they could do that, babe. They need DNA to clone something."

"The Vatican claims to have the robes Jesus was buried in," Cindy replied. "Couldn't they get DNA off the robes?"

"I don't know," Kevin replied giving her a strange look. "Why?"

"Hey," she said shrugging him with her arm. "Don't make fun of me. Think about it. What if a scientist gets DNA off the robes and clones Jesus? How scary is that?"

"Scary?" Kevin asked.

"Yes, scary. Revelations talks about the second coming of Christ. What if the second coming is because man cloned Jesus?"

"Hmmm."

"Hmmm, is right," Cindy continued. "God creates man, and then man creates God. I think they better be careful with that cloning stuff."

"I don't think that is going to happen, babe."

Cindy looked at Kevin and smiled. She took her hand and placed it on his chest, gently running her fingers up and down his stomach. Kevin placed his hand on her stomach, feeling for the baby, and closed his eyes.

Kevin reached down into the dirt of the pitching mound pretending that he was drying his hands. What he was actually doing was trying to give his arm just enough time to rest to throw the next pitch. He looked up at the scoreboard and saw that they were leading eleven to one in the seventh inning. It was the District Championship, and the winner of the game would proceed to the state championship. The ten-run lead would ordinarily ease his mind, but he had just walked two batters, and because the third baseman flubbed a grounder, the bases were now loaded with no outs.

He glanced toward the stands where he knew Cindy was sitting. Despite the fact that they had broken up a week ago, she sat in the stands wearing Kevin's letterman's jacket with her chin resting on her folded hands. She noticed he was looking at her and she shook her head telling Kevin that he had had enough. She knew he would not listen.

"Go to the dugout, baby" Cindy said, knowing that Kevin could not hear her over all the noise of the stadium. She hoped he could read her lips.

His coach was standing at the top of the dugout steps, ready to pounce out of the dugout, approach the mound, and tell Kevin that his work for the day was done. This could not be happening. He had never been pulled from a game. He had pitched eleven innings just a month prior, and three more batters is all he needed. Kevin nodded his head to Cindy that he was okay, and waved to the coach to stay in the dugout. He was going to finish the game, and take his team to the state championship.

Kevin took the mound and waited for the catcher's signals. A curve ball. Kevin doubted that he had the strength to twist off a curve ball now. His arm was dead, past the point of throbbing pain into a numb lifeless state. Kevin shook the sign off, hoping for a fastball or change up. The next sign came, but when Kevin saw that it was a screwball, the pitch that got his arm in the condition it was in, he exhaled and shook off the sign dramatically. The batter called time out and stepped out of the box when Kevin did this.

He knows, Kevin thought. *He knows I don't have shit left.*

Finally, the catcher gave the sign for a fastball, and Kevin nodded to indicate that he agreed with the pitch. He rocked back slowly and with everything he had left, he threw the ball toward the catcher.

The ball arched as it made its way to the plate looking more like a lob ball than a fastball. Due to the lack of velocity, it fell short, landing on home plate and bouncing off to the side, passing the catcher and skipping all the way to the back-stop. Kevin did not even attempt to run to home plate. He lacked the energy. He stood on the mound and watched as one of the runners stomped on home plate, a cloud of dust and chalk rouse into the air.

Kevin instinctively glanced over to the dugout; his coach was walking toward him. The coach looked toward the bull-pin and tapped his left arm, calling in the next pitcher.

"You pitched a good game," the coach said holding his hand out to receive the ball from Kevin.

"I've never been pulled from a game, coach," Kevin replied, refusing to hand the ball to the coach.

"I know," the coach replied. "But, we can win this one for you. Your arm is tired, and I need you for the State Championship."

"Please, coach," Kevin replied. "I can finish this. I promise I won't throw anymore junk. Just fastballs and change-ups. Please."

"No," the coach said taking the ball from Kevin. "Let Jason finish this up. We have a good lead, and this game will go down as a win for you."

"Please, coach," Kevin said, refusing to leave the mound.

"No. Now go to the dugout and ice that arm."

Kevin walked with his head lowered as the fans cheered. He felt defeated for the first time of his pitching career. As he walked, he slapped his glove on his right arm and cursed it for giving up on him. This was his game. He needed no one to finish it for him.

Kevin sat in the dugout and placed a bag of ice on his arm. Michael approached him and patted him on the back.

"Not a bad no-hitter Kevin," Michael said. "Don't sweat it, man. All pitchers' arms get tired from time to time."

"Not really a no hitter," Kevin responded. "They have two runs."

"Not from hits," Michael said and stood on his tip-toes to see what girls may be in the stands.

"Wild pitches and errors are just as bad," Kevin replied.

As Jason Freeman warmed up on the pitching mound, Kevin felt the throbbing in his arm return from the effects of the ice. He wanted to walk up the steps and say hello to Cindy, but felt defeated. He had left her. He had left her and did not know why. And now, he was pulled from the game because he was not good enough to finish. He wondered if he would ever be able to face her again. She was his girl, and he had let her down.

Just as the umpire called the game back into play, Kevin felt a warm liquid hit his hat and spray onto his arms. He paused for a moment, not knowing exactly what was happening, but when he realized it was urine, he threw the ice pack on the ground and ran up the steps of the dugout. He turned to see his father standing on top of the dugout, his penis out of his shorts, and piss spraying all over Kevin.

"You are a worthless piece of shit," Kevin's father slurred, as he swayed trying to keep his footing. "You're a turd! You can't even finish a game!"

Kevin stood on the steps, refusing to wipe the urine from his face and arms.

Kevin's father arched his back and grimaced as he pushed hard to make sure the last of his piss reached Kevin.

Cindy jumped from her seat and ran to the top of the bleachers. She screamed, "You drunk piece of shit!"

Cindy kicked Kevin's father in the small of his back, sending him flying off the top of the dugout, landing hard onto the steps next to Kevin. He groaned as he rolled from side to side, still holding his penis.

Kevin looked up at Cindy and saw her standing, waiting to attack his father. Kevin then looked to his coach and bowed his head. His coach walked up to Kevin's father and picked him up off the steps, struggling to keep him upright and staggering to gain his footing.

The game stopped. Everyone in the stands watched what was happening in Kevin's dugout. An uncomfortable silence followed, and moments later, the stands erupted into laughter.

Kevin, still refusing to wipe his father's urine from his face, stepped into the dugout, grabbed his bat and glove, and walked quietly out of the stadium.

~

Sam pulled his chair around from behind his large metal desk, as he always did when he had visitors, and set it next to the chair Michael was sitting in. Across from him was Kevin, who sat awkwardly in a small metal chair. Next to Kevin was a fourth chair. A chair that should have held the weight of Jake, but there was no Jake. The meeting of three, which should have been the meeting of four, started rather unceremoniously.

"It's been a long time since we've been up there, guys. Do you think we'll be able to find it again?" Michael said, deciding to wait until they were out there to tell his friends about the large truck that sat waiting to be loaded with gold.

"It'll take some time, but yes," Sam replied uneasy. "Unfortunately, I do think we'll find it again."

"We don't have to find it," Kevin added. "We only have to find the son-of-a-bitch who shot you, and whomever he's with."

That is what you think, Michael thought.

"Well, let's talk about that for a moment," Sam added. "What are we to do if we do find the old man? Guys, he's a pretty tough customer. I don't think we can just walk up to him and say, "Hey, go home." He'll put up a fight. He'll put up a damn good fight."

"So, let him," Kevin said.

Michael chuckled. "So, let him? We aren't talking about a keg fight out in the hills. This guy shot Sam ... twice. I don't think we're going to get the chance to go fist to cuffs with the old man."

"Nope," Sam added.

"So, what?" Kevin sat pondering the situation for a moment. "Are you guys talking about killing him?"

"We have to stop him," Sam said. "Hopefully it won't take our having to hurt anyone, but ... yes. If that's what it comes down to, yes."

"Are you guys crazy?" Michael said. "Are we actually sitting here contemplating a plot to go hunt down and kill an old man in the hills? Are you for fucking real?"

"Self defense," Sam replied. "If he attacks first, which he will, you are simply using self defense."

"Guys," Michael said standing from his chair. "I don't practice criminal law, but I don't think self defense works if you actually go hunting the guy down. 'No-no, Judge, it was self defense. We went hunting this old man, minding our own business I might add, and when he got pissed, we killed him in self defense.' Listen to what you guys are saying. This is crazy."

"What if we just watched him?" Kevin added. "It's pretty damn hard to find the gold. There's a good chance that he may never find it."

"For how long?" Michael asked. "I have to get back to New York. I already had to call in and tell them that my father got sick and I would need to stay another week. Work is piling up and ..."

"I have stuff to do too," Sam interrupted, "but, fuck it."

Michael cocked his head with an expression that bordered between comical and confusion. He cleared his throat and said, "Did you just say butt-fuck it?"

"Huh?" Sam replied.

"You just said you had stuff to do … 'butt-fuck it,'" Michael said tilting his head to the other side. "I have been in New York for quite some time, but what the hell?"

"Not butt-fuck it, you jack-licker … but, fuck it. Like … hmmm. Like but, fuck the stuff I have to do." Sam started laughing. "Never thought of it that way."

"We all have better things to do, Michael," Kevin said. "I think it's pretty clear that none of us wants to go looking for that place again."

Michael sat on the edge of the desk. "Okay, I know that I said we had to go looking for it, but now that we're talking about the possibility of killing someone, I'm not so sure. Do you really think those people would come hunt us down?"

They all sat pondering the question, trying to search for some reason why they would not, but no answer came.

Kevin cleared his throat and spoke softly, "I kissed my family good-bye today, guys. I know the risk we're taking by going out there, believe me, it's haunting me. But, I know deep inside that if those guys find it, those people will come looking for us. I don't know if I believe in curses, or witchcraft, or any of that horse shit, but I just know that we'll be held responsible. They'll know how the man that shot Sam found them. They'll remember us."

"But…"

Kevin continued. "They'll remember us as much as we remember them."

Michael's head dropped. He had worked his whole life to get to where he was, and now he was about to throw it all away on a manhunt. He was going. He knew that much, but what he did not know is why.

"We need to play it by ear," Sam said. "We'll find the old man and keep our distance. I don't think we're going to know exactly what to do until we get out there. No plan to kill anyone. No plan at all."

"Okay," Kevin replied. "Okay with you, Michael?"

"Sure," Michael responded.

Kevin stood and strolled to the refrigerator behind him. He pulled out a beer and opened it. "Put this on my tab," he said with a smile.

"You got it," Sam said, acknowledging the fact that he had never charged Kevin for a meal or beer since he owned the place.

"What about the issue of the Gimp," Kevin said and took a drink of his beer.

"The Gimp?" Michael asked, wondering if he had forgotten some part of the story he had lived.

"He means me, Michael," Sam replied.

"What do you mean the issue?" Michael added.

Sam shook his head, "No way, Kevin. I am going."

"Hell yeah, he is going," Michael added.

"Really?" Kevin replied. "How do you suppose you are going to limp around those cliffs and canyons? How do you suppose you will be any help to us with one arm? I remember the area. You will be more of a burden than a help."

"Thanks, Kev," Sam muttered.

"Oh shit," Michael said. "He is right, you know. You won't be able to get up and down, and all around that fucking place. No way."

"Guys..." Sam started.

"You're out, Sam." Kevin said and took another drink of his beer.

The four was now two, Michael thought. *He was friends with a psycho and a gimp. I should cut my losses and catch the next plane to New York. How could those people get to New York? I will leave and never return.*

"I can't do that to you guys," Sam said. "I will manage. I am going."

Michael walked to the old window of the office and mused as the cars drove down Main Street. It was strange that none of the cars were honking at each other. As soon as a light turned green in New York, it sounded as if every car for miles honked relentlessly in hopes of making all the vehicles disappear. When he first moved there, the sound drove him crazy, but now, he would give anything to be back in the noise-polluted streets of the city. He could not help, however, noticing the miniature little version of New York life that was unfolding below him. Across the street was a tiny park only twenty yards wide and thirty yards long with a few metal benches and a small gazebo. It was obviously nothing like Central Park, but it was a little park in the middle of town. Small shops selling jewelry, art, and antiques lined Main Street. A couple sipped coffee in a small deli. He wondered what they might be talking about. This little town was not unlike his big city … just smaller.

"No, Sam," Michael said not turning from the window. "Kevin is right. You'll slow us way down and probably make your injuries worse. Kevin and I will take care of this."

Michael turned from the window and with a very serious look on his face said, "Kevin and I will do this for you, and Jake."

"All for one, and one for all," Kevin said with a smile.

"Oh, Michael, please save Jake and me," Sam pleaded sarcastically.

"Good to be back home," Michael said with a smile. "Sure missed you fucking guys. You truly are the best!"

"Just messing with you, Michael," Kevin said.

"Whatever," Michael replied. "Butt-fuck it."

Sam stood wincing in pain. "Okay, I'll stay. But, that doesn't mean that I'll not be there with you guys. I have some shopping to do. You guys should go to the store and get beer and stuff. I'll get you some other supplies."

CHAPTER 15

October, 1935

A cool October breeze blew through the courtyard of Rafael's estate as the investors sat anxiously awaiting the news from Trabuco. They had heard that the plan was falling into place, and they were very excited to hear the news come from the only man who could tell them all the details.

Trabuco was two days late to the meeting. This was intentional. He knew the investors would wait, and he wanted them to wait. He was in charge, and if any of them thought for a moment that they had anything to say in the matter, they were wrong. He would make them wait. He wanted their minds clouded with fear of losing the investment and of having the plan fall apart.

Trabuco had faced concerning problems with the plan and needed the men to create horrible stories in their heads so that the news would not seem as bad. Despite being in charge, he still needed them to cooperate, or at least think they were cooperating.

The courtyard was decorated with numerous arrangements holding a variety of white flowers. A large lattice alter was being constructed, and workers were cleaning and spreading white tablecloths over tables. He knew this had nothing to do with his visit, and assumed there would be a wedding. He was greeted by his host, Rafael Borega, who welcomed him with a handshake and handed him his trademark mojito.

"Long journey, my friend?" Borega asked.

"Seems to be getting longer," Trabuco said and sat on the edge of the fountain taking a sip of his mojito. "Are you preparing for a wedding?"

"Yes, a cousin," Borega replied. "You're welcome to attend."

Trabuco was not there to attend a wedding, and was not going to apologize for his tardiness. He decided that he would not even speak about why he kept them waiting for two days. Any questions or concerns the investors may have about waiting for two days would have to be left unanswered. This is the way he wanted it, them waiting on him, and him waiting on nothing.

"The news is good, yes?" Carlos Sepulvada asked looking away from Trabuco when he noticed Trabuco had looked at him.

"Professor Morada was right. The Gold Act was passed on January 17th of last year with all the provisions we expected," Trabuco responded. "Our gold, gentlemen, is worth a lot of U.S. currency."

The men exchanged grins to each other.

"However," Trabuco continued, "selling the gold may be far more complicated than we thought."

Professor Morada added, "The U.S. Treasury Department is demanding that all gold be sold to them at the expected value. This we predicted. What we did not predict is how difficult the U.S. Government is being when it comes to large sales. They are aware that foreign investors may try and take advantage of this new law, and the last thing they want is for more gold to be introduced into their market."

Carlos Sepulvada sat his Mojito down on a wicker end-table. "Are you saying that we cannot sell the gold? This is why I voted that we sell the gold a year ago."

Trabuco smiled. "It wouldn't have made any difference. In fact, it's probably good that we have received this information before we tried to sell. We certainly would've been caught if we had sold when you wanted to."

Ricardo Artega turned to Trabuco and said, "I have trusted in you from the beginning. I've deferred all my decisions to you, Trabuco. Please say something that will renew my trust that you're making the right decisions."

Trabuco took a small drink of his Mojito and stood.

"Renew your trust in me?" Trabuco said and threw his drink against the stone fountain. "I have spent over a year transporting your gold. My gold! I have got it safely hidden in the United States without any suspicions at all!"

"Calm down," Borega said as he walked toward Trabuco.

"No, I will not calm down!" Trabuco yelled. "Every ounce of gold I own is buried in the desert up there, and you guys are questioning me? I have more to lose than anyone at this meeting. No, I will not calm down. You will sit! You will all sit and listen to the Professor and me, or I'm leaving. I will leave, and all of you will be on your own."

Rafael Borega sat next to Carlos Sepulvada and looked down at the ground. He had workers he could call on to take care of Trabuco, but then he would not know how to get the gold back. He was frustrated with himself for letting Trabuco become the only person who knew where the gold was buried. He did not trust Trabuco, but he had to give him the impression that he did.

"Sorry," Borega said. "We are just very concerned."

Trabuco sat back down on the edge of the fountain. His hands shook a bit as he fought the fear that was coming over him. He knew the investors could have him killed, and that they probably did not fear him even slightly, but he had to draw the line in the sand. He knew where the gold was, and they did not. That was his card; a card that he would have to keep playing until this whole plan was complete.

"I have contracted some help out of Denver," he said knowing that this was prohibited. "I have an attorney and a bookkeeper working on selling our gold to the Treasury Department. It will take some time as it is certain they will have to sell the gold in small amounts."

"How much will this cost us?" Sepulvada asked.

"I'll pay for their services," Trabuco replied, angry that he had done all the work and was receiving no praise for the progress. All the investors understood the risk, and the problem they were facing was no fault of his own. He did what he promised he would do, and he did it well.

"It will still be very difficult," Professor Morada added, speaking timidly and appearing uncomfortable. He needed to make sure the investors did not blame him for not predicting the problem. "The U.S. Treasury Department is demanding proof of the origin of all gold traded for currency. It's believed that they know of several large shipments from foreign investors. Some Canadians have already been caught, but they managed to smuggle the gold back across the border."

"Then that's what we shall do," Borega said.

"No," Trabuco replied. "If you want your money back, I'll pay you for your loss. No profit. But, I will not transport the gold back."

"Then tell us where it is, so we can go get it," Sepulvada added.

"No," Trabuco replied.

The group sat in silence for a moment. It was a stalemate with Trabuco possessing the next move. He could walk away from them and they would lose everything they invested, but he would not do this unless they forced him.

"Leave us," Borega said loudly. "I want to talk to Trabuco alone."

The men exchanged awkward glances, but eventually they stood and reluctantly moved into the house. Borega sat looking Trabuco in the eyes. He knew he could have Trabuco killed, and more importantly, he knew Trabuco feared this. However, he did not have the desire … yet.

"This is not good news, Trabuco," Borega said softly.

"No. I would've hoped to bring you better news."

"I'm not interested in blaming anyone for his mistakes," Borega continued. "I'm only interested in your succeeding. And this, I trust, you will do."

"Thank you," Trabuco said.

"I trust you will succeed because I trust you know what I will do to you if you fail," Borega added. "I'm not interested in playing any games with you. You yelled at me in front of those men. That was the last time. It was also the last time that you bring me bad news."

"They need…"

Borega cleared his throat and interrupted. "I don't care where you buried the gold. I'm not interested in carrying that responsibility. You chose that responsibility, and you'll be the one to live with that decision."

Borega walked to the fountain and sat next to Trabuco. He looked up into the sky and exhaled.

"Trabuco, you and I have been friends for a long time. For this reason alone, you will walk out of my courtyard today. You'll return to the United States. You'll use the help of the people in Denver, if you need to. You'll be allowed to do this because you are my friend."

"Thank you," Trabuco said.

"Now leave, my friend. Leave, and do not return until you have my money."

Trabuco sat hopelessly on the edge of the fountain as Borega stood and left. He had planned to stay the night at Borega's estate, but he knew he needed to leave, and he needed to leave now.

CHAPTER 16

Almost as quickly as the thought that he might be dead entered his mind, he dismissed it. He knew he did not have time to ponder the question. He was very calm, considering the circumstances, and forced himself to pay attention to what was happening. It was important. He knew it had to be important.

Sheldon floated high above the desert terrain where, just a moment ago, he was standing. He could not immediately see his body, but he knew it was below him somewhere on one of the mesas. He did not care.

The translucent silvery cord attached to him twisted its way toward the earth, and he assumed that it was connected to his body far below. He imagined spreading his arms outward as if to fly in the wind, but he realized that he had no arms or body to cast into the wind. He was an orb. He simply existed.

He considered soaring closer to the earth, and the thought alone caused him to race in the direction of his body.

He heard a hawk cry in the canyon below. This was not good. He did not yet know why.

He fell rapidly as the definition of the mesas got progressively clearer to him. The mesa he was once standing on was now in sight.

He could see his grandfather walking toward his body. Soon he would be shaken and have to return to his physical body. He had little time.

The hawk had to be found.

He could hear the wind blow through him, but it did not seem to have any effect on his ability to maneuver through the sky. The sun was starting to set, and Sheldon knew that he had to find the hawk before it started getting dark.

Quickly, he thought. *Where are you? I am here. Come to me.*

Then he saw it. The hawk was perched on the top of large tree that grew out of the side of one of the steep sandstone cliffs. It feared him.

Sheldon soared toward the hawk and saw that it sat paralyzed, staring right at him. He wondered if the hawk could see him, but he did not care. He had to confront the hawk now while he had the chance, before Lowery shook him back to his body.

As he approached, the hawk spread its wings to begin flight.

No, Sheldon demanded, but no words could be heard.

The hawk appeared to obey.

Something had drawn Sheldon from his body, the creature perhaps. The hawk had answers, and he intended to force the hawk to give him those answers.

As Sheldon grew closer, he noticed immediately that it was in fact not a hawk at all. He could see the natural body of the hawk which possessed sharp talons, dark feathers, and red eyes. He could also see, surrounded by the hawk, a silvery orb. An orb, he assumed, that looked similar to his own image at the moment.

The hawk took flight. It left the tree and started to fly west of the mesa toward the Chushka Mountains. After only a few moments, though, it turned and began to fly directly toward Sheldon.

Sheldon observed his grandfather, who was getting closer to his body, and now wished that Lowery would hurry. He needed no more answers. He knew the hawk would try and sever the cord and disconnected Sheldon from his body.

Dive, Sheldon thought and immediately did.

He hovered just feet above his body, spending very little time looking at the bizarre sight of his body resting motionlessly in the dirt. His grandfather was only yards away now.

He surveyed the sky and could not find the hawk. Still, he knew it was coming.

Sheldon sat himself on the chest of his body and waited as his grandfather approached. He decided that the least amount of cord the hawk could cut, the better off he might be. Then he saw the hawk again. It was diving toward him with its claws wide and talons extended. This was the attack, and Sheldon doubted he could fight back.

The hawk got closer.

Stop! Sheldon thought. *Leave me be!*

The hawk did not stop, but rather gained speed as it tore through the sky toward him.

Sheldon tried to enter his body, but could not. He had been slung out by the creature.

The hawk swooped down and grabbed Sheldon. He expected to feel some type of pain, but pain did not come. He was being flown away from his body, the cord still intact.

Sheldon was helpless as the ground below faded. The hawk had won. Where he was being taken would …

"Told you," Lowery said shaking Sheldon, "you have to keep drinking water. That dehydration will sneak up on you very fast, son."

Sheldon's eyes opened, but he could barely see the foggy image of his grandfather. He swallowed, noticing that he was being given water.

"It is damn hot, and damn dry out here," Lowery said pouring more water into Sheldon's mouth.

Sheldon coughed as he got some water in his airway, trying to swallow the cold water and catch his breath at the same time.

"Here," Lowery said and poured some of the water on Sheldon's face. "This will cool you down a bit."

Sheldon opened his eyes wider and saw his grandfather kneeling beside him. He looked into the sky trying to find the hawk, but could see nothing but the scattered red and purple clouds.

"Lowery," Sheldon said. "I think we should go home."

"What?" Lowery said and chuckled. "Just a little dehydration. You'll be fine after you get some water and rest."

"No, I don't think I will."

"Sure you will," Lowery said and helped Sheldon up to a sitting position. "I have done that several times. Lucky I was here for you, boy."

"I don't think it was dehydration, Lowery. Something very strange is going on. I think we should leave this place."

"Ah, don't be silly," Lowery said. "It's very scary to pass out like you did, but come on, we're here … the starting place."

"Yes, the starting place," Sheldon replied. "But the starting place of what?"

"Son, I won't even pretend to understand what you're talking about. Not sure I care. Look, we'll camp here tonight. Plenty of water and plenty of rest. How does that sound?"

Sheldon took the water bottle from his grandfather and continued to drink. Maybe he was right. Maybe he had just passed out from dehydration and the whole thing was some type of dream. He knew that it was not, but chose to believe otherwise ... for the moment.

"I see you found the trail," Lowery said as he looked down the path. "That's very good. That's very good, indeed."

Sheldon turned his head to look down the path and mustered as much enthusiasm as he could. "Yeah, looks like those rocks were pushed down."

Lowery stood and took a few steps toward the beginning of the path. "It sure does, son. It sure does. Now, tell me ... how does it feel to be standing, well, for you sitting, at the beginning of a road that leads to treasure?"

"Pretty good," Sheldon lied.

"Pretty good," Lowery whispered.

"I have to tell you something, Lowery," Sheldon said. "I know this is going to sound weird, but when we were with the Medicine Man, you told me to tell you everything I thought I saw. Well, I just saw some pretty fucked up shit."

"Fucked up shit?" Lowery replied. "Where did you learn to talk like a sailor ... Harvard?"

"Please, Lowery, listen to me," Sheldon said exhausted. "Come here."

Lowery turned to face Sheldon, and could see that he was very serious. "Okay," Lowery said and sat down next to Sheldon.

"I think I walked halfway down that path," Sheldon said, afraid to look at it anymore. "I found some type of dying dog. I went to touch it, for some reason, and you came up behind me. I thought I was in some kind of trance, and shook my head to get out of it. Next thing I know ... I think my soul got expelled from my body."

"Your soul?" Lowery asked.

"Yes, my soul. I was floating high above us and could see you walking toward my body. A hawk started to attack me. I think it was trying to take my soul somewhere."

"A hawk?"

Sheldon took another drink of water and wiped his mouth with his sleeve.

"Yes, a hawk," Sheldon continued. "But I don't think it was really a hawk. It grabbed me and started pulling me into the sky. I couldn't fight it. I just let it take me away. The next thing I know, you are pouring water in my mouth telling me that I got dehydrated."

"Well, you did," Lowery replied. "That's why I gave you water."

"I know, Lowery. But, something's not right … I really think we should leave."

Lowery lowered his head. "I'm sorry I had us camp with the Medicine Man. I did it because I thought you would find it interesting. There's no magic, no curses, no hocus pocus, no …"

"There is," Sheldon said handing the water bottle to Lowery. "That's my point. The hawk was playing with me. That thing could have torn me apart. It could have torn you apart. It was a warning, Lowery."

"You had a bad dream, Sheldon. When the body passes out from dehydration, the mind can do some very bizarre things. Many sailors know the tricks the mind can play on a man when dehydration kicks in. It is one hundred percent natural."

"No, it was not natural," Sheldon replied, frustrated that his grandfather wouldn't listen to what he was trying to tell him. He had spent the last few years in libraries and lecture halls, and now he was in the middle of the desert with a man who had no education and would not listen to anything he had to say.

Lowery stood and kicked a backpack that lay next to Sheldon. He took his hat off and threw it at the ground cursing.

"Son-bitch!" Lowery yelled. "I thought that perhaps this trip would turn you into a man, but all I am seeing is the wimpy little boy I remember from the past. Mr. Know-it-all. You Harvard Faggot! You fucking pussy!"

Sheldon mustered enough strength to stand, but he felt his legs struggling to keep him upright. He walked over to Lowery and grabbed his shoulder, forcing him to face him.

"Listen, Lowery," Sheldon said. "That's enough. You want me to follow you to the fucking gold ... fine. I told you what happened to me. It was a warning. If you want to ignore it, fine. I'll press on with you, but I swear to God on my father that if you call me a pussy again, I will kick the living shit out of you."

"Really," Lowery said staring into his grandson's eyes.

"Yes, really," Sheldon said spending a moment to return the stare. "Now, get your shit and let's get down this path. We'll camp at the bottom."

Lowery watched as Sheldon took his horse by the reins, threw his backpack on the saddle of the horse, and started making his way down the path.

"Son-bitch," Lowery said just loud enough for Sheldon not to hear.

CHAPTER 17

Michael waited for Kevin to enter the passenger side of his truck and slide into the driver's seat before getting into the truck. Immediately, though, he thought about how dirty the seat probably made his pants. He doubted if Kevin had ever cleaned the truck since high school. Kevin turned the ignition of the truck, and after some protest from the truck's engine, it started. The air-conditioner also started, blowing dust into the cab of the truck.

"Jesus," Michael said as he turned the vents closed.

"It will stop blowing dust in a few minutes," Kevin said as he put the truck in drive.

Sam was off shopping for "things" he thought his friends would need for the trip. Michael and Kevin had no idea what those things might be and were happy to only have the responsibility of grocery shopping. They needed food and beer; lots of beer. The only other thing they needed to get was a license to hunt coyote on the reservation. It was a hunting license that gave them the right to hike anywhere on the reservation, and if questioned by any Navajo, they would simply show them their license and explain they were hunting coyote. The Navajo accepted and appreciated people hunting coyote on their land because it helped protect their sheep and other small livestock. The license would give them free range of the area without having to worry about being hassled.

"So, what kind of beer does a fancy New York attorney want to drink while he's hunting down an old man with a gun?" Kevin asked with a strange smirk.

Michael knew he was being tested. Kevin wanted Michael to give him the name of some fancy beer that probably wasn't sold anywhere in the county so that he could make fun of him. They would end up buying some cheap light beer no matter what. Michael knew this but decided to let his friend have his fun.

"My favorite beer is New Castle," Michael responded.

"I love New Castle, but it may be a little hot for a dark beer," Kevin added.

"Okay, what do you want to drink?"

Kevin smiled, "Ah, I could care less."

"You could not care less," Michael added.

"What?"

"The saying is, 'I could not care less.'"

Kevin looked at Michael and saw that his former friend was staring out the window. They had little in common anymore. What had happened to his friend? Michael used to be a good ball player, fun to be around, and very carefree. Now, his frail friend seemed very concerned about things that were not worthy of concern.

"What?" Kevin asked.

"Hmmmm?"

"I said, 'I could care less about the beer we buy,'"

Michael smiled, "I know. But, the saying is, 'I couldn't care less.'"

177

Kevin thought about the statement for a moment. "No, it's, 'I could care less.'"

"That is what most people say," Michael responded, "but, most people are wrong. The actual saying is 'could NOT care less.'"

"Well, if most people don't throw in the 'not', then the saying does not include a not."

Michael shook his head. "Okay, whatever."

Kevin turned the radio down. "Not going to let you get away with this one Michael. The saying is, 'could care less.'"

Michael decided that Kevin was not going to let this go without either himself admitting Kevin was right or debating him. It was a pastime in which they had not participated in for many years. He chose to debate Kevin.

Michael turned to Kevin, "If you could care less that means that there is room for you to care less which means that you care some. If you could not care less, you do not care at all because you care so little that there is no room to care less. So, when people want to say that they don't care, they mean to say that they could not care less than they care."

"What?" Kevin said throwing Michael an odd look.

"Never mind."

"Maybe you're assuming that I don't care at all," Kevin added. "Maybe you think that I couldn't possibly care less about the beer I drink, but perhaps I don't really care, but care some. Maybe I would be happy drinking just about any beer, but there are a few beers, like King Cobra, that I don't want to drink. Therefore, I generally don't care what beer we buy, but I leave myself open to care if you were to choose a beer that I would not enjoy while hiking around looking for an old man."

"I see," Michael said.

"Well, I thought you would want to walk around drinking a martini or something," Kevin said.

"Here we go," Michael replied. "I was wondering when this was coming."

"Seriously, dude," Kevin said. "What the hell happened to you? You left for college and never came back. You think you're too good for us or something?"

I did come back, you prick. You would have seen me if you had the decency to show up to my mother's funeral.

"Give me a break, Kevin. If you hadn't torn your arm to shit, you'd still be pitching for the Dodgers. You wouldn't give a crap about this place and you know it. The only thing we'd know about the great Kevin Day is what we saw on the sports update on ESPN."

"That's bullshit," Kevin said. "Even when I did make it, I was very humble."

"Really? How many tickets do you give to your friends back in good old Farmington?"

"I'm not like you," Kevin replied.

"Maybe not now, but you would've been."

Kevin felt the sudden urge to put his friend in his place. The frail hot-shot sitting in his truck needed to be brought down from his perch, and despite the promise he made to his other friends to keep the trick they played on him a secret for life, he decided that the timing could not be more perfect.

"Remember in Junior High when we had that slumber party at Jake's?" Kevin asked.

"What?" Michael replied, turning to look at Kevin. "Where did that come from?"

"It was the night you drank Jack Daniels for the first time, and probably the only time you've taken eight shots in one night."

Michael laughed. "Yeah, that was pretty stupid. I got messed up ... bad!"

"Yes," Kevin chuckled. "And the next morning you woke up and said you had to go home immediately. You skipped breakfast, and ran out the door."

"I don't remember that part."

Kevin smiled. "Yes you do. You thought you shit your pants and did not want us to find out. Didn't you?"

"No clue what you're talking about," Michael added.

"Did you ever wonder why you shit a mushy banana?"

Michael remembered waking up in his sleeping bag fighting the fog of a hang over and panic rush through him when he felt the warm sludge in his underwear. He quickly reached for his pants and struggled in his sleeping bag as he put them on. If his friends found out that he shit his pants, he would never live it down. He found his shoes, and without bothering trying to find his socks, he grabbed his sleeping bag and was out the door. When he made it home, he took off his clothes and jumped in the shower, relieved that his friends would never know he soiled himself.

"Still have no clue," Michael proclaimed.

"Sure you do," Kevin said and patted Michael on the shoulder. "When you passed out, Sam said he wanted to put a banana in your tailpipe. So, he went to the kitchen, peeled a banana, and shoved it down your underwear. We laughed for nearly an hour as you tossed and turned in your sleeping bag. By the time morning came, I am sure you had turned that banana into a warm mushy mess. That is why you left so quickly. You thought you shit your pants."

Michael sat quietly staring out the front window, far beyond the road and scenery before them ... the fog of memory played in his mind.

"You're a goober," Kevin said. "You have always been a goober."

"What the fuck?!" Michael shouted. "You tell me you assaulted me with a fucking banana, and then call me a goober? Why the hell are you with me now?"

"Relax. We loved the goober. We hate the pretentious asshole. That is my point."

Kevin had made his point. Whether Michael would ever understand or change, he did not know. Sam and Jake would be furious when they found out he gave up the secret, but he did not care. He missed Michael, and wanted his friend back.

"Banana in the tailpipe," Michael said softly. "Banana in the fucking tailpipe!"

"That's just what Sam called it," Kevin said shrugging his shoulders.

Michael laughed so hard that tears ran down his face. "You guys shoved a banana in my tailpipe. You queer weirdo."

Kevin started laughing.

Michael was laughing so hard that he could barely get the words out. "I was so confused when I saw my tighty-whities sitting on the floor, pasted with some kind of yellowish, brown banana shit."

"We have always wondered," Kevin added.

Michael held his side as he tried to get his laughing under control. "Banana in the fucking tailpipe! Fucking Sam!"

Michael's laugh slowly simmered, and left him with a smile he had not worn in many years. He missed his friends. He missed riding around in a pickup truck talking about nonsense. He had no friends in New York, only a few acquaintances. He would never admit that he was tired of having so-called serious conversations about things that were considered serious only in New York, and he could not help wondering what would happen if he put a banana in Bill Bryant's tailpipe after a night of clubbing.

Michael reached over and rolled the window down, placing his arm on the window sill of the truck. He let his eyes close for a moment, absorbing the smell of the dry desert air, and allowing himself to relax. He was home. "Banana in my tailpipe," he mumbled, and chuckled.

The old truck squeaked as Kevin pulled it off the road and into the parking lot of a grocery store. The few cars that were parked there seemed dirty. It was nearly impossible to keep a car very clean in Northern New Mexico. The wind blew hard, and rain was very rare.

Kevin parked the truck and waited for Michael to exit the truck before sliding out the passenger side. When he closed the door, he knelt to one knee and looked up under the truck's engine. Satisfied that the truck was not leaking oil, he began to walk toward the store.

"We should probably get some whiskey, too," Kevin said. "Takes fewer bottles to get our buzz on which makes it lighter to carry, and sure tastes good by a campfire."

"Sure," Michael responded with emphasis, "I could care less."

"Michael?" a voice said.

Michael looked around to see where the voice came from, and saw a girl loading groceries into the trunk of her car.

"Help, me. I can't remember her name."

Kevin smiled and approached the girl. He gave her a hug and told Michael to catch up with him in the store.

Michael stood awkwardly looking at her. He remembered her, but could not remember why or what her name was. He took a few bags from the cart and helped her load them into the trunk.

"I haven't seen you since high school," she said as she placed the last bag into the trunk.

"It's been a very long time," Michael responded as he closed the trunk.

"What are you doing in town?" she asked.

"Oh, I'm here to check on Sam."

The girl leaned against the trunk of the car and smiled. Michael looked into her eyes and tried again to rack his brain for the girl's name. She was very pretty, and despite having dated most the pretty girls in town, he could not recall dating her.

"That was crazy," the girl said. "I went to the hospital right after he was shot. You know Sam. He was smiling and laughing and making the whole thing a big joke. But, I think he was really scared."

"I think he was," Michael added, "He's doing much better."

"It's hard for Sam to do better, Michael. He's one of those people who's always happy, and always seems to be doing fine."

"That's for sure."

"So, what about you? How are you doing?"

Michael watched as she took a hair pin out of her purse and casually pulled her long blond hair back. She was stunning, and obviously the years had been very kind to her. Michael made sure to look at her left hand for a ring, and when he noticed that there was not a ring, he smiled.

"I'm fine. Just here for a few weeks to get caught up."

"Well, there's not much to get caught up on. I think you'll see that not much has changed here. Pretty boring little town."

Michael leaned against the girl's car, trying to let her know that he was interested in what she had to say, but keeping his distance so she would not feel uncomfortable.

"That's what I like about this town," Michael said.

"Where do you live now?"

"I live in New York. I'm an attorney practicing tax law."

"New York," the girl said faintly. "Were you there when those terrorists flew the planes into the World Trade Center?"

"No. I was at a conference in Pittsburg. But, it really affected a lot of people I know."

"That was horrible," the girl added. "I can't believe how evil some people can be. I cried for a week."

"It was pretty bad," Michael agreed.

Who was this girl? How could he not notice such a pretty girl in this small town? Had he been with her? If he had, she would certainly hate him.

"About a month after that happened," the girl said, "a student pilot crash landed his plane on top of the police department. Guess he just belly flopped the thing right on the roof. Nobody really knows why the lucky guy did not die."

Michael looked deeper into her blue eyes.

"I remember working down at Sam's bar when it happened, and a few cops having dinner got the call on their radios. The police thought it was a terrorist attack."

Michael laughed, "a terrorist attack in this town."

"I know. It was pretty funny looking back, but we were all so nervous. The poor pilot was all banged up, and had to deal with questioning from the police about a possible terrorist attack. Poor guy. I guess we were all a bit sensitive at the time."

"You can't even imagine how nervous people were in New York after the attacks. I didn't know if it'd ever get back to normal."

The girl laughed, "Sam was so cute that night. He looked at me, and for the first time talked to me with a very serious tone. He told me that if we are being attacked, I want you to know that dad and I will protect you and mom. Nobody will hurt our family."

"Deanne," Michael said, his memory jogged.

"Yes?"

Michael stumbled for words. "Deanne….you know Sam would always protect you."

Deanne looked at Michael with an odd expression on her face and smiled. "I know he would. It was just a funny thing for him to say."

"He's a good guy," Michael said, letting his mind wonder back many years to the memory of a skinny Deanne Hewitt. *Nothing had changed in this town, huh?*

"So, do you work with Sam?" Michael asked.

"About two nights a week to help pay bills. I'm getting my degree in psychology through a correspondence course at the community college. There is no money in my field until you get your PHD. So, Sam lets me work when I want to help out. He's a good brother."

"He is, and a good friend."

"They all miss you, Michael. You were a very good friend to them."

"I miss them too, Deanne," Michael said, letting her name glide off his tongue.

Deanne Hewitt took her keys out of her purse and began to play with them. Michael thought that this was not a sign that she wanted to leave, but rather that she was looking for something to say. He had spent many nights at the Hewitt house while he was growing up. It was very rare that he paid any attention to Sam's younger sister. She was three years younger, and Michael only remembered her as a nerdy homely young girl. He could never have dreamed that the girl he remembered could blossom into the beautiful woman who stood before him now.

"Well, I better get in there and help do some shopping with Kevin. We're going hiking for about a week, and if I don't pick some stuff out, I may be in for a very long week," Michael said.

"A week-long hike? That seems like a long time. Is Sam going with you?"

Michael cleared his throat and looked toward the entrance of the grocery store trying to think of what to say.

"I think he's too busy, and his leg doesn't feel so good," Michael responded. "I plan on spending a lot of time with him when we get back."

"Oh, good," Deanne responded with a smile. "Please come to Sam's house for dinner one night. I'm sure he would love to see you before you leave."

"That sounds like fun, Deanne."

"I'll make sure I'm free that night, too."

Michael took a few steps from the car and turned toward Deanne. "It was really good to see you Deanne. I look forward to spending some more time with you."

"That would be nice."

Michael walked to the entrance of the grocery store and turned to watch Deanne get in her car and drive away. He wondered what Kevin would say if he asked him if they could delay the trip by a day so that he could have dinner at Sam's house that night. He decided that it was not even worth asking, and as she drove away, Michael smiled and entered the grocery store.

CHAPTER 18

Sheldon sat by the campfire debating whether his grandfather was right, and that he was simply dehydrated and had experienced a dream. He wanted to believe that he had just passed out, but he could not convince himself of that. He struggled for answers to what the vision could have meant. He did not realistically think that an invisible hawk could really swoop down and grab his soul away from his body. He lacked belief in any paranormal activity. In fact, he lacked any fundamental belief in anything religious for that matter. His parents tried to raise him as a Baptist, and had sent him to several private schools. Still, from a very early age, he had thought faith was all nonsense. He studied all the religions of the world in college, and although he respected the poetic aspects of most of them, he did not find that he had a connection with any religion. He was a man without a church or a god. Now, however, he was concerned about invisible hawks.

Lowery took a long drag from his marijuana pipe and watched as the smoke slowly floated from his mouth.

"Why are you here, Sheldon?"

Sheldon looked at his grandfather for a moment and cleared his thoughts of invisible hawks. Why he was there with his grandfather was a question that he was asking himself more frequently with each passing day. It was a valid question, one to which he was not quite sure he had the answer. He knew why he was interested in starting this trip, but that seemed long ago. So much was changing.

"Not for gold, Lowery."

Lowery smiled behind his pipe. "I know, son. That's why I ask."

"You won't be mad if I tell you?"

"Sheldon, I'm an old man. With that comes the understanding that every man has his motives and his secrets. If you choose to keep yours, that's fine. I'm just passing time. But, I cannot promise you that I won't be mad if you tell me because I have no idea what you will say. If you were to say, for example, that you came on this trip so that you could get me out in the middle of nowhere to slit my throat so that you could inherit my fortune, well....I think that may upset me a bit."

"Well, I assure you, that's not the reason. I'd be too scared to try and slit your throat, Lowery. You'd probably take the knife away from me and spank me with it."

Lowery laughed, choking on the marijuana smoke.

Sheldon leaned a bit toward his grandfather to let him in on the secret. "All right. I wasn't going to say anything because I was afraid you'd make fun of me, but since you do that all the time, I guess I have nothing to lose."

"I make fun of everyone, Sheldon."

"I'm sure you do."

Sheldon pulled a notebook from his backpack and after thumbing through a few pages looked up at his grandfather.

He turned the notebook a bit so that the campfire would give him enough light to see what he had written. "I had to write what is called a thesis paper when I was getting my PHD. It is required of all PHD candidates, and is basically like a scientific study of something. Since I was majoring in Anthropology, the study of ancient civilizations, I had to pick a topic on something in that area of study. In a thesis paper, you have to have a hypothesis, which is really just a question. For example, is the world round? Then you do a bunch of research and studies that try and answer the question. At the end of the paper is the conclusion. For example, yes, the world is round."

"Is the world round?" Lowery asked with an odd smirk.

"I think so," Sheldon responded. "But, that was not my hypothesis. My paper dealt with the question of whether there were ancient civilizations existing undetected within modern civilized societies."

"Sounds very interesting," Lowery added.

"It was to me. In fact, I got so caught up in the question that it took me a lot longer to complete my PHD than expected. I could have just concentrated on South America where there are many uncivilized tribes, but I chose a civilization within the borders of the United States."

"An ancient civilization within the United States? All you had to do was look into the back woods of Arkansas."

Sheldon laughed. "That probably would have saved me a few years of my life, Lowery. I should have given you a call."

"Always here for you, son."

"When the Spanish were exploring the world, they sent a significant number of people to Central America, not only to explore, but to colonize. Like space exploration in the sixties, Europe treated discovery of the new world as a conquest that symbolized power. Simply put, the country that could expand its borders into the depths of our undiscovered world would be the ruler of the world."

"And then came Columbus."

"No. Not talking about Christopher Columbus. I'm talking about the Spanish Conquistadors who settled in Central America and what is now New Mexico. There were all sorts of stories told to the men who explored this area to keep them motivated. Cities of gold, for example. Grand stories designed to keep the men's morale high and feet moving."

"Gold seems to do that to a man," Lowery added.

"I guess you would be a case study on that."

"Don't go writing a paper on me, Sheldon. It'll get you nowhere."

Sheldon chuckled. "It wasn't odd, and in fact common, for groups of these men to gather into large packs and venture in different directions. This is how many modern towns were founded, like Santa Fe, New Mexico. And just as common as these quests, was the detail given to journals and writings. Spain wanted to prove its dominance, and wanted a very detailed record of how it was achieved. That documentation gave me quite a bit of research material to study."

"Have you ever heard of Cliff Notes?"

Sheldon smiled. "Believe me, I am giving you the 'Cliff Notes' version of this. I have to explain this so that you'll understand what I'm talking about."

"It's fine … I'm just having fun."

"It was also common for these large groups of conquistadors to find mates in Indian tribes. Men will be men, I guess you could say. In fact, most of Mexico's population is a mixed breed of natives and Spanish."

Sheldon sat his notebook down and leaned against his back pack. "There was a very large group of Spanish men that left Santa Fe in search of the City of Gold, very well documented up until the time they left. Nearly every journey, whether or not it resulted in death for the men, was documented. This was a priority."

"So?" Lowery replied. "You have told me some of this already."

"So, the men who were to search the area we're in now, were never heard from again. Never left any signs of being here, or leaving here."

"So, they all died."

"No, Lowery. Well, yes. Eventually, they all had to die. But I don't think they died on the journey."

"You don't. Why not?"

"The key word here is hypothesis. A question that does not have an answer. That was the purpose of my thesis paper."

Lowery seemed a bit interested. "And what did you conclude?"

"I concluded that the men submerged themselves into an existing Navajo village and over a period of time, created a new civilization mixed with Navajo and Spanish blood. I don't think they died in the journey. I think they lived."

"Interesting," Lowery said. "If they lived, where did they go?"

"I think they either settled in the Chuska Mountains or the La Plata Mountains. They live a solitary life, undetected by civilized society."

"Lived, or live?" Lowery asked. "You told me when we camped with Ernest that you were interested in the time that the two cultures collided. You didn't tell me that you think they commingled and are still alive."

Sheldon reached into his backpack and pulled out an object that looked similar to a crucifix. He handed it to Lowery and allowed him to study it. It was carved out of a pink stone about three inches in length. Lowery immediately recognized it as a Christian cross. He ran his fingers over the object and sat up, holding the object closer to the fire so that he could see it better.

"Are these swastikas?" Lowery asked.

"No, they're called Whirling Logs, an ancient Navajo symbol that depicts the cyclical motion of life, seasons and the four winds. That symbol is frequently found in Navajo sand paintings and is considered a powerful medicine."

"And this carving on the base of the cross?"

Sheldon reached for his notebook and showed Lowery a drawing. "It's hard to distinguish the detail, as you can see, but that is the Navajo Yeii Spirit. It's considered by the Navajo to be a way to connect man with the Creator."

Lowery now looked very interested. His boring grandson had just handed him a treasure. Not one that he was used to holding, or looking for, but a real treasure of realization: his grandson was a treasure hunter, just like him.

"A Christian cross with a Navajo Yeii Spirit carved on it.... very interesting. You should have shown your mother's father this cross."

"No, I should not have. He wouldn't have liked what I showed him. To you and me, that cross is strange, but I think Ernest, acting as the medicine man, would have thought that stone to be quite a bit more than just strange. I think he would've found it very offensive."

"So, where'd you get this?"

"That cross was found during a class-sponsored dig not far from where we are now. I wasn't on that dig, but I read all the research gathered during the process."

"And, how did you come to possess this cross?"

"Most college students are poor."

"I see," Lowery smiled.

"I think that this cross helps prove my theory that there's a new civilization living near here, that cross being one of their artifacts."

"You think the Navajo people who got tangled up with these Spanish people adopted Christianity and that this is one of their symbols?"

"Much more interesting than that," Sheldon added. "I think that the two cultures colonized together, bred together, and adopted each other's religious beliefs."

"And this cross shows the acceptance of both traditional Navajo beliefs and Christianity." Lowery said. "I must admit, that's fairly interesting."

Sheldon looked satisfied. "That's what my paper's about."

"I see," Lowery said, handing the cross back to Sheldon. "So, you believe that this civilization still exists, practicing a combined version of Navajo and Christian religion?"

"I don't know if they still exist, but if they don't, we're going right to one of the places I think they lived. They may have left more things behind."

Lowery pulled a pouch of marijuana out of his pocket and began to load his pipe with a fresh bowl. "So, you're not looking for gold, but rather for an ancient race or their artifacts?"

"Yes."

"You really are my grandson, Sheldon. I used to think that there's no way you have my blood running through your veins, but maybe I was mistaken. I respect your reasons for taking this trip, but I must tell you that these people concern me."

"Why?"

Lowery took a moment to light his fresh bowl of marijuana. "If you really believe that these people exist and that they may be where we are going, you should be concerned as well."

"Why?"

"I don't know what you learned in your studies of ancient people, but I'll tell you a little something I've learned during my real life experience. Some people just need a reason to be evil. Nearly all of this world's genocide and mass killings of human beings resulted from some religious undertone. The Spanish Inquisition, the Crusades, Hitler, the Middle East, terrorists.... all of those conflicts based on distortions of religious belief."

"But, the Navajo are peaceful people with peaceful beliefs."

"These are not Navajo, Sheldon. These would be a mix of people who have taken religious beliefs and changed them, modified them to accept some things and discount others. A complete mutation of two completely different religions."

"But they could be...."

"And not just creating a religion based on this mutation, but passing it down to their children and grandchildren giving rise to even more perverse interpretation and further mutation of beliefs. The fact is, if they did exist, you have no idea what they believe in. A cross is a Christian symbol that depicts the crucifix of Jesus Christ. That cross," Lowery said clearing his throat "has a Navajo spirit being crucified."

Sheldon looked at the cross and ran his thumb down the carvings. He had been so consumed by the thought of proving his thesis paper correct that he never considered what he would do if he did. His grandfather was right. If these people did exist, would they be peaceful? How would he communicate with them? He assumed that they spoke some distorted combination of Spanish and Navajo. Thinking about that had motivated him to learn as much as he could about the two languages. But, how he would deal with distorted beliefs was not something he had considered. He began to feel like the small fortune spent on his education was quickly becoming worthless.

"Believe it or not," Lowery continued, "I've learned a bit about people during my travels. One thing people are not very accepting of is things that scare them; like a rattlesnake, which strikeout when scared. And, I assure you, nothing scares a human more that something he doesn't understand. I've dealt with people who have had very little contact with civilized people. They don't take very kindly to us, son."

"Do you believe these people are out there?" Sheldon asked as he put the cross back into his bag.

"Hell, no," Lowery responded. "I do believe in fear, though. I need you at your best, and the possibility that these people may exist should frighten you. Fear keeps us alert, our senses acute, and with any luck, alive."

"And the cross?"

"Who knows, son. Hell, could have been some Navajo kid who was getting pressure from a Mormon to convert to Joseph Smith, or something. Maybe a Navajo kid simply thought the shape of a cross was neat. Hell, I don't know. Look, I could pick up a rock and carve something out of it, and leave it to be found a thousand years from now. What I carve could be because of this smoke. I could carve a turtle taking a shit. Doesn't mean I worship turtles or shit."

"Not exactly the same thing here."

"No, it is exactly the same thing. The reason certain artifacts are considered valid or valuable is because of what we know about a civilization. You know that. You studied it in your fancy college. If we'd found one drawing of a cat in Egypt, it would have had no significance if it weren't for all the other information we have gathered. You have a rock that is shaped like a cross that has possible carvings on it. Probably could sell it for a few bucks, but without more information, it really doesn't mean anything, son."

"I simply don't agree."

"Sheldon, I was very excited to hear from your father that you chose anthropology as your study. I guess if I had to go to college, it would be the area I'd choose. Kind of like treasure hunting ancient cultures. And I'll bet you want to prove your theory as much as I want to find the gold. That's good. That will keep us both motivated. But, I don't have to convince you of the existence of gold. I'm going to go look for it anyways."

Sheldon pulled the cross out of the pack again and handed it to his grandfather.

"Look," Sheldon said pointing at the cross in Lowery's hand. "That's not a rock shaped like a cross. Look at the edges. Feel them. It was carved into a cross. Whoever created that cross made it that shape. There is nothing in the Navajo culture shaped as a cross. No structure, no buildings, no cactus, nothing that would suggest that shape to a Navajo hundreds of years ago."

Lowery ran his finger over the edges of the cross and agreed that it had been carved into the shape it now took. It was an artifact; he did not disagree with his grandson about that fact. But, did it have any significance? He didn't know.

"Like I said, it's probably worth some money."

"You can keep it," Sheldon replied. "I think we'll be finding a lot more objects soon. That rock is not indigenous to this area. The local arrowhead hunters call that rock 'Washington Pass.' It was a rock brought by Natives long before even the Anasazi Indian. It is fairly rare to find a rock this size that has not been reshaped by the Anasazi into their form of arrowheads."

Lowery leaned back against a rock and continued to look at the cross. "And what about the Navajo? Did they make arrowheads out of this rock?"

"The Navajo rarely made arrowheads. They were farmers and traders, not hunters like the Anasazi or the natives who lived thousands of years before them. The traditional Navajo believe that ancient arrowheads are rocks formed when horny toads chewed on the rocks. They sometimes crushed them into dust and used it for medicinal purposes, but they rarely carved arrowheads or rocks into shapes like you hold now."

"So there is no way that a Navajo could have been bored one day and just carved this thing out of a rock?"

Sheldon realized that he would not convince his grandfather. "No. I don't believe that would happen. People have lived in this area for tens of thousands of years. A rock like that would likely have been used for an arrowhead, or sold. Nothing in my studies gives any explanation as to why a rock would be carved like that. Nothing."

"I see," Lowery said as he slid the cross into his pocket. "I hope you're wrong, son. I hope for both our sakes that we don't run into these people. But, thanks for the cross. I hope it protects us on this journey. I'll pray to both Jesus and the Yeii Spirit."

CHAPTER 19

Trubuco did not particularly like the attorney he had hired in Denver, Colorado. He was very smug and arrogant, and Trubuco was convinced that if the attorney believed him, he would try and take as much of the gold or money as he could. However, he knew had no other options. His last attempt to get outside help to retrieve the gold nearly got him killed. He had approached the German Embassy in Mexico City, and they held him for days, claiming he was a spy for the United States trying to set up Germany to lose its Embassy in Mexico. Once released, he realized he needed someone from the United States to negotiate directly with their government. After a year of research, he chose a former assistant U.S. Attorney in Denver by the name David Lockley.

David Lockley sat in a large leather burgundy chair and read through some of his notes, occasionally making a moaning sound as if he did not approve of what he was reading. Trubuco sat quietly, admiring the art in David's office. He could not wait to get back to Mexico, but promised himself that this time he would stay in the United States until all the issues were resolved.

"I need to know who all my clients are," David Lockley said, breaking the silence.

"Just me," Trabuco responded. "My gold has been in the United States for about 15 years. I think it's time I either get it back, or get compensated for it."

"I see," David Lockley responded. "However, you have multiple investors...do you not?"

"I did."

David Lockley flipped through some of the pages of his notes, and asked, "Where is Rafael Borega?"

"He died in his office in 1939," Trabuco responded.

"Died of what?"

"Heart problem."

"And Carlos Sepulvada?"

Trabuco cleared his throat, "he was killed in a drunk-driving accident in 1940."

David Lockley took his glasses off and sat them on his desk. He leaned back in his chair and took a deep breath. "And, what happened to the workers who William Elliot testified about? Where are they?"

"What workers?" Trabuco replied, shrugging his shoulders. "I don't know who you are talking about."

"William Elliot testified that you had a few workers who helped you move the gold from the landing site to your hiding spot. Where are they?"

Trabuco looked up at the ceiling, appearing to try to receive knowledge from above. "Ahhh, yes. I do remember now. I did have two men help me move the gold. Where they are, I do not know."

"Can they be found?" David Lockley asked.

"I don't know," Trabuco replied. "Their names are Juan and Jose. I'm sure you can find them in Mexico."

"Do they have last names?"

"I'm sure they do, but I don't know them."

David Lockley sighed, "So, everyone is gone."

"If you think I killed my partners, you're wrong. In fact, I paid off the Sepulvada family for their losses. I also ..."

"I don't care," David Lockley interrupted. "You hired me either to get your gold for you or to have the Treasury Department buy it from you. This will not be easy."

"But it's my gold," Trabuco replied.

"Our government passed the gold act to reduce the amount of privately owned gold in this country and to make the value of our currency stronger. Our government is not going to reward a foreigner for smuggling more gold into the country. What you did was contrary to what the government was trying to accomplish."

"There's a lot of gold. I'll sell it at a discount," Trabuco said.

"What would prevent our government from simply contacting William Elliot again and compensating him in exchange for his information regarding the gold's location?"

"Because he's dead," Trabuco replied.

David Lockley tossed the papers he had been fingering onto his desk and stood. He paced over to a mahogany cabinet and picked up a bottle of scotch. "Would you like a drink, Mr. Trabuco?"

"Sure."

"You have to appreciate the difficult position you are in, and even the more difficult one I will be in, trying to negotiate for you," David Lockley said as he poured two glasses of scotch. "You smuggled gold into the United States, and now everyone is dead except you."

"I didn't kill anyone," Trabuco replied, taking the glass of scotch being handed to him. "William Elliot was shot down in the war. How could I have anything to do with that?"

"I see," David Lockley said returning to his chair. "The Treasury Department doesn't regard you as innocent in any of this, and even if all the deaths really were accidental or overseas, they simply won't believe you."

"What do you mean the Treasury Department doesn't regard me as innocent?" Trabuco asked. "How do they even know about any of this?"

"You've contacted many private buyers. One of those buyers disclosed your story. And, like I said, William Elliot already testified. He gave them your name."

Trabuco drank his glass of scotch and sat it on Lockley's desk, feeling pleased that the man he trusted was shot down. *He is lucky I didn't get a hold of him,* Trabuco thought.

"The Treasury Department wants to offer you a deal."

"What's the offer?" Trabuco asked obviously upset that the U.S. government had too much information on him.

"They claim that you have violated both Mexican and United States Law, and if you turn over the gold, they will not prosecute you."

"And what will be the compensation?" Trabuco asked.

"Your freedom," Lockley replied.

"My freedom," Trabuco said.

"I'll continue to negotiate for you, but I don't…"

"My freedom," Trabaco stated again. "How will they prosecute me for smuggling gold into this country if they can't even prove that I did?"

"I guess they feel that they'll find the gold eventually."

Trabuco smiled, "They won't find the gold, and even if they did, they won't be able to get it."

"What is that supposed to mean?" Lockley asked.

Trabuco rose from his chair. "I would rather the gold stay right where it is than to give it to the United States government. If you are a chess player, Mr. Lockley, you will understand what I'm saying. This is a stalemate. We all know that I can't get the gold. Now that they're watching, it would be impossible. On the other side, they know they won't find it without me. And, like I said, even if they do, they can't get it."

"I agree," Lockley said, "for now it appears there is a stalemate."

"You can tell the Treasury Department that there is approximately 20 million dollars of gold in this country, and I'm the only person alive who knows where it is. If they want to make me a reasonable offer, I'll listen. Otherwise, I'll take the secret to my grave."

Trabuco knew, however, that he could not take it to the grave. He had left his bull with the final shipment believing that it would be safe. He doubted that they would ever find his bull, but he missed it terribly. He needed it back.

There was also the story his workers had told him. Trabuco had sent them up the mountain to check on the gold a year after they completed the transport, and they returned with a story about people with white faces moving the horde. He dismissed the story immediately, assuming the workers created the story with the intentions of stealing the gold one day. He believed they were trying to frighten him and give an explanation for why the gold was missing when Trabuco finally returned to the hiding spot.

He disposed of the two workers, never giving them much thought. However, he longed for his bull.

CHAPTER 20

"Does this look familiar, Michael?" Kevin asked as he began to slow his truck down at the end of a dirt road.

"Not really," Michael replied. "I guess it doesn't matter, as long as we find the trail at the base of the mountains. Just stop here and let's look around."

Kevin drove the truck down a hill with no road and pulled the truck behind a tree so it would be out of sight. Kevin and Michael exited the truck and walked to the edge of the mesa. Several miles away to the southeast loomed a large rock formation called Shiprock. They both tried to use Shiprock as a reference, trying to pinpoint where they had found the trail leading up the Chuska Mountains directly west of them.

"I remember walking down this canyon," Kevin said pointing to a large canyon with a dry riverbed at the base.

"Me, too," Michael added. "I think we should leave the truck here and hike until we make it to the base of the mountain. Maybe we'll start remembering when we get closer to the trail."

"Sam bought us a G.P.S. locater," Kevin said. "It would have been a lot more useful if we had it back then, and flagged our position."

"Sam bought us a G.P.S. locater? Why?"

Kevin smiled, "I guess so we don't get lost. I don't really know. Obviously he's worried. He bought us the GPS, a first aid kit, a snake bite kit, rope, a survival knife, and other items."

"Don't tell him, but we'll probably have to leave half that crap in the truck. It's quite a hike," Michael said.

"I was thinking the same way. Come to think of it, we may want to leave all the beer too. I forgot how far this hike will be. We should just take the whiskey."

"No kidding," Michael agreed looking across the canyon and the distance to the base of the Chuska Mountains.

After they packed their large hiking packs with supplies, they took a moment to drink a few beers, realizing that they would have to leave most of it in the truck. They sat on the tailgate of Kevin's truck drinking in silence. They both knew the other was scared. There was no need to ask. Michael thought about telling Kevin about the Bull he had in his pack, but decided against it.

"They say uncertainty is man's biggest fear," Michael said, breaking the silence. "This would be a lot easier if we didn't know what we're walking into."

"All we have to do is find the old man, and get back. We don't have to go all the way."

Michael jumped off the tail-gate and picked up his hiking pack. "Then let's get going. We need to find him soon."

Kevin chugged the rest of his beer and threw the empty can into the bed of his truck. "I agree."

Hiking down into the canyon was difficult as the two tried to keep their footing on the loose dirt. The heavy packs did not help things either. When they did falter, they had to land on their backsides and slide, holding the rifles they were carrying into the air so they did not get dirt in them.

Once they got into the base of the canyon they took the packs off and rested. It was frustrating that they had to climb deep down into this canyon knowing that they had to climb right back up the other side. However, there was no other way for them to get to the trail than to cross the canyon. At least, that is what Kevin thought. What Kevin did not know is that a few days ago his hiking partner had driven a large oil truck and parked it near the base of the mountain.

Michael would have preferred simply to have told Kevin about the road than to have made the hike down and back up the canyon, but he knew he could not explain why he knew the road existed. He doubted that Kevin would have been pleased that he had learned of the road by being given an aerial photograph of the well site from a goon in Michael's Father's kitchen. Michael figured the hike would be less painful.

As Kevin rested his backpack against a large sandstone rock, Michael could not help staring at the rifle Kevin was carrying. Michael's rifle was no bb gun. It was a bolt action 30/30, but Kevin's was a bit much. Michael was not sure of the caliber or make of the gun since he really knew nothing about them, but the scope on the rifle seemed very large and expensive.

"Is that a normal size scope?" Michael asked.

Kevin wiped the sweat from his forehead. "It's a pretty powerful scope."

"How far can you see with it?"

Kevin smiled, "You can see a long way, but I'm no sniper. Not like I can hit something from 4,000 yards or anything."

"How far?"

"Far enough."

Michael took a drink out of a canteen, and said, "You and Sam planned on killing the old man, didn't you? You really want to take him down like a deer, huh?"

Kevin shook his head, "No. I don't want to shoot anyone. I want to catch up to him and try and talk him out of what he's trying to do. If that doesn't work, well....I just don't know."

"You can't kill him."

"Fuck!" Kevin yelled, stood quickly and kicked his hiking bag. "I don't have a clue why we're even here. I should be home!"

"Just promise me that you won't shoot him, okay? Promise me I'm not going to be asleep and wake to a loud gun shot and you telling me that we can now go home. Please."

Kevin picked up his pack and put it on his back. "Let's go."

"Promise me. Please. I can't be an accessory to murder."

"I promise I won't shoot anyone until I tell you I am going to first....happy?"

Michael paused, not responding, and then picked up his pack.

They did not speak much as they crossed the dry river and climbed to the top of the other side of the canyon. They spent most of their time wondering what the other one was thinking, and what they were really going to do when they found the old man. Kevin thought that he could talk him out of searching for the gold, and if that did not work, he would use physical force. He had no plans to use the rifle. Michael, on the other hand, knew he had to delay finding the man until they got to the location of the gold. He needed Kevin, and if they stopped the old man, Kevin would be going home.

After they made it to the top of the west side of the canyon, the hiking got much easier. The terrain was mostly small hills and flat valleys, and as they got closer to the base of the mountains, the bushes were being replaced by pinon and cedar trees. Despite the landscape being fairly flat, they had no luck spotting the old man. The land was very desolate without signs of any human presence. They would see an occasional cattle trail as they walked, but they could no longer see any dirt roads, power lines, or any signs of civilization.

The sun began to set behind the Chuska Mountains, and they decided to set up camp for the night.

"Should we build a fire?" Michael asked.

Kevin looked around. "We can if we camp in that crevasse over there. Anywhere else, you could see the fire for miles."

"I say, we go camp in that crevasse," Michael said. "I don't want to get eaten by bugs tonight, and the smoke will keep them off."

"Bugs?" Kevin laughed. "You're worried about bugs?"

"You know … mosquitoes."

Kevin laughed again. "Okay. Let's set up camp there."

They hiked another hundred yards to the crevasse and began collecting firewood. They spent a few hours talking about high school and drinking whiskey, but they were both very exhausted and found themselves nodding off. Somewhere in the middle of a conversation, they both fell asleep.

When Michael first opened his eyes, he saw the fire and assumed that the cracking sound was the cedar logs burning and popping. Just as he began to close his eyes he heard the cracking sound again and realized that it was not coming from the fire. He tried to look around, without moving his head, so that whatever it was did not know he was awake. The sound came again, and Michael immediately recognized it as something walking through the trees and sage brush. They were not alone.

Michael reached slowly out of his sleeping back and grabbed a small pebble. He flicked it with his fingers, trying to hit Kevin to wake him. He could not tell if it hit Kevin as Kevin lay on the other side of the fire, and his body was barely visible. He thought of yelling out Kevin's name to wake him, but he became overwhelmed with fear.

He heard more breaking of limbs and twigs even closer now, and then movement caught his eye. He saw something moving very slowly in the shadows just yards from the fire. Michael squinted his eyes trying to make out the figure, and slowly started to unzip his sleeping bag without making a noise. He did not know if the figure could see that his eyes were open, but if he had to act, he wanted to act fast and with surprise.

He thought about his rifle, but remembered that it was tied to his back pack. By the time he got the rifle untied and ready to fire, he would be dead. That is, if it were something that wanted to kill him. Michael, heart pounding and adrenaline pumping through his veins, believed that whatever it was, it was there to kill them.

Michael had to close his eyes tight and reopen them as the figure made its way slightly out of the shadows. He was not sure what he was seeing, but disbelief began to overtake his fear.

It was man, a very pale looking man walking almost cat-like toward their fire. He had no shirt or shoes on, just denim jeans. The man was not carrying any weapons, and did not look as though he was trying to harm them. He moved and acted as if he were simply curious, creeping quietly upon them to see what they were doing. Michael recognized the face and tried to speak, but as he was still overcome with fear, a sound would not escape his throat.

"Jake?" Michael barely squeaked out above a whisper. He took a deep breath and tried louder, "Jake?"

Jake stood blankly, staring at him. Michael wondered if Jake thought that he could not be seen.

Michael remained frozen as Jake stood motionless, breathing very deeply, his eyes staring straight through him.

"What the Fuck, Jake?!" Michael said, sitting up in his sleeping bag.

Kevin jerked, and mumbled something.

"Kevin, wake up!" Michael shouted.

Suddenly, Jake turned and ran back into the shadows.

"Wake up!" Michael yelled again.

"What!" Kevin said.

They heard the sound of breaking tree limbs and tumbling rocks as Jake ran away from the camp site.

"What the hell was that?!" Kevin asked as he sat up quickly. "Get your gun."

"No, wait." Michael said getting out of his sleeping bag and standing.

"What was that?" Kevin asked. "What's going on?"

"I saw Jake," Michael replied.

"You saw Jake."

"Yes, he was standing right here. Watching us sleep."

Kevin unzipped his sleeping bag and grabbed his rifle. "Don't fuck with me, Michael."

"I'm not. Dude! I saw Jake standing right here. He was only wearing blue jeans. He was staring at me!"

Kevin took the safety off his rifle and held it in both hands at this hip. "Are you sure we're not sleeping?"

"Wake up!" Michael demanded. "You had to have heard his running away. You had to have heard all that noise."

"I heard something running away," Kevin replied, "but…. Jake?"

"I wasn't asleep. I lay awake listening and watching for awhile. He came right out of the shadows and stood right the fuck here. He was staring right at me!"

"And his eyes?"

"Not red. It was him. He was damn close!"

Kevin looked at Michael for a brief moment. He could tell that Michael was not making up something just to scare him. He knew that Michael was acutely aware that he would get the worst ass-kicking of his life if he tried to pull something like that. Kevin walked to where Michael was standing and yelled, "Jake!"

Michael also yelled out, "Jake! Come back. What the hell, dude! Come back!"

They both stopped yelling and stood in silence. They could not hear the sound of anything moving anymore. They strained themselves to hear any sound at all, but all they could hear was the sound of the crackling fire.

"Where's the whiskey?" Michael asked.

"By my sleeping bag," Kevin replied. "Grab the flashlight while you're at it."

Michael grabbed the bottle of whiskey and a flashlight. He handed the flashlight to Kevin and took a long drink of the whiskey. Kevin moved the light slowly as they tried to find some sign of Jake. As the light moved, the shadows of the trees shifted making it appear that everything was moving.

"Get your gun, I'll be back in a minute," Kevin said.

"What? What do you mean, 'you'll be back?'"

"I'm going to look for Jake. Stay here and watch our stuff."

Michael took another long pull of the whiskey. "Screw you! You aren't leaving me alone right now."

"We can't let our crazy friend wander around half naked. I'm going to go get him."

"Let's get him in the morning," Michael replied. "He's obviously pretty good at getting around if he found us here in the middle of the night. He doesn't even have shoes on!"

"So?"

"He is walking around here at night without shoes on? What the hell?!"

Kevin grabbed the whiskey bottle from Michael, took a drink, and handed it back. "I'll just walk in that direction for a little bit. If I don't see or hear something soon, I'll come back. Okay?"

"Not okay. Stay here."

Michael searched in his back pack for a flashlight as Kevin staggered in a sleep induced haze in the direction Jake ran off. Michael could see Kevin's flashlight moving around in the trees as he walked, and as it got further away, he realized he was alone. He quickly took his hands out of his back pack and picked up his rifle. He used the bolt to chamber a round in the gun and sat on a sandstone rock waiting. He continued to drink whiskey as he waited, watching as the flashlight got further and further away.

"Fucking, Jake," Michael said looking around the campsite. He heard a sound behind him and jumped, letting out a high pitched chirp of a scream. After realizing that it was nothing, he prayed that Kevin did not hear him.

Fifteen minutes passed, yet it seemed like hours until Kevin returned. Kevin placed his gun back on safety and rested it against a rock next to his sleeping bag.

"No, Jake?" Michael asked.

"Oh, he's out there," Kevin replied. "I saw him. You definitely were not dreaming."

"Did you talk to the fruitcake?"

"Couldn't get close enough to him. Yelled at him a few times, but then he would just run off like a madman."

Michael sat his gun down and handed the bottle of whiskey to Kevin. Michael looked around the campsite again and said, "So, we have to worry about an old man, crazy monster people, Skinwalkers, rattlesnakes, and now Jake!"

"He's not right," Kevin replied.

"No, shit. Nothing about this is right!"

"Just go to bed. We'll look for him in the morning."

Michael reluctantly got in his sleeping bag and tried to fall asleep.

"What's going on?" Michael asked.

"What do you mean?" Kevin replied, obviously barely awake.

"What happened to Jake?"

"I don't know," Kevin replied. "I guess he just couldn't deal with what he saw that night."

"So, he is crazy?"

"I don't know," Kevin replied. "Go to bed."

"He is stalking us in the middle of the night, in the middle of the desert half naked, and you want me to go to bed?"

"Yep."

Michael lay quiet for only a moment then asked, "Do you believe the story about the hat?"

"Nope," Kevin replied.

"Good," Michael added. He closed his eyes and remembered Jake claiming he was cursed because his hat was stolen and placed into something that looked like a jar. He had done some research on the issue, and discovered that some Navajos believe a person can be cursed if a skinwalker places an article of that person's clothing in a jar. He remembered vaguely the belief that the soul would be captured, and despite not many Navajos accepting the story as true, it seemed so to Jake. He concluded that he was "different" since that night because either they took his hat, or because he took their bull. Michael believed that it was the trauma of that night that changed Jake, but could not help from being scared of the possibility that Jake was correct.

CHAPTER 21

Sheldon and Lowery got an early start, leaving their camp before the sun had finished rising in the east. They reached the base of the Chuska Mountains, and after telling their guides to leave and take the horses, they were now alone on foot. Although they were unaware of the two men tracking them at the time, Lowery knew that someone would be coming. He expected that when he shot the boy in the bar, either law enforcement or others would be on their way. He figured, by the popularity of the boy, it would be both. He did not mind. His plan was to get enough of the gold as he could carry, and be off, back to his island that belonged to a country with no extradition.

Sheldon, he thought, would have to deal with his own problems. He is a grown man now, and if he gets himself into trouble, he has to get himself out.

The hiking was getting very difficult as there were no roads or trails to follow. Lowery was spending his time looking for a road or a trail, or for signs of where one might have been. If Trabuco had driven the gold into the Chuska Mountains, they should see the remnants of some sort of path. Time would not have changed the fact that Trabuco could not have driven his truck over cliffs or large unmovable rocks. It was a clearing he was looking for. He instructed Sheldon to do the same, but he doubted that he would have a trained eye for such a thing.

Lowery sat on a large rock and pulled a canteen out of his backpack. Sheldon took his pack off and stretched his back. Lowery smiled as he took a sip of his water.

"What?" Sheldon asked.

"Nothing," Lowery responded. "Just wondering how good of a treasure hunter you are."

"Really?" Sheldon replied. "Well, I guess this is my first treasure hunt, so this one will prove it either way."

"I guess it will."

Sheldon sat on a rock next to his back pack and started looking in his pack for his canteen.

Lowery began to laugh.

"What?!" Sheldon asked.

"My god, son. Look at the ground next to your feet."

Sheldon looked down and saw an old can.

"An old rusty can. Is that what I'm supposed to see?" Sheldon asked.

"How much money did you spend on your fancy degree?"

"I guess not enough. What am I supposed to get from this can?"

Lowery smiled. "Throw it to me."

Sheldon picked up the can, took a brief look at it, and tossed it to Lowery. Lowery looked at all sides of the can and tossed it back.

"Let me ask you something, son," Lowery said looking around, "how can you explain an old oil can lying way out here?"

"Oil can?"

"Why sure," Lowery replied. "Look at its size. Look at the punch holes in the top of the can. That there is an oil can."

"You see trash like this all over the place."

"You do, son," Lowery replied, "but not out here. The only explanation for an old oil can being out here is that there was something out here that needed oil."

"Don't talk to me like I'm three-years-old, Lowery."

"And even more interesting to me, at this particular moment, is an oil can from 1933. The year Trabuco moved the gold."

"You can tell the year of this can by the rust? Is that what you are telling me?"

"No," Lowery replied, "I'm just playing with you. I don't know the date of the can. But, I do know that it is old, it's an oil can, and it's many miles from any place a car or truck has ever been. Or, ever should've been."

"Look, Lowery," Sheldon said. "I found the trail off the top of the mesa by finding an oil can. I know you think, because my mother was Navajo, that I am stupid. I also know that you think my college studies are worthless, and your experience far exceeds anything I've learned in my studies. As far as experience, I'll give you that. But could you please stop talking to me like I am an idiot? My mother was very intelligent. You would know this, if you would have taken time to meet her. There are a lot of things you would know, if you hadn't stayed hidden most of my life."

"Hidden, huh?"

"Yes, hidden."

"Sheldon Lowery," Lowery said, "the Irish Navajo. Ya Ta Hey, I'm telling ya."

"You're an ass," Sheldon said. "You're a sad old man."

"Yep," Lowery replied.

Sheldon glanced around and realized he had to agree with Lowery about the can. They were many miles from even a dirt road. There would be no reason for someone to hike an oil can to the base of the mountain and leave it. It was definitely out of place. He agreed with him, but did not need to be told the obvious.

"Look," Lowery said pointing toward the mountain. "Not a road, but awfully flat. Appears as though someone made a clearing, right up into the trees, wouldn't you say? Kind of hidden, I think."

Sheldon looked in the direction Lowery was pointing. It was not immediately apparent, but as he regarded it carefully, it did appear that a path was cleared at some point. And, it ran back the other direction toward the landing strip. There were not any obvious signs such as tire marks, dirt tracks, but something had made a path.

Sheldon studied the oil can again, "I could have found this without you."

"Keep telling yourself that, son."

Exactly 1,327 yards away, Kevin watched Lowery and Sheldon through the scope of his rifle. Kevin placed the tiny red dot between the two so that he could see both of them in his scope.

"You promised me that you would not just shoot him," Michael said.

"I'm just watching him. Calm down," Kevin said softly, trying to keep the rifle steady. "He's not alone. He has another guy with him."

"Just one?"

"All I see is one," Kevin replied. "They're just sitting there talking."

"Right at the base of the trail … great."

Kevin slowly reached up and turned a dial on the scope. He exhaled deeply and remained quiet, not breathing, for over a minute. He took in a deep breath and looked away from the rifle and said, "The old man has a small machine gun, I think. It looks like an MP5, or something. Like the one we shot at the range that day. Remember?"

Michael remembered going to the shooting range with Kevin and his dad several times. Kevin's father was an ex-marine and would take him and his friends to the shooting range to fire a variety of different weapons. Michael could not remember which gun was the MP5. All he could remember is that he spent more time watching than shooting, as the guns usually scared him.

"I don't remember that one," Michael replied.

"You've seen movies where they refer to a gun as an Uzi, right? Well, that's what it is. It shoots 9mm rounds, and can either be automatic or semi-automatic. It doesn't have very good range at all, and is not very accurate, but if you get close, it can do a lot of damage."

Michael motioned for Kevin to hand him the rifle, and when Kevin did, Michael took a look down the scope. He spent several minutes trying to find Lowery and the other man, but all he could see was shifting blurs of unfocused colors. After trying his best to hold the rifle still and find the two men, Michael finally gave up and handed the rifle back to Kevin.

"Well," Michael said very matter of fact, "looks like we go back and call the police."

Kevin sat thinking, gazing toward the mountains without the aide of the scope. He did not know how to respond to Michael's statement. The old man had a gun. Not a big surprise since they were only days removed from their friend being shot by the man. He expected that the man would be armed, and was not surprised that the man would be armed with something like an MP5, but now reality began to sink in. They had found the man, and he sat at the base of the mountain to which Kevin vowed never to return. His pregnant wife came to mind. He could pick up his rifle and end this right now. He was sure he could make the shot.

"Kevin," Michael said in a stern voice, "let's go."

Kevin continued to stare at the mountains. He looked above the two men and to the south, and thoughts ran through his mind so fast that he could not make sense of them. He recalled the excitement of the four of them when they found the gold, the smiles, the cheering, and all the emotions of the find that were mixed with the horror of what then found them. Being tied to a cross, drugged and semi-unconscious, seeing his friends tied up to crosses as well. White faces, with wild eyes, coming out of the darkness with wicked smiles.

"Kevin!"

"Shut up!" Kevin yelled and turned his head to glare at his former friend. "I don't want to be here either, goddamn it!"

"So, let's go!"

"Go where?" Kevin said as he stood. "See that?" He said pointing toward the east.

"See what?"

"Less than an hour's drive that way is my fucking home! I don't get to jump on an airplane and fly to New York, cocksucker!"

Michael looked dumbfounded. "You believe the warning, don't you?"

"I have to believe the warning! I have a wife, a child, and another on the way. I have to believe the warning so I don't have to think that what happened to us might happen to them."

Michael stood and noticed that Kevin looked scared, a look he had only seen on Kevin's face once, the night that changed their lives. .

Michael turned and surveyed the mountains. He said softly, "How could they find you? How could they get all the way to town? Kevin, how in the world could they harm you?"

"I don't know," Kevin replied. "I've thought about that since that night. While you were living large in New York, I spent countless nights lying awake. Do you know what it's like to jump at every creak, every sound outside your window? You don't know because you were thousands of miles away from this."

"So, move."

Kevin took a deep breath trying to calm his nerves. "This is my home. Even if I had the money to leave, which I don't, this is my goddamn home!"

"So, every time someone comes to look for the gold, you're going to chase after them in fear that those people will come and get you and your family?"

"Yes!"

"That's insane!"

"I guess it is, Michael. All I know is that Sam said there was only one copy of the tape the old man took. If I get the tape and destroy it, maybe all this will end."

"He has a gun!"

"So do I," Kevin replied. "And, if you want to leave, go ahead. I expected you to anyway."

Michael watched as Kevin picked up his backpack and placed it on his back. Less than a month ago Michael was drinking martinis with lawyers and wealthy clients, wearing Armani and Versace suits, on the short list at most of the exclusive restaurants and clubs in New York. Now, he was dirty and tired as he was hiking across the desert after a crazy old man with a machine gun, just miles away from a horror that he spent his life trying to forget.

Who am I? He thought.

Michael looked around trying to see a sign of Jake. Jake should be the one that is about to hike back into the Mountains. He is the one that thinks his soul was stolen. He was the one who had his hat put in a bottle.

I did not work this damn hard to get shot or tortured in the mountains, he thought.

"Do you really believe they'll come after you?" Michael asked.

"I wouldn't be here if I didn't," Kevin replied.

"Alright," Michael said and picked up his backpack. "We got into this mess together, I guess we have to try and get out of it together."

Lowery smiled as he watched Sheldon look up and down the old clearing. He smiled because he enjoyed watching his grandson see history come to life, but he also smiled knowing that the two men who were following them were not yet willing to shoot them.

The two men were in range; he knew this. He half expected to hear a bullet shatter a rock or the wood of a tree, but none came. It was a good place to rest, but it was the last time they would be in the open. It would be the final opportunity the men following them would have to take them out with the long range rifles. They did not seize it. This told Lowery that the men following were either law enforcement, or cowards. Either of the two pleased Lowery. He could deal with either.

The only concern he had about the men was that they were tracking them so quickly. He had taken steps not to leave a trail, but yet, they were hot on their trail. This, as all things he could not explain, troubled him.

"So, it's just up this clearing somewhere?" Sheldon asked.

Lowery felt resentment simmer in his mind.

My dumb shit grandson didn't even know he had a red dot on his head.

He knew, however, that he needed Sheldon, and despite the fact his grandson was oblivious, he could carry gold. He was a donkey.

"I think so, son." Lowery replied. "I am sure we'll be able to follow this clearing for awhile until the terrain gets too steep. Then, I'm assuming, there will be some sort of hiding place just off the path, a cave, a hole, or something."

"And then what?" Sheldon asked.

"Then we empty our packs and load as much gold as we can carry, and leave."

"There's no way to take it all."

Lowery nodded his head condescendingly, "No, shit. I don't want to take it all, son."

"Why not?"

"I have plenty of money and have never really felt good about taking all the treasure from a site."

"Why?"

"I guess it's like a code I created for myself. I'm a treasure hunter, and it feels as though we're a dying breed. I'll take what I need to stake a claim, and move on to the next."

"But you've said to me several times that you've spent a good part of your life looking for this gold," Sheldon said.

"I've spent a good part of my life looking for lots of different treasures. I guess you could say I get bored with just one project. You need to come visit me sometime at my estate. I think you'd enjoy my library. I continuously work on many projects, some of which I think you would be very interested in."

Sheldon had never been asked to visit his grandfather. The invitation to Lowery's estate, although Sheldon had no clue where it was, made him feel good. He was on a treasure hunt with his grandfather and for the first time in his life felt like a grandson.

Lowery stood and turned in the direction the two men once were. He acted as though he was stretching his back and spent that time trying to find the men. His eyes were still good. So were his instincts. The men were on the move again, and thus, so should they be.

CHAPTER 22

Sam struggled at appearing comfortable and confident as he sat on the cold metal chair with chipped gray paint. Up in the corner of the cold lifeless room was a small hole in the ceiling for a camera. He had seen this room before, but never from the inside. A good friend of his had promoted quickly in the Sheriff's office, and on a few occasions, had let Sam watch videos of interviews. The videos were usually of a drunk or a meth user and would have been quite comical if it were not for the criminal undertone of the interview.

Now, Sam found himself in this same room staring into the eye of the camera, remembering watching others in the same situation. He had often wondered how he would respond or act if interviewed by the police.

People did not necessarily act nervous because they had anything to hide, but rather because the room was very cold, uncomfortable, and unfamiliar. Next to his metal chair was a gray metal wastebasket that had nothing in it. Just next to the wastebasket was a table made of the same chipped, gray metal like all of the other furniture in the room. On the other side of the table was an empty chair that matched the chair Sam was sitting in. The only other items in the room were a notepad and a mechanical pencil.

He knew from what he had seen that they make the interviewee sit in this cold lifeless room for a very long time. In the room next to him would be a more comfortable room that had an overwhelming smell of stale coffee. The video screens taping him would be viewed by several different officers and detectives, all discussing his mannerisms and trying to find something in his body language that suggested his guilt or innocence. And despite knowing that he was not guilty of anything, he still could not help but be nervous. He could not keep from looking at the empty chair, the empty wastebasket, the pencil, the camera, and wondering what would be asked, and more importantly, what he should say.

Quite still, trying not to fidget and to remain calm, he wanted to give the people in the next room nothing to be suspicious of. He waited for nearly 30 minutes when he finally looked up at the camera and said, "I have to be at my restaurant for the dinner rush, so if you want to talk to me, let's get going."

A few moments passed, and the silence was broken by the heavy metal door squeaking on its hinges as it slowly opened.

A young detective whom Sam did not recognize walked in holding a file under his arm. He wore jeans, a white shirt, a cheap tie, and an empty holster on his hip. He carried two small Styrofoam cups of coffee and held a pen in his mouth. He set a cup of coffee in front of Sam and sat himself in the chair across from the metal desk.

"I didn't know if you wanted coffee or not, so figured I'd just bring you a cup so we can get started," the young detective said.

"Thank you," Sam replied, refusing to look at the cup.

"Do you know why you were asked to come here today?" The young detective asked, sliding the notepad toward himself and writing down the date and time.

"I was told that you guys wanted to talk to me about my case," Sam replied.

"That's correct. My name is Detective Peterson, I don't believe we've met."

Sam smiled, "As you must know, my name is Sam. A pleasure to meet you."

"We want to ask you a few questions very quickly so you may be on your way and back to work," Detective Peterson said as he sat back in his chair holding the notepad so that Sam could no longer see what he was writing.

Then why did you make me sit here for half an hour, Sam thought.

"I want you to know that we're still looking into leads on the man who shot you. As you know, there were a lot of witnesses, and interviewing them all takes time."

"Okay," Sam replied.

"The reason we wanted to talk to you is that we know a couple of your friends are in town, and they have now gone."

"Kevin lives here, but Michael is in town from New York," Sam said immediately questioning whether he should have said their names. "I don't know where they are now."

"We have witnesses saying that they were purchasing camping supplies and ammunition."

"Okay," Sam replied, trying not to look up at the camera.

"It's not hunting season, Sam," Detective Peterson added.

"I told you, I don't know where they went. I know that Kevin likes to hunt coyote, and it is always hunting season for coyote."

"Sam," Detective Peterson said, setting his notepad on the table, "what happened to you is a very bad thing. Nobody would disagree with you on that. But, if your friends are going to go do something stupid, it'll hurt a lot of people, and they'll go to prison for the rest of their lives."

"I don't know where they are or what they're up too," Sam replied.

"You were with them the other night at the Drip Tank?"

Sam was surprised that they had this information. He began to get a bit nervous. If they knew that, what else did they know? Surely they did not know about the tapes.

"We were," Sam replied. "Just catching up a bit."

"Old friends just hanging out, huh?"

"Guess so."

Detective Peterson opened his file which Sam figured was just a prop. He watched as the Detective thumbed through a few pages and wondered what it was that he could be reading.

Sam cleared his throat, "You know, I was the one who got shot. I'm the victim in this. Why are you treating me like a criminal?"

"Nobody said you were a criminal, Sam. We're just a bit worried. You get shot, your friend from New York flies in, and two guys who can't stand each other leave town on a camping trip together. It all worries us, that's all."

Sam felt himself begin to sweat. How did they have all this information? He thought of leaving the interview and calling Kevin and Michael to call the whole thing off, but he knew that they were already in a place that had no cell phone reception.

"I don't know anything," Sam said.

Detective Peterson looked up at the camera and stood. Sam wondered if the interview was over when he noticed that the Detective was giving a signal to someone in the other room. The Detective told Sam to stay seated and made his way out of the room.

Great. Another half hour. Sam thought.

It was only a few minutes before the large door opened again, but it was not Detective Peterson who walked in this time, but a very large Navajo man wearing a suit. Sam immediately recognized the man as Under-Sheriff Travis John. He was a friend of Sam, Kevin, and Michael in high school. As a very tall Navajo who was an all-state tight-end for the football team, he was expected to go away on scholarship to just about any school he wanted. He was very smart, and was an even better football player, but Travis decided to go to work for the Sheriff's office right out of high school, never attending college.

Sam had followed his career. He had spent several hours with Travis at his restaurant trying to convince him that his expedited promotions were not thought by most to be based on his race, but rather on his ability. Sam had also spent many hours in his restaurant listening to those who disagreed. In any event, Travis was a friend, and Sam was very proud of his success and secretly felt comfortable being the friend of the number two ranking man at the Sheriff's office. He never asked Travis for a favor, but he knew that there were plenty coming.

"Hey, Travis," Sam said feeling a bit more relaxed.

"What's up, Nutz?" Travis said, calling Sam by his high school nick-name that was coined when Sam blocked a field goal with a less desirable body part than his hands. It was Travis who carried him off the field, whispering the name to Sam for the first time. It was a name that only Travis called him by since high school. "I told them to turn the camera off."

"Okay," Sam said matter-of-fact.

"What's going on, Sam?" Travis asked.

"I don't know what you're talking about."

Travis picked up Sam's cup of coffee and took a sip. He looked at Sam with tired eyes.

"Don't make me do this, Nutz."

Sam shifted in his chair a bit and said, "Do what?"

"Don't make me spend all night telling you what I know so that you'll tell me what you know. We go way back. Please tell me what's going on."

Sam saw that Travis was truly concerned.

"I don't know...."

Travis raised his voice a bit and said, "Stop ... look at me. Cindy is pregnant."

Sam looked up at the camera; he immediately knew that she was one of the people in the other room watching the video screens. He imagined her face, a tear running down her cheek.

"Well, it's not mine," Sam replied, shrugging his shoulders.

Travis smiled, and fought the urge to laugh. Unlike most people, he actually liked Sam's sense of humor. 'The kind of guy who would rip off a loud fart at a funeral,' is how Travis would explain him. Well, Sam just ripped out his fart, and Travis had to shake it from his mind. He was at work now, and he had to stop what they all thought was going to happen.

"Do you want me to bring Cindy in here, and let you tell her that you don't know where her husband is?" Travis said looking toward the door.

Sam thought about this for a moment. Usually humor got him out of situations, but he was beginning to realize that it would not work this time. They were truly concerned, and if they did have Cindy, they had a lot of information.

"Not here....not like this," Sam said soft enough that the microphone could not pick up his voice.

"My boss is watching, Nutz. The Sheriff is in the next room. There are a lot of people around here who think it's very peculiar that you never ask us how your case is going. Not once have you asked if we found the man. Then, Michael shows up from New York, buys a bunch of supplies for camping and hunting, and leaves with Kevin, who can't stand him. A hot-shot New York lawyer and an assistant baseball coach go off camping together? All of this shortly after you're shot."

Sam's mind was racing with thoughts. He wanted to try running for the door. They had no reason to hold him, did they?

"And Jake is missing," Travis said in a strange voice.

"What do you mean Jake is missing?" Sam asked.

"We sent a few guys up to his trailer to ask him some questions, but he wasn't there. All they found was a strange calendar, and written on it was…."Travis flipped through some notes, "'Jake to get hat back,' and then a line drawn through every week for the rest of the calendar year."

Sam took a deep breath and tried to think of what to say. He wondered if Kevin and Michael picked up Jake before they left and was very concerned about the mess he may have caused.

"I don't want to talk here, Travis," Sam said looking up at the camera.

"I don't care. If Kevin and Michael have gone off to do what we think they are doing, we need to stop them before a lot of people's lives get ruined."

"I need a drink," Sam said.

"What?"

Sam spoke louder, "I need a drink, Travis."

"What would you like?"

"Belvedere."

Travis knew that such a request was against protocol, and he would certainly hear about it from his boss, but he looked at the camera anyways and simply nodded.

They sat in silence waiting on the vodka.

When Sam was handed the bottle of Belvedere by a young rookie cop, he was asked if he wanted a mixer. Sam smiled at the awkwardness of the question, and simply poured it into a Styrofoam cup. The rookie police officer looked at Travis expecting to receive some type of reprimand, but when Travis nodded, the young officer left the room and closed the door.

Sam was into his fourth drink before he began to speak. His words were slow and deliberate, and he tried to keep his answers as short and vague as possible.

"Okay," Sam said after a long drink from the cup.

"What's going on?" Travis asked softly.

"They're not going to get some kind of revenge. They're just trying to find the man."

"Why?"

"Why, what?" Sam replied.

"Don't do this," Travis demanded. "We'll be here all night if you try and be evasive. Just answer the questions and let's get through this, Okay?"

"May need more Belvedere," Sam replied.

"Fine, but for now, tell me why they're trying to find the man."

"They're trying to stop him."

Travis picked up the notepad and prepared his pen for writing. "Stop him?"

"You don't have to take notes, Travis. You're recording this," Sam slurred.

"You don't want me to take notes, fine."

"They're stopping him from finding Hell," Sam said and poured another drink.

"Hell."

"Yes, from finding Hell and releasing its fury on us."

Travis looked concerned. This was not Sam's nature at all. He was a smart-ass, sometimes a bull-shitter, but Travis knew that Sam would not intentionally create drama. It was his nature to do the opposite.

"Nutz, I need you to tell me what the hell is going on, and we don't have time to play word games. That man shot you, and there is no reason to believe that he won't shoot Kevin or Michael. Kevin's pregnant wife is crying in the next room, and you're telling me that they went to stop this man from going to Hell and releasing its fury? You're not making sense."

"None of this makes sense," Sam replied and poured another cup of vodka. "The bottle is half gone, Travis. Tell your camera man to go get another."

"Go," Travis said to the camera. "Now, tell me what's going on. Please."

"When I was in high school, I found these weird tapes. Remember, when I worked at the radio station? Well, I found these reel-to-reel tapes that said, 'interview of navy officer' or some shit like that. I transferred the reel-to-reel to regular cassette tapes, and then listened to them. It was an interview of a pilot who was flying one of those sub-finder planes, and was talking about what his radar showed. I think the person asking the questions was trying to prove that a U.F.O. crashed near here or something. Anyway, we were all hanging out at the station drinking beer one night, and I played the tapes for Jake and Michael. I didn't think anything much about it, but you know Jake. He got obsessed with the damn thing."

Travis watched as Sam finished another glass of vodka and poured another.

Sam continued, "So, Jake did a bunch of research and found this story about gold being illegally transported and hidden near here. Some of the information was verified, and some of it was bullshit, I think. But, small town with nothing much to do, so fuck it, right?"

"Slow down a bit," Travis said as he watched Sam chug another cup of vodka.

"Shut up," Sam replied. "I'm talking. So, we became little gold searching fuckers. Jake figures out some coordinates from the interview, we take what little information we had, and we went off looking for 17 tons of gold."

"17 tons of gold," Travis said bluntly.

"Shut up," Sam slurred. "After graduation, we packed up some camping stuff and went off looking for our gold. Hell, at the time I considered it a senior trip. I didn't really think we'd find anything, but knew that some of us were going to college and shit, and figured, what the hell. So, we go out into the reservation, and lucky us, we find the goddamn gold."

"You found 17 tons of gold."

"That's right. Write that down. We found 17 tons of gold. Well, actually, I didn't fucking weigh it, but we found a bunch of gold. And, I don't know what 17 tons of gold looks like, but it was within a couple of goddamn tons!"

"Calm down," Travis replied.

"You calm down. We find the gold, we get all happy, we high-five, we jump around like a bunch of little girls, and then night falls."

Sam tried to pour another cup of vodka and knocked the cup off the table. He laughed when it hit the floor. "Pointless little fucker," he said and drank from the bottle.

"What happened when night fell?" Travis asked.

"Oh, good," Sam said as the young officer walked in with another bottle of vodka.

"What happened when night fell, Sam?" Travis asked again.

"Give me a minute," Sam replied. "I need a few more before I tell you the best part."

Travis sat patiently as Sam drank the first half of the second bottle, realizing how far Sam's alcoholism had progressed. Sam was swaying in his chair and Travis was getting concerned that he would pass out. He knew, however, that if he stopped Sam from drinking, the interview was over. He would have to be patient and deal with him. Hopefully, he would be able to make sense of all of this.

"What happened at night fall?" Travis whispered.

Tears swelled in Sam's eyes, his speech now very sloppy. "We decided to camp at the gold. There was so much of it. So many different sizes and types. We didn't know how to move it. So, we thought it would be fun to camp at the site and celebrate what we had found. We were all rich!"

Sam caught himself before falling out of his chair.

He shook his head as if to sober up a bit. "So we sat by the fire drinking," Sam said almost in a whisper, talking very slow. "When we first started to hear noises, we tried to freak each other out. We all thought it was just animals, so we started telling stories to scare each other. Then Jake said something. We all started to laugh. Then he said it again, and again. The look on his face. My God."

"What did he see?" Travis asked trying to keep the story going.

"He said that he kept seeing faces in the darkness. White faces with black hair. He said they kept popping in and out of the shadows."

Sam closed his eyes and rubbed out some tears. "We didn't believe him. We thought he was just trying to scare us, but … the look on his face."

Sam paused and stopped speaking.

"Sam," Travis said. "Hey, you're doing well, bud. Come on."

"These people," Sam said with a tear running down his face. "These people came out of the darkness. There was so many of them; yelling, chanting, coming from every direction. We tried to fight them. We couldn't fight them off."

"People? What people?" Travis asked.

"Evil people. They had white stuff painted on their faces, they all had long black hair, crazy people … I don't know."

"Skinwalkers?" Travis asked.

Sam did not reply.

"Sam," Travis said, "I'm a traditional Navajo. I don't even believe in Skinwalkers."

"They weren't Skinwalkers!" Sam said and threw the vodka bottle against the wall. "They weren't anything! They looked like demons. They spoke a weird language. I don't know!"

"Okay, Sam," Travis said raising his hands motioning for Sam to settle down. "What happened?"

"They took us away to a clearing. They tied us all to crosses." Sam took a very long deep breath. "They took Jake away for a long time. I don't know what they did to him. They cut us with sticks and sharp stones. They drank our blood. They rubbed grass and dirt on our bodies. They..."

Sam stopped and looked at the floor.

"Keep going. Come on, Sam."

Sam placed his head in his hands and rested for a few minutes. "They told us if we, or anyone, ever returned, they would torture us."

"I thought you said they spoke a weird language," Travis added.

"They did. That's what Jake told us when they brought him back. We were still tied to the crosses. Jake looked up at us, almost like he was possessed. He screamed at all of us. Yelled, over and over, if we or anyone returned, we would be tortured."

Sam took another deep breath. "That is the last thing any of us remembers."

"What was the next thing you remember?" Travis asked.

"Waking up at the base of the mountain."

"What mountain?" Travis asked.

Sam looked up at Travis and pointed at him. "Ah, ha! You want me to tell you were the gold is, don't you?!"

"Sam, stop it, I want to know where Kevin and Michael are."

"Kevin and Michael are going to stop that man from finding those people. That is where Kevin and Michael are."

"So, the man knows about the gold?"

"Lots of people know about the gold. Fuck, everyone knows about the gold. They just don't know where it is."

"Does the man know where it is?" Travis asked.

"He does now," Sam replied. "Got a couple of wounds that proves that. He has the tapes and is headed to hell. I tried to stop the poor son-of-a-bitch."

"Why didn't you tell us?!"

"Tell you what?" Sam replied. "Tell you I was shot by a treasure hunter who's on his way to a bunch of unknown demon-people? Ha!"

"Do you want some coffee?" Travis asked.

"Hell no!" Sam shouted and then looked up at the camera. "So, there you have it. Kevin and Michael went to stop a crazy old man from finding the demon-people. Is that what you were expecting? If not, you can shove it up your ass!"

The door to the interview room opened as Sam took another drink from the bottle he did not throw against the wall. Standing at the doorway was Cindy. She was crying and her hands were shaking nervously. Sam expected her to run up and hit him. He would make no effort to block her punch.

She walked slowly up to Sam and stood looking down on him. She started crying harder, shaking uncontrollably.

"I'm so sorry, Sam," she whimpered. "I'm so sorry."

Sam tried to speak, but the words would not come out. He had known Cindy her whole life, but had never known how good-hearted she was. He had just sent her husband off possibly to be killed, and she was consoling him. It was more than Sam could take.

"I can't do this anymore," Sam slurred and tried to stand. He fell, knocking over Cindy and the metal table.

Cindy got herself to her feet and her expression changed.

"Listen, Sam," Cindy said in a stern voice, "tell me where Kevin is, NOW!"

"He went off after…"

"I know he went off after the old man, and I know what is out there. I heard your story. I don't give a shit!"

Sam stood and tried to look Cindy in the eyes without falling over.

"I don't know," Sam responded.

"I want you to tell me right now!" Cindy screamed. "I don't give a shit about anything else but where Kevin is!"

Cindy began pounding on Sam's chest with her fists.

"He is all I have in the world, Sam," She said in a shaky voice. "Please, tell me where he is. Please."

Sam shook his head again to sober up. "I can't explain it."

"Try!" Cindy yelled.

"I can't explain it, but I might be able to find it," Sam slurred.

"Find it!" Cindy yelled again. "Take them and go find it, now!"

CHAPTER 23

Lowery was not surprised that his wimp of a grandson could hardly keep up. In spite of this, he increased the rate of his hike. He knew that the two men would eventually catch up to them. He actually wanted this to happen, but he had to find the right place for the confrontation to occur. The clearing of the path would not last much longer. Lowery assumed that the terrain would get too steep. The hiding place for the gold would be close, and he wanted to confront the followers before the site was found.

Lowery could hear Sheldon gasping for air behind him and fought his desire to look back at his tired grandson. He kept his eyes fixed on the ground to avoid turning an ankle or falling down. He was in unusually good shape for his age, but a fall would still be a big problem for him. He doubted that Sheldon had the physical or mental strength to keep the hunt alive if he were injured.

It was because he was concentrating so hard on keeping his footing that he jumped when he saw the man standing in front of him.

Lowery stopped and quickly grabbed his MP5, aiming at the man's chest. The man was extremely skinny, standing before him, staring blankly and wearing nothing but denim jeans. The man was frail and pale, his eyes wide and seemingly unconcerned that a gun was pointed at his chest.

"Get the fuck out of our way, boy," Lowery said raising the gun to the man's forehead.

Sheldon stopped twenty yards behind Lowery and stood panting. He was thinking of reaching for the gun Lowery had given him, but decided that the MP5 Lowery was pointing at the man would take care of any trouble the man might try to cause. Sheldon noticed that the skinny man had nothing in his hands, and that the man's arms hung lifeless by his side. He noticed the man's feet were bare, and wondered how this man could be walking on these rocks and bushes without shoes.

"Who are you?" Sheldon asked, barely loud enough for Lowery to hear.

"Shut up, Sheldon," Lowery said as he took a few steps closer to the man.

"Believe me, boy," Lowery said in a voice familiar to Sheldon, "it would be in your best interest to get the Hell out of here."

The man stood very quiet and still, his eyes fixed on Lowery's eyes. Lowery had pointed many guns at many men, but this was the first time he could recall that the man on the receiving end of the gun did not even glance at the threat.

"Don't," the man said as if it took all the energy he could muster to get the word out.

"Don't what?" Lowery replied. "I won't shoot you if you get the Hell out of here and mind your own damn business."

"Don't go any further," the man said, still staring at Lowery's eyes.

Lowery chuckled and said, "Look, we have business here, and our business is none of yours, so take your boney little ass and get out of our way."

Lowery knew that there was plenty of room to get around the man, and did not see that he could pose a threat, but how and why this man was out here bothered him.

"You don't know what lies ahead," the man replied. "Please turn around and go home."

"Are you alone?" Sheldon asked.

"Shut the fuck up, Sheldon!" Lowery shouted.

"I've always been alone," the man replied.

Lowery had killed a man, and shot several more, but he was not a cold-blooded killer. The killing of the man was declared by the court in Barbados as self defense, and the shooting of the other men was intended to intimidate, not to kill. He knew that he would not pull the trigger sending this man to his death, but he had to make the man believe he would. He was beginning to doubt that this man was in his right state of mind, and was convinced that he cared very little if Lowery did squeeze the trigger.

Lowery and Sheldon watched as he slowly turned and walked to a large rock. The man sat on the rock and stared up, looking in the direction Lowery and Sheldon were heading.

"Please don't go up there," the man said, staring up into the forest.

Lowery turned and looked at Sheldon, motioned with his head for Sheldon to walk up to him, and then turned back to the man. Once Sheldon reached Lowery, Lowery passed the man slowly.

"We're going now," Lowery said keeping the gun pointed at the man's head. "Do not try anything stupid, and definitely don't try and follow us. I promise you, I'll cut you down."

The man did not reply.

Lowery picked up his pace as he passed the man sitting on the rock, and Sheldon used all his effort now to keep up with him.

"Don't go," the man said again as Lowery and Sheldon pressed on.

"Don't respond," Lowery said to Sheldon. "Mindless men deserve no reply."

Lowery attached the MP5 to a clamp on his backpack and continued to walk as if nothing had happened, never looking back at the man. Sheldon stumbled several times over the next half hour, continuously turning back to see if the skinny man was following them. Lowery smiled awkwardly every time he caught Sheldon looking back, trying to make Sheldon think he was wasting his time concerning himself with the man. However, Lowery was deeply concerned about the man. He had seen countless oddities in his life, but until now he had never encountered a nearly naked man in the middle of nowhere with no concern that a gun was pointed at his head.

They had traveled far enough up the mountain that the path was no longer ascertainable, and more significant to Sheldon, they were a good distance from where they left the man sitting on the rock.

They heard a voice echo through the mountainside.

"I tried to stop them! I tried to stop them!"

At the base of the mountain, Michael and Kevin heard the yelling voice, and recognized it to be Jake's.

"What the hell is Jake doing?" Michael asked Kevin.

"How am I supposed to know?" Kevin replied.

Kevin sat on the same rock where he had observed Lowery sitting through his rifle's scope, took off his backpack, and drank some water. He smiled when Michael chose to sit on the exact same rock he saw the companion of the old man sitting.

"We didn't stop him in time," Michael said.

"We still have time," Kevin replied. "We still have several hours before the sun starts to set. We should leave our packs here, and take only our guns and water. We can catch up to them."

"You really intend to go up into the mountain?" Michael asked.

"Yes," Kevin replied as he untied his rifle from his backpack. "We'll hike fast, and if we don't find them before the sun starts to set, we'll hustle back down the mountain to our packs."

"And if the people follow us?"

"We have guns this time and will be ready."

Michael reluctantly untied his gun from his pack and stood. He took a moment to look back in the direction from where they had come. The miles of desolate landscape to the east was their safe zone. He would go up the mountain with Kevin for a few hours, and if there were no sign of the man, he would jog down the mountain and into the desert with or without his friend.

He chose to leave the Bull in the backpack. There was not enough time to find the man and return it to the site. He decided to wait until that night to tell Kevin about the Bull, Jake's belief that it may be cursing him, and his promise to return it to the people. Tomorrow morning, with plenty of time to do so, he would hike back up the mountain with the Bull and do what he promised his friend. Hopefully, he would not be doing it alone.

Michael surveyed the northeast and tried to see the well site where he had left the truck. When he dropped off the truck, he thought it was closer to the path than it really was. He concluded that there was no way he was going to be able to load the truck with the gold. He thought that if Kevin protested, he would be able to load the gold slowly during the day by himself. He now realized that there would be no way to do this, even if Kevin did help him. He also knew that when he did not deliver the gold, his life would drastically change.

Butt-fuck it, Michael thought.

Chapter 24

Sam had finished his third cup of coffee, and after chugging many glasses of water and forcing himself to throw up, he was beginning to sober up a bit. He shook his head violently to gather his senses as Cindy paced in the break room of the Sheriff's office. He could not believe what he had just told Travis John in the interview room, and doubted that the video had really been off. The people had warned them what would happen if he or anyone ever returned, and now, he had just informed everyone about the gold and the people. He was ashamed of what he had just done, but knew he had to go get his friends.

Sam walked up to Cindy and led her into an office so that they could talk alone.

"I will go get Kevin," Sam said, his slur improving.

"Then go," she replied.

"Okay, Cindy. Just know that whatever happens, I promise I'll bring Kevin back."

Cindy tried to smile at her drunken friend and gave him a hug.

"I hate you for this Sam, but I'll forgive you if you bring my husband home," she said, pushing away from him.

"I will," he replied.

Sam staggered out of the office and looked at the six officers who waited for him in the break room. *There are not enough of them,* Sam thought.

"So," Sam exclaimed, "what kind of gun do I get?"

"Funny," Travis replied.

Sam leaned against the sink, folded his arms, and said, "It's time to go get my friends, but I'll only go and show you where they are if it's just me and Travis."

The room exploded in conversation and protest, mostly from Cindy who started crying again. Sam slapped his hand down on the countertop to break the commotion.

"We'll return with Kevin and Michael, but I'll only go if I go alone with my friend Travis. Despite all the goodwill everyone in this room claims to have, there's a lot of gold out there and even more danger. I will not bring the temptation or threat upon anyone I don't completely trust, and the only person I trust in this room is Travis. So, it's either that, or I'm going to go back to my restaurant to prepare for the dinner rush."

"Sam," Travis replied, "If those people are really up there, we need as many guys as possible."

"It won't matter," Sam replied.

"Really?" one of the officers asked sarcastically.

"Really," Sam responded. "Look, I'm not going to argue about this, and we're wasting time. Travis and I'll go get them, and if anyone tries to follow us, it's over."

Travis shook his head, obviously not approving of Sam's demands, as the two drove in an unmarked police car westward out of town.

"There are not many mountain ranges around here, Sam," Travis said breaking the silence.

"I know," Sam replied. "Don't worry, they're not far."

"If you can drive to the location, why did they need so much camping gear?"

Sam shook his head, "We're not going to the location. We're going to the end of the closest dirt road. Once we get there, we'll try to get in contact with them and get them to come back to us."

Travis reached over with his right hand and began to type on a laptop that was attached to the middle console of the car. Sam took long deep breaths as Travis typed surprisingly fast with one hand. Sam thought about asking him what he was typing, but decided against it.

"Lots of cool gadgets in this thing," Sam said looking around the interior of the car. "Guns, radios, laptops, handcuffs, mace, all the cool cop shit is in here."

Travis chuckled as he continued to type. Sam leaned forward placing his hand on his stomach.

"Are you okay?" Travis asked still typing.

"Yes, I'm fine," Sam replied taking in a deep breath.

Travis stopped typing and placed his hand back on the steering wheel.

"Are we going toward the La Plata or Chuska mountains?" Travis asked.

"Just drive," Sam replied.

"I am driving," Travis said. "I need to know if I'm turning north or continuing west."

Sam leaned forward again, placing his hand on his stomach. He looked up and saw that the turn to head north to the La Plata Mountains was a few miles away.

"What's wrong with you, Nutz?"

Sam took a long deep breath and said, "I guess I'm not done puking."

"Need me to pull over?"

245

Sam nodded his head, indicating that he needed the car pulled over. Travis slowed the car and pulled it into an empty dirt lot just before the turnoff to the La Plata Mountains. Once the car came to a stop, Travis put the car into park and placed his hands back on the steering wheel.

"Okay," Travis said, "do what you…"

Suddenly, Sam lunged toward Travis, and since he would have never expected his friend to do anything, his guard was low. Travis knew immediately what had happened when he felt cold steel press against his wrist, followed by the sound of short repeated clicking sounds. His first instinct was to backhand Sam with his right wrist; but that was stopped by the handcuffs that now attached his wrist to the steering wheel. It also stopped him from preventing Sam from quickly pulling the keys out of the ignition.

"What the hell are you doing?!" Travis yelled.

Sam did not respond immediately. Sam opened his door and quickly slid to the edge of his seat so that Travis could not reach him. Sam then reached down and pulled the CB microphone until it was unplugged.

"What the fuck?!" Travis yelled and tried to grab Sam as he threw the keys and microphone out of the car.

Travis quickly reached for the laptop and began typing something with his left hand when Sam slammed the lid shut on Travis's hand. Travis pulled his hand out from the grip of the laptop lid and quickly pulled out a can of mace.

"Stop, Sam!"

"You spray that shit, and I'll close the car door on you when I get out. You'll be sitting in here coughing and choking for a very long time."

Sam leaned forward and grabbed the wires to the laptop, and just as he had hold of them, he felt Travis grab him by the back of the neck. Travis's grip was extremely strong, but Sam pulled the wires several times not concerning himself with trying to break free of Travis until they were disconnected. Finally, on his fourth pull, the wires ripped free.

Sam struggled in Travis's grip for a moment, twisting and slapping at Travis until he finally broke loose from his grip.

"Have you lost your fucking mind?!" Travis yelled.

Sam slid out of the car and knelt down so that he could look Travis in the eyes. He rubbed the back of his neck and tried to get control of his breathing.

"Don't kick my ass for this later," Sam asked panting.

"What the hell are you doing, Sam?!"

"I can't take you there, Travis. I don't have time to explain. Hopefully one night, over a beer at my place, you'll let me explain all of this."

Sam began to stand when Travis said, "This is a fucking felony, Nutz."

Sam paused, and after a few moments, returned to his kneeling position.

"What felony?" Sam asked.

"False imprisonment for one."

"Huh," Sam replied and thought for a moment. "What level of felony is that?"

"It's a fourth-degree felony."

"And how much time would a guy serve for a fourth-degree felony?" Sam asked.

"18 months, why?"

Sam continued to rub his neck and said, "With good time?"

"Shut up and let me go."

"I think with good time, I'd serve 9 months," Sam said.

"Something like that, that's not the point. Why don't you trust me? I'm trying to help you."

Sam stood, "And I'm trying to help you. 9 months, huh? Fuck it."

Sam slammed the door shut and started walking toward the road. He knew that there would be sheriff's officers coming very shortly, so he needed to find a car fast and make his way to the back roads, off the major highways.

Sam began waving his arm and jumping in the air frantically as an old pickup truck came toward him. The truck was slowing down and he began to limp toward the truck, holding out his hand demanding that it stop. When the truck stopped, he could see that the driver was middle-aged oilfield man who had a look of concern on his face. Sam went quickly up to the driver's side window and gasped, trying to catch his breath.

"I am Detective Sam with the Sheriff's office, and my partner is having a stroke or something. Do you have a cell phone?"

"What do you…"

"I need the phone now," Sam said still panting. "Please, help us."

The oilfield man quickly handed a cell phone to Sam and reached for the ignition keys.

"No!" Sam yelled. "Leave it running. Come on; help me load him into the bed of the truck. We need to get him to a hospital."

"Why not drive him?" the man asked.

"We don't have time for this! The car won't start … come on," Sam said and started walking as quickly as he could toward the police car.

The man climbed out of the truck and began following Sam. Travis tried several times to yell for the man to stop, but the man obviously could not hear him. When Sam and the man got halfway between the truck and the police car, Sam dropped the cell phone, and when the man reached down to pick it up, Sam turned and tried to run. With his injured leg stiff from the brace, he ran awkwardly, like he had a wooden leg that was a foot longer than the other. The man picked up his cellular phone, and stood for a moment trying to comprehend what Sam was doing. When the man's senses came to him, he started chasing after Sam. For a moment, the man thought he might catch up to Sam, but just as the man reached the tailgate, the truck sped off, leaving a large cloud of dust.

Sam shook his head and took many deep breaths, continuing his efforts to sober up. He was still drunk and knew that his whole plan would be finished if a police car stopped him for swerving.

He turned north, heading toward the La Plata Mountains. He knew that Travis would be watching the direction he headed, and when the other Sheriff's officers arrived, Travis would send them in that direction. He planned on taking the road north for about ten miles, and then he would take a dirt road he used to go four-wheeling on for another 25 miles. There would be no traffic on the road, and Sam had never seen a police officer patrol it.

Sam did not know how long he had before there would be cops all up and down the highway. He assumed the man called 911 immediately after the truck sped off, and since they were not far out of town yet, it would not take the police long before they were on top of him.

Sam breathed some more to steady himself and placed his hands in the ten-and-two position on the steering wheel. He made sure that he drove at least the speed limit, having been told by Travis several times that most drunks drive too slowly. He watched the center line, and tried his best to maintain a fairly straight driving path. He turned the air conditioner on high, and rolled down the windows, thinking that the influx of air would bring more oxygen into his lungs and speed up the sobering process.

When Sam finally reached the dirt road he looked down either side of the highway to ensure that there were no flashing lights of police cars that could see him make the turn. He saw no cars at all, and after a few hundred yards of driving down the dirt road, he was over a hill and out of the sight of anyone driving on the highway.

Sam loudly sung a mess of the words of the Hank Williams song *Lost Highway* as the truck rumbled down the dirt road.

CHAPTER 25

Kevin knew they were hiking far too quickly if they were hunting an animal, for whatever they may be hunting could hear them coming from a long distance away. They did not, however, have the time to properly stalk their prey slowly and quietly. They had only until the sun began to set, and if they did not find the man, he knew Michael would demand that they retreat immediately.

Michael held his gun at his waist as he hiked, as if he was ready to blast off a round at the first thing that moved. He found the surroundings strangely familiar as he hiked behind his friend. What had happened years ago now seemed to have just occurred days or weeks before. Back then, he and his friends had made their way up this path, laughing and telling each other what they would do with all the money if they found the gold. Now, he was wondering what they were supposed to do if they found the old man. Choosing to believe that Kevin must have some plan, he decided that he would let Kevin take the reins.

"Do you think when Jake was yelling that he was trying to tell us that he tried to stop the old man?" Michael said, keeping up the very quick pace.

"No," Kevin replied, breathing easily.

"You think he was trying to tell the people?"

"Yes," Kevin replied, "Now stop talking. You're wasting your air."

Michael obeyed as he followed his friend up the rough terrain. He tried to keep his attention focused in the direction they were headed, but he felt compelled to keep his eyes out for Jake. Although he agreed that Jake had probably lost his mind, Michael also felt that he could help them and bring additional safety to their hunt.

"I'm really sorry about Cindy," Michael said as he tried to keep up with Kevin.

Kevin took a few more steps and stopped, placing the butt of his gun on the ground and holding it by the barrel.

"Sorry about what?" Kevin asked.

"I'm sorry about what I did," Michael replied, stopping next to him and breathing hard.

"You already said you're sorry."

Michael cleared his throat, "I know. I wanted you to know that I really am sorry. Not a drunk apology, but a real one. I really fucked up."

"That was a long time ago," Kevin said.

"It was, but it still bothers you. I can never go back and change what I did, but I want you to know that if I could, I would."

Kevin nodded his head and took a drink of water from his canteen.

"I know you don't like me. You think I'm just a chicken-shit New York lawyer who once tried to steal your girlfriend. But you know what? We were once good friends."

Although Michael had achieved the life he wanted, he missed his hometown, and missed his friends even more.

Kevin glared at Michael, "You're fucking right we were friends. And the one guy-code that can never get broken is a friend screwing with another friend's girl."

"I know," Michael said.

"Like I said, it's in the past. Cindy and I are married, and she's having my kid."

"You've never let go of that anger," Michael said stepping closer to Kevin. "It takes a big man to admit he was wrong and apologize, but it takes an even bigger man to accept an apology and forgive."

Kevin quickly punched Michael on the bridge of his nose and watched as Michael fell backwards, landing on his back in some bushes.

"I forgive you," Kevin said.

Michael lay for a moment, holding his nose as blood ran from each nostril. Kevin stood over him and watched as Michael spit blood on the ground beside him.

"And, I'm very happy for you and Cindy," Michael said spitting more blood.

"What?"

"I don't think I told you congratulations or anything."

Kevin smiled, "Yes, you did."

"Oh, good," Michael said and pushed himself into a sitting position.

"Damn, I'm sorry," Kevin said extending his hand and helping Michael to his feet.

Michael took his hand, and when he got to the standing position he said, "Listen to this ... I forgive you."

Kevin shook his head, "You knew I was going to hit you, didn't you."

"One day," Michael replied. "I was kind of hoping it had been back in school and not halfway up a mountain with crazy people running around."

"Well, I'm very…"

"Damn good punch," Lowery said.

Kevin and Michael turned to see the old man sitting on a log pointing the small machine gun at both of them.

"Drop your guns," Lowery said and watched as they both dropped them on the ground.

"Look, we're not here to harm you," Michael said.

"Well, no shit," Lowery said. "Looks like I'm the only one who could do any harming right now. Both of you walk up there away from your guns."

Kevin and Michael both walked slowly away from their guns, and watched as Sheldon walked over and picked up the two rifles.

Kevin put himself between Lowery and Michael and said, "Look sir…."

"Sir!" Lowery yelled. "Ain't never once been called Sir. Never once. Now stop talking for a moment. I have some questions. You guys just became my donkeys, but what good is a donkey without a pack?"

"We left them at the base of the mountain," Kevin replied.

"Why?" Lowery asked.

"We knew we could hike a lot faster if we weren't carrying our packs," Kevin replied.

"Oh, well, that just opens up a whole set of new questions," Lowery replied pulling his pipe out of his pocket.

Kevin and Michael exchanged odd looks at each other as they both smelled the marijuana smoke when the old man lit the pipe.

"I'm assuming you wanted to hike faster so that you could catch up to me and Sheldon. So, obviously, I'd like to know who you two fellas are?"

"I'm Kevin, and his name's Michael. We're friends with the guy you shot in town."

"I see," Lowery said smoking his pipe. "Good friends, obviously, or you wouldn't have come after me to avenge him."

"We're good friends, but we're not here to avenge him," Michael added.

"And the skinny fruitcake?" Lowery asked.

"What?" Kevin asked.

"That boney naked freak down the path. Who's he?" Lowery added.

"His name's Jake," Kevin answered. "He's a friend of ours, but we don't know why he's here."

Lowery chuckled, "Sure you do. He's here for gold."

"No, he's not," Michael said. "He's probably here for the same reason we are. To stop you, and get the tape back."

"So you can have the gold," Lowery said, making a circling motion with his pipe.

"No, we want to destroy the tape and stop you from being here at night," Michael replied.

"What do you think your chances are of stopping me now that you have no guns, and I'm holding this?" Lowery said lifting the gun.

"The same as they've always been," Kevin said. "You saw us when I had the scope on you. You know we're not here to kill you."

"Ah," Lowery said, "a worthy tracker. So, you're going to hang your hopes on convincing me not to take the gold. Very interesting. Well, you've both walked a long way to talk to me, so let's hear it."

"The gold is very close," Kevin said. "It's about five-hundred yards from us right now. I won't even try to lie to you about that, but you have to believe me when I say, you don't want to find it."

Sheldon laughed.

"You don't want to find it because there are these people," Kevin continued. "These crazy people who come out at night."

"What people?" Sheldon asked.

"Shut up, Sheldon," Lowery said letting a cloud of smoke from his mouth. "I've been all around the Caribbean, South America, jungles of Africa, Asia, and so on, and every time I look for antiquities or treasure, there's always a local story intended to scare people like me off. Hell, I've been cursed, hunted by magical creatures, anything you can think of. Voodoo, black magic, sacrifice, all of it. I've heard and seen it all, fellas."

"This is not a story," Kevin replied. "We've seen these people. We were captured by these people. Our friend said he tried to warn you. Think about it. If there weren't something up here, why in the hell wouldn't we have come back for the gold."

Lowery continued to smoke his pipe, thinking.

"What did the people look like?" Sheldon asked.

"They had white…"

"Here's what we're going to do," Lowery said. "We're going to camp here tonight. It's approaching sundown anyways. If we don't get eaten by evil people, then in the morning you two will get your packs and help us get as much gold as we can out of here."

"No way," Michael said. "No fucking way."

"Yes, fucking-way," Lowery said pointing the gun at Michael.

"Look, we're not lying to you," Michael said. "We need to get out of here now, or something very bad can happen to all of us."

"I don't think I'm going to let that happen," Lowery replied. "If the evil people don't eat us tonight, we will …"

"No," Michael said and started walking down the path. "You might as well shoot us."

"Fine," Lowery said and sent three rounds into Michael's left wrist and hand.

Michael fell to the ground holding his hand, blood oozing from between his fingers. He nearly slipped into unconsciousness when he looked at what was once his hand.

"Okay," Kevin said raising his hands in the air. "Okay. Don't shoot anymore. Please."

"I don't want to shoot," Lowery said still pointing the gun at Michael. "You dumb-asses made me shoot one of my donkeys. Now I have a donkey with only one good hand. That doesn't make me happy."

"Lowery," Sheldon said softly, "can I talk to you, please?"

"Talk, son," Lowery replied.

"Away from them, please."

"Whatever you have to say to me, son, you can say in the presence of our new friends," Lowery replied.

Sheldon looked at Kevin, "Just do what he asked, and everything will be fine. I promise."

"We'll do what he asks, but you guys are not getting it," Kevin replied. "Everything will not be fine. We're not lying to you, and things are going to get very fucked up tonight."

CHAPTER 26

After Sheldon had cleaned and wrapped Michael's wounded hand and wrist, he offered him a prescription pain pill. Michael refused, knowing that he needed a clear mind once night came. The bones in his wrist and hand were shattered which made it difficult for Lowery to tie him up, but by night fall, both Kevin and Michael sat up against a large log with both their legs and arms tied securely.

Lowery provided food for his prisoners not because he felt sorry for them, but because he needed his donkeys strong in the morning. He allowed Sheldon to feed them dried meat and bread, and even allowed Sheldon to give them each a few drinks of whiskey. It was not the first time Lowery had tied men up and then proceeded to use them to carry artifacts or treasure out of a location. However, it was the first time that his captives could speak English. This, Lowery thought, added more entertainment to the whole situation.

Once Sheldon had finished giving the men food and whiskey, he sat next to Lowery. He threw a few logs on the fire and grabbed his grandfather's pipe. He expected Lowery to hit him or say something demeaning, but nothing came. He put fresh marijuana in the pipe and began smoking as the fire grew and darkness fell.

"What are you doing, Lowery?" Sheldon asked.

"Fixing to go to bed, you?"

"You can't kidnap people, shoot people ---- this is all wrong."

"You do things your way, I'll do things mine," Lowery responded taking the pipe away from Sheldon.

"Please untie us," Kevin asked. "I promise on my unborn child, we will not leave. Please untie us, so when they come, we can fight."

"No," Lowery responded.

"What people?" Sheldon asked. "Please tell me about them."

Lowery laughed, "You believe them, huh?"

"Just campfire talk, Lowery. You do things your way, I'll do them mine," Sheldon responded.

"Ok, but if you can't sleep because the ghost stories scare you, don't come crying to me," Lowery added.

"What did they look like?" Sheldon asked.

"They had white stuff on their faces, long black hair, looked like Native Americans, but a lot of them had blue eyes," Kevin replied.

"Did they speak?" Sheldon asked.

"Yes, but we couldn't understand them," Michael answered. "It was like a strange version of Spanish. We think our friend Jake could understand them enough to figure out what they were saying, but we don't know. We have never talked about what happened that night."

Sheldon admired the small stone cross he carried with him. He turned his back to Lowery so that he could not see it.

He had given the cross to Lowery, but had changed his mind and thought it would be easier if Lowery thought he had lost it than if Sheldon had asked for it back. He ran his thumb gently along the pink rock that had been carved into a cross, wondering if the person who carved the Navajo Yeii Spirit onto the cross had long black hair and a white painted face.

"Did you see anything like this?" Sheldon asked holding up the rock.

Kevin and Michael both looked at the rock and refused to reply.

"It's dark now," Michael said, "please untie us."

"No," Lowery responded, and then tapped Sheldon on the shoulder. "Nice rock, thief."

"You may not trust us, but when they come, you'll want us able to help you fight them off," Michael added.

"And even if these people do exist, what makes you think they're still here, and will come get us tonight?" Lowery asked.

"We don't know that," Kevin replied. "But if they do come, you will want us to help you fight them off."

"I got this," Lowery said raising the small machine gun.

When Michael heard the first sound of snapping wood, he did not say anything, hoping that what he had heard was not what he thought was coming. More snapping and sounds from the surrounding forest came, and when Michael noticed that Sheldon had heard something, he motioned for him to cut the ties off them. Sheldon looked away and stared into the darkness that surrounded them. He thought about telling Lowery about the sound he had heard, but decided against it, knowing he would just be chastised for the comment.

Sheldon thought he heard someone breathing behind him, and spun to try and see what it might have been. Kevin noticed Sheldon's startled reaction to something and struggled to undo his ropes.

Sheldon's heart jumped when he saw what he thought was a white face protrude from a shadow behind a bush that lay several yards behind Kevin and Michael. He froze as the face slowly pulled back, disappearing into the shadows. He reached slowly for his gun and looked at Lowery who seemed only interested in watching the flames of fire dance around the logs.

"I saw a face, Lowery," Sheldon whispered.

"You saw what?" Lowery responded in a stern voice.

"I'm not screwing around. I saw a face, right behind them by that bush."

"You're letting your mind play tricks on you, son," Lowery responded. "Let me guess. It was white."

"It was," Sheldon replied. "Get your gun. I'm going to untie them."

"I'll get my gun, but the hell you are," Lowery replied picking up his MP5. "If there's a bunch of white-faced evil people around, they won't like the sound of this very much."

Lowery held the gun over his head and held the trigger down running through half his magazine before stopping. The loud explosion of bullets made Michael jump and Kevin began squirming harder in an attempt to get out of the ties.

"Stop moving, or the next set of bullets will not be shot into the air," Lowery said as he stood, pointing the gun at Kevin.

"He saw one of them," Kevin said, "listen to him. They're here, and there will be a lot of them."

"Well, I have a lot of bullets," Lowery said patting a pouch on his hip that contained several magazines filled with 9mm rounds.

"Please cut us free," Michael asked Sheldon.

Sheldon pulled out his knife and started toward Michael when Lowery shot off a few more rounds.

"Enough with all this bullshit!" Lowery yelled, "I am not going to listen....."

They did not immediately know what had stopped Lowery from yelling at them. It was not until Lowery turned to the side that the light from the fire showed the long spear the protruded through his chest.

Lowery began coughing and staggering as his left hand grabbed the spear that extended from the middle of his chest. Sheldon lunged forward with his knife and started cutting the ropes around Kevin's feet. Lowery stumbled and coughed blood down the front of his shirt as his grip tightened on the spear, trying to pull it all the way through his body. He swayed as he started shooting randomly and aimlessly into the trees.

"Mother Fuckers!" Lowery yelled, choking on blood.

Sheldon got through the ropes around Kevin's feet, and started on his hands when the magazine in Lowery's gun ran out and the loud sound of gunfire stopped. Sheldon turned his head to look at his grandfather; his heart skipped a beat when he saw a second spear hit Lowery in the back of the head, sending him falling forward into the fire. Sheldon dropped the knife and grabbed his grandfather by the arm, trying to pull him off the fire.

"You have to get…."

Darkness.

CHAPTER 27

Sheldon had been unconsciousness for quite some time, but once he started to awake, his senses ignited very quickly. He remained quiet with his eyes shut in the event he was being watched so he could listen and absorb his current situation. He felt himself hanging from his arms which were out-stretched above his head, and his ankles were tied to what felt like wood. He could surmise by the weight of his body that he was upright, and from the position he was in, he assumed he was tied to two trees or on a crucifix.

He slowly opened his eyes. He opened them only enough that he could see without anyone noticing that his eyes were open. His heart hammered in his chest and his breathing got short and rapid when he saw his grandfather lying lifeless on some type of altar. Resting on Lowery's body were some pine needles, sage brush, and what appeared to be some type of rosary. Standing next to the body was a small man with a white face and long dark hair saying something very softly and motioning his hands as if he were blessing Sheldon's grandfather.

Sheldon slowly positioned his hands so that he could feel what was tied to his wrists. It was thick twine, possibly made out of the hair of an animal. He pulled several times at the twine, but realizing that he could not rip free, he let his hands go limp as if he were still unconscious.

He turned his head slowly to the left, still keeping his eyes nearly shut, and saw Kevin and Michael tied to large crosses facing the altar. He felt the urge to scream, and stopped himself just before he let any noise escape. They were in the middle of the mountains, and Sheldon knew that there was no one to hear his cry.

Kevin and Michael were stripped of all their clothes except their pants, and painted on their chests were some markings of crosses, three wavy lines, and a circle with red lines emitting from it. They were conscious and trying to talk to two men and a woman who stood below them, all with white faces and long black hair. One of the men held a long spear and a very long shield that Sheldon immediately recognized as an old Spanish shield.

Sheldon's grandfather was sprawled out on the altar which was made of stacks of gold bars. Around the altar were a few huts made out of trees and bushes, but if it were not for the several fires that were burning near them, they would not have been detectible. The people went in and out of the huts casually, walking up to the altar and placing various items on his grandfather's body. Sheldon knew that he could not get free from his ties, but he also knew that if he did not do something, he would soon be on the altar with his grandfather's body.

Sheldon lifted his head upright and opened his eyes. His body twitched violently when he first saw that there were two men standing in front of him, one holding a spear and the other a Spanish sword. He tried to pull at the ropes as the man with the sword approached, saying something in what sounded like broken Spanish. The man placed the tip of the sword on Sheldon's chest, motioned his free hand like he was blessing him, and ran the sword downward, cutting Sheldon.

Sheldon screamed in pain as the sword made its way down to his stomach, and just when he thought that the man was going to drive the sword into his stomach, he turned and walked away. Sheldon felt his warm blood run down from his chest to his thighs. He imagined the cut to be very deep, his guts spilling from his stomach. Sheldon looked down at his body and a brief, unsavory feeling of relief came over him when he saw that the cut was not deep, just enough to make him bleed.

The man with the spear approached Sheldon. He was holding a small clay bowl in his other hand. He stopped a few feet away from Sheldon, laid his spear down, dipped his fingers into the bowl, and then started rubbing his fingers on Sheldon's chest and stomach. Sheldon felt helpless and violated as the man drew similar shapes to those he saw on Michael and Kevin.

"Wait, please," Sheldon said trying to clear his mind of the haze that still filled it.

The man did not respond.

Sheldon could hear Michael and Kevin pleading to the people in front of them.

"Please, stop, let us down and we will go," Sheldon begged.

The man did not respond.

Sheldon tried to determine what these people meant to do with them. He could not recall either Spanish or Navajo ever engaging in sacrificial ceremonies.

"We're not here to harm you. We'll leave without taking your gold. Please let us go," Sheldon said looking at the man standing further away and holding the sword. He then looked down at the man painting on his chest and said, "Please let me go. I will leave this place. Please."

The man did not respond.

"*Permitama por favor para ir,*" Sheldon said.

The man painting Sheldon's chest stopped looked at the man holding the sword. He put the bowl down and picked up his spear, slowly backing away from Sheldon as he pointed the tip of the spear at Sheldon's chest. The man with the sword lowered his weapon and his face contorted in confusion.

Sheldon heard the two men speaking to each other, but he could not understand what they were saying. He strained to understand a few words, as they sounded like Spanish, but it seemed that the words were out of context, or were Spanish words combined with a different language.

"They think we're criminals," Sheldon said loud enough for Michael and Kevin to hear. "They are descendents of Spanish and Navajo people, and I think they have us on crosses because they're acting out the crucifixion of Jesus."

"How do you know?" Michael responded.

"I'm an anthropologist. I studied the possible existence of these people in school. I think they've learned the story about Jesus, and over the years, the story was distorted."

"If you studied these people, tell us how to get the hell out of here!" Kevin pleaded.

"I didn't study them, I studied the possibility of them," Sheldon replied. "I think they speak a mixture of Spanish and Navajo. They seemed to respond when I asked them to let me go in Spanish. Does either of you speak Navajo?"

Michael and Kevin both replied that they did not.

"Didn't Jesus hang from the cross for days until he died?" Kevin asked.

Neither Sheldon nor Michael responded. Sheldon felt a jolt of fear shoot through his body as Kevin's question sank in. That was exactly what these people were doing. There was nothing that could stop them.

"We are not criminals," Sheldon said. "*nosotros no somos los criminales.*"

The man holding the spear said something to the man holding the sword, and the man with the sword walked away and into a hut on the other side of the altar. A few moments passed, and an older man wearing an old Spanish helmet emerged from the hut. The man with the sword pointed it toward Sheldon, and after the older man examined him for a moment from a distance, he paced over to Sheldon to get a closer look.

The man stood staring into Sheldon's eyes. Sheldon wondered if this man were some kind of leader, shaman, or wise man. In his thesis paper, he discussed at length the two different beliefs of the Spanish who settled in New Mexico, and the Navajo who migrated from the North not long before the Spanish arrived. The Navajo, who were passive in nature, believed in medicine men, healing ceremonies, and to some extent, in magic such as Skinwalkers. The Spanish had traditional Catholic beliefs. They were Christians with precise order and a commitment to the Church and the Pope. He concluded that in this culture, as in many commingled cultures, the two groups had colonized together and adopted portions of each other's beliefs. The man standing in front of Sheldon was dressed in such a manner and had body painting that seemed to prove his theory. He wore an old Spanish helmet, his body was painted with markings of Navajo symbols, while his physique, black hair, blue eyes, and a slightly dark complexion showed evidence of the mixture of blood.

The man spoke, but Sheldon did not understand what he said.

Sheldon repeated, "*nosotros no somos los criminales.*"

The man pointed at Sheldon and yelled something as he threw his arm to his right and pointed toward Michael and Kevin. Again, Sheldon could only understand familiar sounds but could not identify any of the words. As the helmeted man spoke, another man exited one of the huts wearing the carcass of a coyote draped down his back, its skull resting on his head. The man hunched over, making the head of the coyote head appear to be his own head. The Coyote Man slowly danced around Lowery's body, and as he did this, more people appeared and circled around him to watch. The man wearing the Spanish helmet observed the dance, stopped talking, and joined the circle that was forming around Lowery's body.

As the people circled the body, Kevin took the opportunity to struggle with the twine, trashing back and forth with as much effort as he could. After a few moments, Kevin fell limp, hanging from the cross. The Coyote Man pulled a handful of dust and ash from a pouch he wore at his hip, and began tossing it into the air above Lowery's body. Sheldon remembered the Skinwalkers, and tried to focus on the man's eyes. They were blue.

"He's acting out some type of Skinwalker ceremony," Sheldon said to Michael and Kevin.

Sheldon heard a loud snapping sound on a tree a few feet from his stomach, and looking to see what it was, and saw a large spear sticking out of the tree. He tried to determine where the spear had come from, and clinched his body in expectation of a second spear finding its target in his chest. The crowd continued with the ceremony, and a second spear did not come.

The Coyote Man then jumped up onto the altar and crawled animal-like over Lowery's body. He established a position with his head was just above Lowery's, and started to breathe inwardly with long exaggerated breaths. The crowd began to chant and cheer as the breathing got deeper and more exaggerated. Sheldon thought of screaming out for them to stop, but knew that a second spear would follow, its destination not being a tree.

They are acting out the stealing of his soul, Sheldon thought. *Why would they perform a funeral with rosaries that was intended to send him to heaven, and then try and steal his soul?*

Sheldon thought he heard the cry of a hawk to his right and it caused him to look away from the altar and into the trees. The forest seemed unnaturally dark and calm. Just as Sheldon began to look away, he saw a man emerge from the shadows. The man stopped when he got to the point where complete darkness and the light from the fire consumed each other. He was tall, had a dark complexion, and did not have a white painted face. He was not one of these people.

Sheldon's mind was still foggy, but he was able to recognize the man. The man was wearing ceremonial clothing, had a stern face, and a bold and confident stature. It was all now clear in Sheldon's mind; he was the man he had seen the night he camped with his grandfathers. Sheldon thought that his grandfather had fooled him into believing he had a spirit guide, but the sight of this man standing here now gave him a slight sense of hope.

The spirit guide moved. No, something behind the spirit guide moved.

Sheldon closed his eyes tightly, and reopened them to see that the spirit guide was fading into the shadows. He was leaving.

"Wait," Sheldon whispered, "don't leave."

More movement came behind the fading image of the spirit guide. Soon, the spirit guide had faded from sight, and standing behind where he stood, was another man. The man crouched next to a tree, a Caucasian man wearing a red baseball hat. Sheldon quickly turned to see if Kevin and Michael noticed the man at the edge of the trees, but they were both watching the bizarre ceremony that was being performed on Lowery. He looked back toward the forest, and after struggling to find the man again, saw the man moving slowly in the shadows toward him. He crawled on his hands and knees, and Sheldon could see that he was not wearing a shirt.

Sheldon turned his attention to the ceremony. The people continued to huddle around the altar, the Coyote Man still performing strange rituals on the body. Sheldon wondered how many men there were, worried that there were too many of them to fight off. He imagined a battle breaking out, and he would have to watch helplessly as he hung from the cross, his body exposed and an easy target for another spear.

Sheldon tried to think of a way to get Kevin and Michael's attention without attracting the attention of the people around the altar. He tried several times to whisper something to the two men on crosses, but realizing they could not hear him, started to wiggle his body.

He did not know if the wiggling caught Kevin's eye, or if he simply chose to look toward Sheldon, but when Kevin did look over, Sheldon began to motion with his head toward the forest to his right. Kevin looked toward the forest and shook his head as if he did not know what Sheldon was trying to convey to him. Sheldon turned his head and looked into the forest, and could not see the man anymore.

Sheldon spent several minutes squinting his eyes, desperately trying to find the man again, and when he failed to find him, he let his head sag in despair. Just as he began to think the spirit guide and the man were a fragment of his imagination, he felt the ties around his ankles loosen and fall to the ground below him.

"When I undo your wrists, stay in the same position," Sheldon heard a voice whisper from behind him. "They can see your body from where they are, but it is too dark to see the ties."

Sheldon whispered to the voice behind him that he would do as he was told.

"I'll free the other two, and you'll know when to run."

Sheldon's left wrist was freed, and he struggled to keep himself in a similar position as he hung from only his right wrist. He did this for just a moment, as his right wrist was freed, and he fell a few feet to the ground. When he landed, he quickly recovered and stood motionless, his feet and legs together with his arms outstretched above his head.

He thought about running the instant he was freed, but realizing it took all his strength just to keep his arms above his head, he feared that he would not make it far before he was caught by the people. He kept his eyes on the circle of people. He decided that if one of them started to walk toward him, he would have to run.

Who is this man? Sheldon thought. *God, I hope he is not alone.*

Sheldon was close enough to Kevin and Michael that he could see that neither their wrists nor ankles were bound anymore. They were all free now ... no, they were only free from the twine. Sheldon wondered what the man had meant when he said, "you will know when to run." He wondered if that meant, when they were all free. Was he supposed to start the escape?

His arms began to burn in agony as he stood in the awkward position, holding his arms outstretched above his head. He debated in his mind whether he should start the dash into the dark forest to his right. He felt his arms falling from the position he was holding them, and grimaced as he used what was left of his strength to lift them a bit higher. He could not hold the position much longer, and the ceremony would end eventually with a few of the people returning to check on them.

He looked to the forest to his right, calculating how long it would take him to get into the darkness. Once he got there, then what? He assumed that Kevin and Michael would have to run in the same direction, as the forest behind them was further up the mountain, and any other direction would send them straight into the people. They would have to follow, and if the people caught up to them, they would catch Kevin and Michael first. He wondered how long they could fight the people off. Would it give Sheldon the time to distance himself from them enough to get to the base of the mountain?

Just as he had decided to try and make a run for the forest to his right, something caught his eye. Near the tree where he had seen the spirit guide and then the man, he saw a figure. It moved swiftly in the shadows, crouching behind trees and bushes. It appeared at first to be wearing a coyote carcass like the man on the altar, but Sheldon realized that it was not a carcass. Sheldon's arms dropped to his side when he saw that the figure's red eyes looked directly at him.

Kevin saw Sheldon drop his arms to his side and a rush of adrenaline and panic overwhelmed him. *Was that the sign?* Kevin thought.

The people around the altar jumped and stood motionless for a moment when the sound of a short burst of gunfire rang out from the forest to the north of the ceremony. Sheldon turned and saw the people scramble for weapons, talking softly to each other as they organized. Another short burst of gunfire echoed from what seemed a bit further away down the mountain. The area erupted with yelling and the people chaotically scrambled around the altar, in and out of huts, more people emerging from the border of the trees.

The people crouched in unison, and appeared to float into the darkness of the forest toward the gunfire. They moved quietly into the trees, but the quickness of them was frightening. They were nearly flying into the darkness. Only a few moments had passed before all the people were gone, leaving Sheldon, Michael and Kevin standing alone facing the altar. Sheldon looked back to the forest to his right, and could not find the red eyes.

"Let's go," Kevin whispered as he walked up to Sheldon.

Sheldon was hesitant to run into the forest in the direction of the Skinwalker. He gazed longingly at his grandfather's body on the altar and began to walk toward it.

"Are you fucking crazy?" Michael said, grabbing Sheldon's arm.

Sheldon pulled his arm away from Michael and ran to his grandfather. He took his arm and wiped away the dust, rosary, and other items that lay on Lowery's chest. When his grandfather's body was free from anything but his clothes, he leaned forward and kissed him on the forehead.

"You're lying on an altar of treasure," Sheldon whispered in Lowery's ear. "Thank you for everything."

Sheldon expected that when he turned away from his grandfather, Kevin and Michael would be gone, but they were standing at the edge of the darkness waving for him to hurry up. He took a deep breath, another brief look at his grandfather, turned, and hurried toward Kevin and Michael.

They ran as fast as they could toward the south, making their way gradually down the mountain. They struggled in the darkness, falling and stumbling as they moved clumsily in the opposite direction from the gunfire. Sheldon fought the urge to take his eyes off the ground at his feet, trying to ignore that he had seen a Skinwalker in the forest.

The gunfire was gradually getting more faint until eventually they could hear it no longer. The lack of the occasional gunfire concerned Sheldon, as he imagined that the man who freed him must have been captured or killed, and that would direct the peoples' hunt toward them.

Michael stopped and leaned against a tree. "Hold on for a second," he said, panting. "I need a second."

"We don't have a second," Kevin replied. "Come on!"

"I need to rest too," Sheldon said, stopping next to Michael. "We've been running in the opposite direction for awhile. We have a second to catch our breath."

Kevin looked frustrated as he approached them.

"Only a second," Kevin demanded.

"Do you think Jake is ok?" Michael asked.

"I don't know," Kevin replied, turning to look in the direction they last heard the gunfire.

"Jake?" Sheldon asked.

"The guy who freed us," Kevin replied. "We know him."

"Is he …"

"Let's go," Kevin demanded, and started jogging down the mountain.

Their jog eventually slowed to a quick hike, and as they neared the base of the mountain, they walked briskly, paying more attention to the difficult terrain, and trying not to fall and get injured. When they finally reached the tree line at the base of the mountain, they could see the sky to the east illuminate as the sun began to rise.

They hiked out of trees without talking, and after walking into the desert a few miles, they stopped. Michael fell exhausted to his back, lying on the ground staring into the sky above. Kevin sat on a sandstone rock and put his head in his hands, while Sheldon remained standing, looking at the two of them.

"Are we safe?" Sheldon asked.

"For now!" Kevin responded.

"What do you mean?" Sheldon asked.

"He means that they will not come out into plain view, for some reason," Michael replied. "So as long as we are out of the trees and the sun is up, we don't think they'll come after us."

"So, we're fine," Sheldon said.

"For now," Kevin said keeping his head in his hands.

"We have all day to hike out of here," Sheldon said. "We'll be long gone from here by the time night falls."

"You don't understand," Kevin replied. "We've been here before. We tried to warn you. They said they would hunt us down if anyone ever returned."

"Hunt you down?" Sheldon said looking to the east. "How could they do that if they don't want to be seen?"

"I don't know," Kevin said, lifting his head from his hands. "Move at night, hide … hell, I don't know. All I know is that I live in the town just to the East of here with a wife and child and another on the way, and now I have to live in fear of those crazy fuckers coming to get us. I have to live in fear because you and your grandfather would not listen."

Sheldon thought of suggesting that he did not think there was any way that those people could, or would, make it all the way to town to evoke some type of revenge on Kevin. He chose not to say anything. Kevin was very angry, and if he provoked him anymore, Kevin may attack him.

Sheldon reached into a pocket in his cargo pants, and felt the small container his grandfather had given him. Lowery told him only to open the container in the event that everything went bad, and he needed help. He opened the container, and saw inside a piece of notebook paper and a strange looking phone. Sheldon unfolded the paper and saw that it was a note from Lowery. It read;

Sheldon,

If you are reading this, I must be gone or things have gotten out of control. I did not want you to know about this phone unless it was absolutely necessary. This is a satellite phone that can get service anywhere in the world. Hit speed dial #1, and my helicopter will come get you in less than an hour. You do not need to tell the pilot where you are because the phone has a GPS homing device on it. I do not want to waste your time with a good-bye. I have left my entire estate to you, and hope that you continue my legacy in searching for lost treasure. You will find in the island library maps and my research of many more treasures. Please go after a few of them. But please find a woman. Your grandmother was my entire life, Sheldon. I was truly happy that your father found love, and my one regret is that I let my prejudice and pride get in the way of celebrating their love. All the details of my estate are waiting for you on the island. Please, make some of the same mistakes I made. You will enjoy your life if you do.

Lowery

Sheldon folded the note and placed it back into the container. He felt the desire to start heading back up the mountain to his grandfather. He fell to the ground in a sitting position, took a few deep breaths, and pressed speed dial #1 on the phone.

Michael said, "There's no cell phone reception out here."

"It's a satellite phone," Sheldon replied and waited with the phone to his ear.

Kevin looked at Sheldon.

"Come now," Sheldon said into the receiver of the phone. "Lowery is dead. We need you to come now." Sheldon paused for a moment. "We are near the base of the mountain making our way east."

Sheldon returned the phone to his pocket and closed his eyes.

"We should keep walking east away from the mountain," Sheldon said. "We have a helicopter on the way."

Kevin and Michael remained motionless as Sheldon stood and limped toward the east. Kevin remained standing as Michael followed Sheldon, and after only a moment, he reluctantly followed as well.

"It's not going to fucking matter anyways," Kevin said as he caught up to them. "Michael, you'll be off to New York, and you, whoever you are, will be off to wherever the hell you're from."

Sheldon stopped and turned toward Kevin.

"My name is Sheldon Lowery, and I live in Boston," Sheldon said, extending his hand.

"Have you lost your goddamned mind?" Kevin said. "I'm not shaking your fucking hand!"

Kevin continued walking past Sheldon and Michael, taking the lead and heading east. Sheldon stood with his hand still extended, and Michael, elevating his wounded hand, shook his head, disapproving of Sheldon.

It was nearly noon when they heard the faint sound of the helicopter, and only a few moments passed before they identified a small speck in the sky as it approached. Sheldon looked to the west, and being satisfied that they were now a safe distance from the mountain and no one was following, he stopped walking.

They waited in awkward silence as the helicopter approached. When they heard the sound of breaking limbs and falling rocks from a crevasse less than a hundred yards away to the north, Kevin picked up a rock and slowly started to back away in the opposite direction.

"I returned the Bull," Jake said as he hiked out of the crevasse.

Kevin dropped his rock and smiled as he saw his friend come toward them.

"I also found my hat," Jake continued.

When Jake reached his friends, he gave them both a hug.

"Thank you," Michael said, fighting off the urge to cry. "Thank you."

Kevin and Michael patted Jake's back and took turns giving him hugs. Sheldon knew that this must have been the man who freed them.

"Yes," Sheldon said. "Thank you."

"Who's this?" Jake asked.

"His name is Sheldon," Kevin replied. "This is the son-of-a-bitch who got us into this mess."

Jake smiled, "We got us into this mess, if I recall."

"We tried to warn them," Michael said. "They wouldn't listen."

Jake smiled as he took off his hat and wiped sweat from his forehead.

"It wouldn't have mattered," Jake said. "While you were trying to warn them, you were completely surrounded. That's when I went up there, returned the Bull, and found my hat."

"Returned the Bull?" Kevin said.

"Yes," Jake replied. "I found your packs at the bottom of the hill, and searched them for a pistol. I found the Bull in one of the packs. The people had left the site when they were hunting you, so I took the Bull and returned it. My hat was in a jar that was sitting on that alter."

"What bull?" Kevin asked. "What the hell are you talking about?"

"You didn't tell him about the Bull?" Jake asked looking at Michael.

"No," Michael replied. "I told you I wouldn't."

"Thanks, Michael. You saved me," Jake added, putting his hat back on his head.

Jake pointed to the sky as the helicopter, less than a mile away, started making its descent toward them, and said, "What is that?"

"A helicopter for us," Sheldon replied.

"Mind if I catch a ride?" Jake asked.

Sheldon smiled. "Sure, but I'd love to hear about the Bull," he said.

CHAPTER 28

A man dressed in a black suit strolled slowly along the rows of warehouses in the industrial part of Farmington. When he had received the text message from Michael that most of the gold had been transported and placed in a warehouse, he left his motel immediately. He had decided to leave his car on San Juan Boulevard and walk the remaining distance to where three warehouses stood. With the information that the gold was waiting for him, and that all he needed to do was dial the combination to the lock to the large sliding doors, his pace quickened.

When he reached the warehouse, he paused for a moment to see if anyone was watching. He had made a mistake wearing his suit to this part of town. He knew that he stood out and would evoke curiosity from anyone who saw him, but he was overtaken by the excitement. He rushed out of his hotel so quickly that he even forgot his cell phone on the night stand.

His hands trembled as he spun the dial to the lock, whispering the numbers as he set them in place. When he completed the combination, he paused for a moment and then pulled at the lock. It opened. He slid the lock out of the metal loops of the door very slowly as if the slightest of sounds would awaken some terrible giant that would rob him of his fortune. Images of the stacks of gold came to his mind as opened the door just enough so that he could fit side-ways into the room. Once inside, he slid the door shut and reached into his pocket for a small flashlight.

The air in the warehouse was stale and thick with dust. The light from his flashlight quickly danced around the interior of the building. He did not see anything but steel walls and rafters. As the beam of his light moved to the middle of the room, though, he jumped, startled by the figure of the man he saw in just a brief moment of light. The image burned into his mind, and he could see it almost as clearly in the darkness as if the light were still shining on it. He quickly reached for this gun.

"Don't," a voice said calmly. "Calm down and come here."

The man, not knowing how many people were in the warehouse, knew he should not pull his weapon.

"Alright," the man said as he returned the light to the figure. He saw the large man with the dark complexion sitting in a small chair in the middle of the room.

The man in the chair pointed to an empty chair. "Have a seat, Mark."

Mark thought of trying to open the door again and make a run from the warehouse. His idea was quashed when he heard the sound of several cars pulling up on the dirt lot outside the doors.

Mark took a step toward the man in the chair and the lights to the warehouse came on in a violent flash, his little flashlight now useless in the fully lit space. He stopped and noticed that there were a few other men in the warehouse. One man, lying in the rafters, had a rifle with a scope pointed directly at him.

"What the hell's this about?" Mark asked and continued toward the chair. When he got to the chair he stood motionless.

"Sit."

Mark turned off his flashlight and placed it in his coat pocket. He took a defeated gulp of air and sat in the chair.

"My name is Travis John," the man in the chair said.

"Okay…"

"And your name is Mark Jennings," Travis added.

"That's right," Mark replied.

"I am the Under-Sheriff for San Juan County. That's the county you're in now."

"Okay," Mark added. "We know each other now. So, what's this all about?"

"No, we don't know each other, now. Not yet," Travis said and smiled. "I know your name. I know you used to be an analyst for the C.I.A. with low grade clearance and that you showed really little promise as an agent. I know that you left the agency about five years ago, and despite claiming on your website to be a very good consultant, have not filed a tax return or claimed a residence in that time period."

"Times have been rough," Mark replied.

"So rough that you are willing to blackmail and resort to attempts at extortion."

Mark adjusted himself uneasily in his chair. "If you're arresting me, I want an attorney."

"Oh, I'm not here to interrogate you. I really don't care what you have to say. This conversation is more for me. Guess you can call it a stroking of my ego."

"So stroke," Mark replied.

"That's almost funny. I'll give you that. You see, I'm sure that you're quite pompous. Probably think that the fact you had a small stint with the C.I.A. makes you far more clever than us country folk, especially a small-town Navajo Under-Sheriff. That for some reason or another, your past experience will allow you to wiggle your way out of the situation you've created for yourself."

"Still stroking?" Mark said with a sideways smile creeping across his face.

"Yep. You see, Michael O'Brian is a friend of mine. He's the fella you tried to force into stealing all the gold. Now, I don't believe the gold is out there. Not really the point. But, Michael is a very protective person. Despite what he may come across as, he has a deep devotion and would do anything to protect the people he loves."

"Don't know who Michael O'Brian is?" Mark mumbled.

"No, you certainly do not," Travis added. "If you did know Michael, you would have known that when he moved to New York, he felt very bad for leaving his aging parents behind. You'd know that he has only returned to his hometown a few times since leaving for college. One of his trips was to attend his mother's funeral. I spent a night with Michael after his mother died, and he was damn close to calling his law firm and quitting his job. The thought of leaving his dad alone in this town was almost unbearable for him."

"Will you just do what you plan on doing and spare me the speech?" Mark sighed.

"Sure," Travis said as he stood from his chair. "You stay seated."

Travis stretched his back and bent his legs to get circulation flowing and said, "Been sitting here in the dark for about two hours. I sat here wondering if you would actually come. I'm not sure I know everything that's going on, and I may never know. It's in those times when you have nothing to do but think that your mind really starts playing with you. You know what I mean?"

Mark refused to answer.

"Sure you know what I mean. Hell, being a C.I.A. agent and everything. So, when you're sitting in your cell, I just wanted to give you a few things to think about. First, a recommendation. It's quite obvious from your past that you have few friends, if any. I would suggest finding a few. A true friend would do anything for you. I know, kind of mushy. Just trust me on that. Second, a lesson. No matter how smart you think you are, always assume you are overlooking something."

"Okay, Mr. Under-Sheriff, what did I overlook?"

Travis smiled, "Oh, good, you want to hear. Okay. You see, before Michael returned to New York after his mother's funeral, he had several discussions with his father regarding why he didn't want to leave him alone. His father is quite a stubborn man. They argued for days, mostly due to their grief over their loss, but family, like friends, eventually work things out. Michael demanded that he would only leave if his father allowed him to install a security system on the house."

Travis sat back in the chair and stared Mark in the eyes. "Michael, despite being young, is quite wealthy. He didn't go buy a motion detector at Radio Shack. He purchased the most expensive and fanciest system I have ever seen. Probably nothing compared to the systems you have seen as an agent. In any event, it took me, three of my men, and an electrician two solid days installing the damn thing. It has everything, breach alarms, glass breaking sensors, alarm calls to the Sherriff's office and some outfit out of Georgia, and so on. I'm sure you noticed it when you walked in, and probably noticed that it was not armed."

Mark's face was expressionless. He felt anxiety beginning to flow through him.

"Like I said, Michael's father is stubborn. The minute Michael got on the plane to return to New York, his father unarmed the alarm. It has been unarmed this entire time." Travis chuckled. "The whole thing unarmed, except ... the video and audio recording. The damn little cameras and microphone are in every room in the house, and send the information to a computer that stores it for a year. Can you believe that? Kind of creepy if you ask me. I'm sure Michael's father didn't know that his whole life was being recorded. Quite an invasion of privacy, I would think. I'm sure Michael and his father will have words about it one day. But, Michael will explain that nobody can access the database without a subpoena. So, one day his father will probably understand that nobody has watched him do … well, whatever an old man does. However, some people, me being one of them, have watched a small portion of the tape."

"The kitchen talk," Mark said, defeated.

"Yep, the kitchen talk. As I'm sure you are aware, Mr. Under-Sherriff, as you refer to me, has the ability to subpoena things like video tapes. Just takes a judge's signature, and since the Judge is Sam's uncle, it really didn't take too much persuading to get the thing pushed through quite quickly."

They sat in silence for a moment. Travis allowed the story to sink in.

"Can I ask one question?" Mark mumbled.

"Sure."

"Where's the gold? Did they get it?"

Travis stood laughing. He waved at his men and motioned for them to place Mark under arrest.

"There is no gold," Travis replied as his officers placed handcuffs on Mark's wrist.

"Yes, there is," Mark replied.

"No leprechauns on the reservation, bud," Travis said. "Have fun in prison."

CHAPTER 29

Sheldon looked up from the nautical map that lay on the large, hand carved mahogany desk, and glanced out the window of the library. A large mass of dark clouds was quickly making its way toward the island. He rose from the desk and rubbed his temples. He knew that he needed to make his way around the estate, ensuring that all the windows were securely shut before the storm hit. The library was packed with artifacts on shelves and hanging from the walls, but the most precious of them all was a pendant that hung from Sheldon's neck. It was a translucent pink rock carved in the shape of a cross with tiny carvings of the Navajo Yeii Spirit on it. To him, it was far more valuable than anything in the room. He rubbed the stone between his thumb and index finger, a habit he had recently developed.

He left the library and made his way down a long hallway, stopping at the doorways of rooms as he passed, noting that the windows were shut. He entered a large sitting room and saw a man wearing a baseball hat talking on the phone. He quietly walked over to one of the windows and closed it, fastening the latch. He looked over at the man and smiled.

Kevin laughed and said into the phone, "You're my hero."

Kevin paused, listened for a moment, and started laughing again.

"Tried to come save us, and got arrested for D.W.I.," Kevin continued. "Unlawful taking of a motor vehicle?"

"Ah, shit man," Kevin said into the phone. "Well, I'm glad Travis let that slide."

Sheldon got Kevin's attention and pointed to the clouds through the window to show him that a storm was coming. Kevin nodded and held his finger up indicating that he would be off the phone shortly.

Sheldon strolled out of the room as he heard Kevin say into phone, "I know they're looking for us. When you get out of rehab, we'll come get you."

In the hallway Sheldon was greeted by a fat man with a dark complexion, wearing white pants and a silk flowered shirt.

"The storm is coming, Lowery," the man said.

"I know," Sheldon replied. "I'm making my way around the estate to be sure all the windows are closed. Please make sure Cindy and the others get inside, and have them help me secure the place."

"Yes, sir," the man replied and started to walk away.

"Excuse me," Sheldon said and waited for the man to turn around. "Please do not call me Lowery."

The man smiled, "I'm sorry. Just a habit, sir."

"I understand," Sheldon said and turned away.

Sheldon went through the main entrance of the estate out onto the beach, and found Jake standing waist-high in the ocean wearing cargo pants, no shirt, and a strange-looking cowboy hat. High above Jake's head was a fly line, passing back and forth in a rhythmic fashion. Jake was a conductor, the orchestra of the ocean and approaching storm obeying him obediently.

Michael approached Sheldon and said, "I didn't know you could fly-fish in the ocean."

"I didn't either," Sheldon responded.

"Guess if there's a way to fly-fish the ocean, Jake would figure it out," Michael added. "I'm leaving now. We're taking the sea plane out of here before the storm hits."

"Okay," Sheldon said and shook Michael's hand.

"My immunity lasts for thirty days," Michael continued. "I'll tell them what happened, sell Sam's bar, and wrap up a few things in New York. Pretty sure I can get Sam out of the criminal charges. I don't think the police want the paper to know that the alcohol that got Sam drunk was given to him by their department. I'll have lunch with the Sheriff, and I'm sure Sam will be freed. Not to mention Travis and Sam are friends."

"And then what?" Sheldon asked.

"There's a girl named Deanne. I'm going to try and make a life for myself. But, whatever happens, I'll be back in a month. There's a treasure we have to attend to."

Michael picked up a small duffle bag and went to the dock. Sheldon was unsure if he would see Michael again because he would probably work things out at his firm and settle the police down enough so that he could continue with his life as he had known it. Whether Michael would return, he did not know, but there was plenty of money to go around, and he would welcome him back at any time.

Sheldon whistled at Jake, and when Jake turned to look at him, he waved for him to return to the house. Jake nodded, but turned back to his casting. Sheldon smiled and returned to the house as Kevin hung up the telephone.

"Michael's leaving," Sheldon said.

"I know," Kevin said. "I hope that plane gets back soon in case Cindy goes into labor."

"It'll be back in a few hours," Sheldon said. "Don't worry."

"So, now what?" Kevin asked.

"Come to the library and I'll show you," Sheldon said with a smile. "According to Lowery's notes, we need to start making plans to head for the mountains of Belize."

Kevin shook his head, "Any crazy, lost tribes in those mountains?"

"Guess we'll find out," Sheldon replied. "We have a library full of clues that could lead to many lost treasures. Let's go get another one."

Kevin pondered the statement for a moment. "We didn't get the last one."

Sheldon smiled and said, "Yeah, but what the hell else is there to do?"